CURSED GOLD

Slade looked into Catheryn's eyes. Yellow flecks of firelight danced in the deep blue of her irises. He felt a tightness in his throat. He swallowed. The sudden urge to impress her overpowered him. He said, "Where I come from in Arizona Territory, there's a valley with a chimney of solid gold that rises two hundred feet up the side of the canyon."

Catheryn caught her breath. She had heard claims like this, but she had never before met anyone who had firsthand knowledge of the location of such a bonanza. She laid her hand on his arm. "Tell me about it," she whispered, her voice courting him.

Her fingers tightened on his muscular forearm. "Please."

His eyes held hers for several long seconds.

"Please," she implored again.

"Why? It'll do you no good to know. It's far away, and if you did go there, the Apache would stop you. And if they didn't, the curse would."

His words puzzled her. "What curse?"

"The curse that goes with the canyon—the curse of the chimney of gold…."

Kent Conwell

Chimney
of Gold

LEISURE BOOKS NEW YORK CITY

A LEISURE BOOK®

November 2005

Published by

Dorchester Publishing Co., Inc.
200 Madison Avenue
New York, NY 10016

ISBN 0-8439-5622-4

The name "Leisure Books" and the stylized "L" with design are trademarks of Dorchester Publishing Co., Inc.

Printed in the United States of America.

Visit us on the web at www.dorchesterpub.com.

CHIMNEY
OF GOLD

ONE

The squirming lawman lay on his stomach in the blistering sand, his hands bound behind his back and his feet cinched up to his wrists. His close-set eyes blazed with anger while the young half-breed snugged down the last knot. "I'll see you in hell for this, Slade."

With a grunt, Jake Slade rose and stared down at the hogtied Texas Ranger. A frown knitted his brows. "Just be glad I got business up Santa Fe way, Jack, or else I might decide to have me some Apache fun with you." He pushed his slouch hat back on his head, revealing deep-set eyes under a broad forehead. His dark hair was cut short like the white man's.

"I'm giving you a break this time, Jack." He hooked his thumb over his shoulder, indicating two dark figures perched among the granite slabs a hundred yards up the mountainside. "They'll make sure the stage stops for you." He paused, then added coldly, "It was a fair fight back in Texas. Stop hounding me. Next time, you're a dead man."

The lawman ceased struggling against his bonds. His eyes blazed with hatred. His voice shook with anger.

1

"One of these days, you'll look around, and I'll be there."

"I figure on that, Jack. Lawmen like you are bought by them with the deepest pockets. And that rancher down on the Texas coast has mighty deep pockets." Slade stared coldly at the prone man. If ever a man deserved killing, Jack Barker was the one. The star on his chest meant nothing where money was involved.

With a shake of his head, the young half-breed swung onto his buckskin. He had a long piece to travel and not much time to get there. "Stay out of Arizona, Jack." Slade dug his heels into the buckskin's flanks and the short-coupled animal broke into a mile-eating gallop in the direction of Santa Fe.

Jack shouted after him, "Go to hell!"

Slade kept his eyes forward. Around the first bend, out of the lawman's sight, he cut east to the Texas Panhandle. Information awaited him there that could lead him to the men who murdered his mother and kidnapped his sister years before.

Two weeks later, Slade reined his buckskin to an abrupt halt. He studied the vast prairie of rolling hills beyond the Staked Plains. Something, or someone, was out there. He saw nothing, but it was there, a disturbing presence.

Heeding his Apache upbringing, Slade wheeled the buckskin and heeled the animal into an all-out sprint back to the cottonwood grove he had just departed.

He dismounted, and then he smelled them, a stench of rancid buffalo fat. From deep in the cool shadows of the cottonwood grove, he watched a band of Indians wend its way, single file, over the crest and down the side of a sagebrush-covered sand hill to the east.

Slade recognized the tribe instantly. "Kiowa." He growled the word through clenched teeth.

Garish stripes of red and yellow decorated the chest and ribs of the Kiowa warhorses. Brothers of the Wolf. Looking for blood.

Slade rubbed his broad jaw thoughtfully. Maybe the rumors were true. Maybe Kicking Bird had lost his say-so. For months, the lid on the Kiowa pot had been rattling. Maybe Big Tree had won out. Looked like it was all primed to blow off. For whatever reason, the Kiowa had finally painted themselves into a fighting mood.

Why? Kicking Bird's counterpart, the inflammatory Big Tree, who advocated war? Or the ignorance of the U.S. Cavalry?

The muscles in Slade's jaws stood out like new whipcord. He shook his head. To hell with the reason. Let someone else worry about it. This time, nothing would prevent him from running down the Comancheros he had sought for so many years. Not even a full-blown Indian war.

He slipped the rawhide loop from the hammer of his .44. A war club and a double-edged knife rode on his other hip.

He glanced at the buckskin standing motionless beside him. Below the fender of his double-cinched Texas saddle rode an elmwood bow in a deerskin case, with two dozen iron-pointed arrows in a matching sheath. The other fender cradled a Winchester Model 66 in a deerskin case.

A wry grin curled his thin lips. He was well armed. With Jack Barker behind and now the Kiowas ahead, the young man could very well have need of all his weapons, perhaps even the slingshot he carried in his shirt pocket.

The sleek buckskin caught the alien smell of the Kiowa. The animal started, nervously stamping its feet in the sandy soil. Slade held the bridle and pinched the wide-eyed animal's nostrils. The buckskin steadied.

Without emotion, Slade surveyed the rolling short-grass prairie. Unlike the Staked Plains he had just crossed, the undulating sand hills covered with purple balls of sagebrush offered solid cover for an ambush.

Slade could not afford to be careless, not now, not this close to the end of years of searching. He had failed before. More than once he had failed. But not again. This might be his last chance to find his sister—if she still lived.

His eyes on the Kiowas, the wiry young man considered his buckskin, wondering if the animal could handle the rigors of an all-out race against the Kiowa war ponies.

"Yeah," Slade muttered to the buckskin. "If the Kiowas see us, boy, we're going to be up to our necks in buffalo chips."

A blast of hot air rolled across the prairie and slapped his sun-darkened face, tightening the skin across his broad cheekbones. He turned his eyes back to the sagebrush and grass prairie.

Disdaining any effort at concealment, the line of Kiowas rode over the top of another sand hill and dropped out of sight beyond the crest.

Slade waited ten minutes and then swung into the saddle and pressed his knees into the buckskin's ribs. The animal responded immediately, heading north. Later, Slade would cut east. Zeb Walker's ranch and the eagerly sought news of his sister were only a few hours away.

The sand hills dotted the boundless prairie like warts on a toad-frog, different shapes, different sizes, some high, some low, all held together by the wiry prairie grass and the tenacious roots of the sage.

Slade rode along the base of the sand hills, staying well below the horizon. The sun burned through his heavy denims, baking his legs. He removed his hat and dragged his forearm across his sweaty forehead, grateful for the southerly breeze blowing across the prairie. His leather vest flapped in the wind.

The buckskin's ears pricked forward. Slade felt the tightening of the animal's muscles, but the animal's gait never faltered. Without changing his posture, Slade cut his eyes in the same direction the buckskin stared.

Ahead lay another sand hill.

Because of the buckskin's reaction, Slade decided to give this sand hill a wide berth. He squeezed with his right leg, and the buckskin obeyed by sidestepping to the left, widening the distance by which Slade would skirt the hill.

He jerked the buckskin to a halt. Directly in front of him, a set of wagon ruts cut into the sandy soil. The conveyance that made them was heavy, likely a Conestoga. The ruts led toward the very hill he had planned to avoid. Between the ruts appeared to be the tracks of two yoke of oxen.

Although the sand had filled back into the ruts, leaving only shallow depressions, Slade quickly read the sign. A few feet farther away, a thin S-shaped snake sign crossed the tracks. Probably during the night. Snakes weren't like people. They were smart enough to stay out of the Texas sun. That meant the trail was about a day old.

He shook his head. Whoever made the tracks was either a fool or a greenhorn, or both. No one with any sense wandered through the Texas Panhandle by himself in a bulky, ponderous Conestoga.

A crooked smile curled his thin lips. The only people out here were idiots like Zeb and him, and a whole passel of crazy Indians.

Slade studied the sand hill. The backside swept to the left in a semicircle, forming a cul-de-sac around a large patch of scrub oak. He nodded. That's the only place the wagon could be, in the middle of the oak thicket.

He muttered to himself. "That damned fool should say his prayers and thank his blind luck that it was me that stumbled across his tracks instead of the Kiowas."

He nudged his heels into the buckskin's flanks. The animal crowhopped. "Whoa, boy. Take it easy. Let's just see if I'm right." Slade rode lazy, slumped against the cantle, but the intensity in his dark eyes searching the wide-open prairie belied his casual manner. He had learned well the Apache trick of disappearing into a barren stretch of soil, a trick other tribes knew also. The only way a jasper could survive on the prairie was to spot the other hombre first.

At each step, he expected to be hailed, but the only sound was the scratch of sand against the buckskin's hooves and the squeak of the leather saddle. He held the reins in one hand. The other hand lay on his thigh, ready to palm the Remington army .44.

His steady gaze tracked the wagon ruts into the cul-de-sac. Slade nodded with satisfaction. He had been right. Whoever the tenderfoots were, they had holed up in the oak thicket. A hundred yards from the oaks, he drew up.

The years with the Apaches tugged at him, warning him. A white man would ride right in, stopping before entering to call out, but the Apache would slip in, see what he wanted to see, and then, if he chose, depart—unheard, unseen.

The Indian in Slade won. Pulling the buckskin around, he rode around the sand hill until he reckoned he was directly behind the thicket. Ground-reining his horse, he dropped into a crouch and slipped through the sage. He paused halfway up the hill. A strange smell touched his nostrils—sweet, like the lilac water used in that fancy Yankee hotel that his unit had overrun in Chattanooga during the war.

He crept forward. Just below the crest, he dropped to his belly and slithered through the sage until he spotted the thicket below. "Well, I'll be damned," he muttered, surprised at the scene before him.

TWO

Down below among the oak shinnery, an emaciated man was unloading the wagon while a striking blond woman in a blue calico dress and puff bonnet looked on. Slade pressed his lips together. That was where the sweet smell came from, the woman.

He saw in an instant that the iron rim had been thrown from a rear wheel. Two yoke of oxen stood tied to a scrubby oak. The thin man struggled to drag a leather-strapped trunk from the wagon and then took a long pull on a bottle of whiskey. The woman said something, but the man shook his head angrily and continued unloading the wagon. That they needed help was obvious, but the delay chafed at Slade's patience like a green mustang jerking at the snubbing rope.

Zeb Walker had information about Slade's sister, and that information was the most important thing in the young man's life. But he couldn't just ride off and leave two people, especially greeners like these two, in desperate need of help—not out in the middle of a Texas prairie that was thick with Kiowas and Comanches.

He studied the area below him for several more minutes. Satisfied the two were by themselves, Slade rose to a crouch and slipped silently down the hill. Both the man and woman were too engrossed in the job at hand to notice him.

The oxen did. One bawled, but neither tenderfoot paid heed.

Slade grimaced to himself. Damned greenhorns. Not even the good sense to listen to their animals.

When he was twenty feet from them, he stood upright, keeping his hand near his revolver. "Howdy."

His greeting startled them. The woman spun, her slender hand pressing against her breast. Her lips parted in a scream that never came. The thin man cursed and scrabbled for his rifle.

Slade spoke quickly. "Leave it alone, mister. I'm nobody for you to be afraid of."

The man ignored him. Slade pulled his revolver and cocked the hammer.

The man froze at the sound. He looked around at Slade, who nodded. "I said, leave it be. I don't figure on hurting nobody unless I'm pushed to it." He glanced at the woman and added, "I saw that you might need some help."

Tall and skinny, the man had a mop of black hair and a wild, glazed look in his eyes, but the woman met Jake's eyes with a gaze as steady as his own. "Do what the gentleman says, Phillip." Her soft but clearly commanding statement cut through the tension sharply.

Phillip's eyes darted between the woman and Slade. He hesitated, then nodded.

Slade dipped his head and holstered his .44. "Name's Jake Slade. I didn't mean to put a scare into you folks, but out here, a man who plans on staying alive makes it a point to see others before they lay eyes on him. You folks are lucky." He hooked his thumb over his shoulder. "A party of Kiowas passed through not two hours back."

The man looked around sharply, but Slade's words did not alarm the woman. She smiled and offered her hand as she took a step closer to Slade. "My name is Catheryn Dubuisson. This is my husband, Phillip. We're from Philadelphia, and we'd be most grateful for any help you can give us." She stared curiously at his sun-blackened skin.

A strange feeling came over Slade when he took her hand. The sweet smell of lilac enveloped him. She was a handsome woman. No, she was downright pretty, and she filled out her blue calico dress in all the right places. It seemed to Slade, however, that she would have been more suited to one of those fancy ballroom dresses he had seen fine women wearing at the officers' dances during the war.

But the only dance she would find out here would be attended by rattlesnakes and Indians. Yep. She belonged back in Washington or Atlanta at some fancy tea social, Slade figured. "Yes, ma'am," was all he said, suddenly aware that he was holding her hand too long.

Awkwardly, he dropped her slender hand and glanced at the broken wheel. "We can fix that easy," he mumbled, failing to notice the sly smile on Catheryn Dubuisson's full lips as she glanced at her husband.

Drawing himself erect, Phillip retorted, "I can repair the wheel." He took another long slug of whiskey.

Slade nodded. Here was a waddy who didn't think much of himself. "I reckon you can. I'll just give you a hand if you don't mind. That way, you can get back on the trail," he replied in an effort not to make the man look bad in the eyes of his wife. "And I can get on my way."

After bringing his buckskin in, Slade built a small, smokeless fire to heat the rim. Phillip attempted to help, but he proved more of a liability than an asset; nevertheless, Slade gave him simple tasks to shore the frail man's self-respect before his wife.

As Slade wrestled the hot rim over the wheel, he asked idly just how they had come to find themselves in such a godforsaken place all alone. "Seems like you folks should be traveling with a train."

Catheryn Dubuisson had seated herself daintily on the trunk. She nodded and replied for the two of them. "We were. We came out on the Santa Fe Trail from Independence. Outside of Fort Dodge, we turned off for Adobe Walls."

Slade grunted and glanced at Phillip, who stared back at him with unconcealed dislike. "You folks buy a spread around here?" He leaned the wheel against the wagon.

Phillip laughed. "Not likely." He shot a smug glance at his wife. "There's more out here than dirt farming or ranching."

"I reckon there might be, but if there is, I never heard of it." He glanced around. "Any grease?"

"You never heard of gold?" Phillip replied, his words slurred, his tone mocking as he ignored Slade's question. "I always heard tell that you Western gents know just about all there is to know."

Catheryn snapped, "That's enough, Phillip." Anger flashed from her eyes and twisted her face. "Get the grease for Mr. Slade."

Phillip glared at her, fists clenched. A test of wills ensued. Phillip lost. He rummaged about the wagon bed and tossed Slade a container of tar and tallow.

The anger fled her face as she turned to Slade. "Please excuse my husband. He's had a long day." She cast a sidelong glance at the whiskey bottle. Her lips curled with disgust. "We both need some rest."

"Rest, hell." Phillip snorted, his eyes bright with whiskey. He nodded to the south. "I'm figured—I mean, I'm fine. I figure to push on soon as the wheel is fixed. That gold is just laying there waiting for us."

Slade knelt, and using a branch broken from a sagebrush, he spread a generous layer of tar and tallow on the axle. Now he understood why the couple had been so foolhardy as to leave the train and push into Kiowa country all alone. He said, "I never heard of any gold-bearing veins in this part of the country."

A self-satisfied glow of satisfaction lit up Phillip's red face. "It's there." He patted his shirt pocket. "I know exactly where it is. I got a map in my pocket."

Slade suddenly realized just what gold the man was talking about. He forced a laugh. "You're not looking for that wagonload of Spanish gold that's supposed to be stashed along the North Fork of the Red River, are you?" He shook his head and slid the wheel on the axle, packed more tar and tallow inside the hub, and spun the nut and tightened it with a wrench. He turned to face them. "I've been hearing that old wives' tale ever since I been coming to this part of Texas, and I reckon I've seen more than a dozen waybills showing the hiding place, each one different."

Catheryn Dubuisson caught her breath and cut her

eyes to her husband, whose face darkened. "Phillip," she gasped.

Phillip took a threatening step toward Slade. "What are you saying? Nobody knows about that gold."

Slade's eyes narrowed into slits of ice. Phillip jerked to an unsteady halt. "Just what I said, Mr. Dubuisson. I reckon everyone around here has heard about the Spanish gold that's said to be salted away in one of those caves along the Red. It's just talk." For their sake, he hoped they believed his lie. "That's all, just bunkhouse talk." He heaved the tool trunk back into the wagon and fastened the tailgate.

For several moments, Phillip Dubuisson stared dumbly at Slade, who, despite his impatience with the man's foolishness, felt sorry for him and his wife. They had been suckered. No two ways about it. The gold was there, but they would never find it. No one would.

Any waybills the Dubuissons might have seen were purely speculation as to where the gold was first buried by the Spanish aristocrats at the turn of the century. What they didn't know, what no one knew, was that the precious metal had been moved within the past ten years, and no one who had helped hide the gold would have dared revealed its location.

Kicking sand over the fire, Slade said. "I'm sorry I had to break the news to you folks like that, but that's an old game out here." He hesitated. Slade didn't like to hurt people's feelings, but they were better off having their feelings stomped on than getting themselves killed.

Catheryn climbed up on the wagon and plopped down in the seat.

Slade removed his hat and dragged his shirt sleeve across his sweaty forehead. "Look. I'm not one to go sticking my nose in other folks' business, but it seems to me you two are out here in the middle of bad trouble. No offense intended, Mr. Dubuisson, but you're greenhorns. And what might seem innocent enough to you back east can prove downright dangerous out here."

Slade glanced over his shoulder, his conscience wrestling with itself like a bulldogged steer. Zeb's place was a half-day's ride, but he couldn't turn his back on such innocents. He tugged his slouch hat down on his head. "For some reason, there's a lot of Kiowas moving around. Something's in the wind. Something big. You're asking for pure old trouble out here by yourself."

Slade gestured to the horizon. "Now, I got me a friend who has a small ranch a few hours' ride to the east. If you like, we'll go over there for a solid meal and a good night's rest, and then one of us will take you back to Adobe Walls. From there, you can hitch up with some wagons back to Fort Dodge."

Catheryn Dubuisson tilted her chin. "You seem to know a great deal about the Indians, Mr. Slade."

He heard the challenge in her voice. He grinned crookedly. "Probably because I'm part Indian myself, Mrs. Dubuisson."

Phillip's eyes grew wide, but Catheryn Dubuisson's expression remained unchanged other than her eyes, which flickered to the moccasins on his feet. "Oh? What tribe?"

"Nez Percé, but I was raised by the Apache."

"You don't talk like some I've heard. You speak as an educated person."

"I reckon that's because I've spent the last seven years with the white man."

She nodded. "So, you believe we're asking for trouble if we go on?"

"No two ways about it. Like I said, all you folks will find out here are rattlesnakes, Kiowas, and wolves, one as bad as the other. So what do you say to a meal and night's lodging?"

Catheryn replied sweetly, "Thank you, Mr. Slade. But we prefer to continue our trip."

Slade shrugged. He backed the yoked oxen over the wagon tongue. He looked at Phillip and Catheryn. His eyes darted from one to the other, then rested on the woman. "That isn't the smartest decision I ever heard, Mrs. Dubuisson."

She leaned forward, her jaw set and a defiant expression on her face. Her voice remained soft and pleasant. "Perhaps not, Mr. Slade, but Mr. Dubuisson and I are meeting a certain man where the Fort Sill trace crosses the Red River. We intend to be there when he arrives." She offered her hand. "We want to thank you. And please be assured that we are certainly most appreciative of your assistance and your offer of additional help. We know that you are sincerely concerned for our safety, but Phillip is more than capable of taking care of us."

Phillip Dubuisson smiled smugly as he clambered up on the seat beside his wife and reached for the whip.

Jake Slade studied the two for a moment. Damn fools, he told himself. But if someone doesn't want to be helped, you can't do nothing for them. He nodded and took her hand. He stared into her blue eyes.

"Whatever you say, Mrs. Dubuisson. Just remember about the Kiowas." He dropped her hand and swung onto the buckskin. He stared down at them for several seconds before touching his fingers to his hat brim. "Take care."

Ignoring Slade, Phillip cracked the whip at the off leader and shouted. "Git now. Hey!"

Slade shook his head at their ignorance as the couple moved out toward the Red River. With a click of his tongue, he turned the buckskin east. The damned fools didn't even know how to drive oxen, riding on the seat instead of walking beside them with a Moses' stick. "What the hell. I got better things to do." Pushing the pair of fools from his mind, he glanced at the sun dropping in the West. He kicked the buckskin into a running walk, and the miles fell behind. The sun burned the back of his neck. He turned up his collar and settled down into his saddle.

Repairing the wheel had taken him longer than he had expected. Or was it that he had deliberately worked slowly just so he could be in Catheryn Dubuisson's presence longer? He had to admit a man could do a lot worse than that woman. Just being around her made a jasper feel good. And it made him feel kind of sad when he left her, a lot like the time he had left behind the little White Mountain Apache girl.

That had been on the return trip from moving the gold on the Red River. The band of Chiricahua braves had stopped for a few days with a tribe of White Mountain Apaches, some of whom were relatives—cousins, uncles, aunts, even brothers—of the Chiricahua. Slade was twelve, a pony jingler along with his Apache brother, Nana, named after the indomitable subchief Nana. Slade met a beautiful young maiden and was immediately overwhelmed by her comely smile.

She felt as he, for the two strolled the night away through the moonlit mountains. They spoke of the future, and how Slade would return as a brave, and how he would speak to her father.

The next morning, the Chiricahuas moved out. Slade rode behind, herding the remuda before him. He looked over his shoulder at the last bend.

Standing tiptoe on a boulder, the young girl waved. Slade waved back. He felt empty, as if part of his insides had been pulled out. And now that same feeling disturbed him again.

The sun slipped below the distant sand hills as the gray dusk tugged the full moon over the eastern horizon. Slade eyed the white globe warily as it balanced on the horizon before beginning its long journey overhead. Indian Moon. At least, that's what the white people called it. He couldn't resist a wry grin at their ignorance. The Indians had given it a more suitable name, Hunter's Moon.

His thoughts drifted back to Catheryn Dubuisson. He could still smell the lilac perfume and feel her soft skin. For several moments, he permitted his thoughts to revolve around her.

He shook his head and scolded himself for letting his attention wander. That was as foolish as the Dubuissons insisting on continuing their trip. Keep your eyes open if you want to keep your hair, he reminded himself as the full moon climbed higher in the dark sky and lit the sage and grass prairie with a cool glow. As the night deepened, the sage became black splashes of pitch standing out in stark relief against the white sand.

The buckskin picked its way between the bushes. The hair on the back of Slade's neck prickled. He trained his ears, but the sounds of the night continued uninterrupted. Crickets chirruped. In the distance, an owl hooted. A dark shadow swooped from the sky. A rabbit shrieked.

Slade's eyes quartered back and forth across the prairie, never locking onto one object but gazing to the horizon, his peripheral vision searching for some interruption, some movement that did not belong within the panorama of black splotches that dotted the prairie. Everything seemed normal. That was what concerned Slade. Too normal. Abruptly, a sagebrush at his feet erupted into a wild cry. At the same instant, Slade jerked the buckskin around, slamming the horse's neck into a leaping Indian, knocking him off-balance. Keeping the buckskin in a spin, Slade aimed a kick at the brave's head. He felt bone give under the impact of his heel. With a grunt, the brave dropped.

Two other shadows rushed him silently. Kicking his heels into the buckskin's flanks, Slade charged the two. He grabbed the war club. The smooth elmwood handle felt good in his hand. He spun the club over his head and yanked the buckskin toward one of the dark shadows.

The charging animal slammed into the second Indian. At the same instant, Slade swung the spinning club. He felt it crush into the skull of the third brave.

Behind him, an angry cry cut through the silence of the dark night. Without hesitation, Slade urged the buckskin into a dead run, angling to the north away from Zeb's place.

He leaned low over the animal's withers and neck. A blood lust rushed to his head as the Apache eagerness to engage the enemy coursed through his veins. He resisted the fierce desire to turn and fight.

Silent as the wind, the buckskin raced through the night, the sand muffling its hooves. The only sounds that reached Slade's ears were the rhythmic grunt of the straining animal and the squeaking of saddle leather. There was no sign of pursuit. He grinned to himself. Probably young bucks trying for a coup.

Slade pulled up at the base of another hill and studied his back trail. Nothing moved. He reined the buckskin around, still heading north.

Sometime later, Slade glanced into the northern heavens. About ten, he figured, noting that the handle of the Big Dipper pointed up. He cut southeast.

It was almost midnight when Slade reined up on the crest of a hill. Below was a deep valley, Zeb's valley, an offshoot of the Canadian River valley. Shining like quicksilver in the moonlight, a narrow creek twisted and curled the length of the basin, looping in the center like a silver horseshoe. In the middle of the shoe sprawled the black shapes of the ranch house and outbuildings.

Slade suppressed the excitement growing in him. Too many times he had been disappointed in his search. No sense in building expectations this time either, he cautioned himself. But his heart refused to listen. Hope surged wildly through his veins.

THREE

The stockade-walled ranch house lay silent in the darkness. Slade pulled up at the hitching rail. He remained in the saddle, his head even with the roof of the squat building. The moon shone over his shoulder, illumining the homemade slab door. Between the door and the jamb was a dark shadow less than three inches wide.

He pushed his slouch hat back. "See you're still a spooky old coot," he said to the narrow strip of darkness.

A cackle of laughter sounded from inside, and a croaking voice said, "Reckoned it was you ridin' up. Don't know of nobody else tetched enough to ride Kiowa country at night." The dark strip widened as the door swung in on leather hinges. "Put your animal in the barn while I rustle up some coffee."

The yellow light from the coal-oil lamp lit the main room of the ranch house. Slade leaned his elbows on the table and watched Zeb Walker busy himself in front of the fireplace. The pungent aroma of brewing

20

coffee filled the room, and the popping of buffalo grease told him that the fried venison would soon be ready.

Zeb glanced at Slade. "How's Bent?" he asked, referring to Slade's partner back in Tucson.

"Still yanking the ribbons."

"Any trouble with the law this time?"

Slade told him of the incident with Jack Barker.

The older man cursed. "Seems like they'd give up after all this time."

"Not likely," the younger man replied. He pulled out his revolver and dismantled it. "Money and family pride make it hard for the old man to forget about a half-breed killing his son."

Zeb snorted. "The little bastard deserved it. He drew first."

Slade ran a thin cloth down the barrel. "Maybe so, but Little Rivers was his town. That makes a difference."

"Looks like they plan on hounding you wherever you go," warned Zeb.

"Then I'll go back to the Apache," the younger man replied, his gray eyes dancing with laughter. "No lawman will ever come into Apache territory and live." He reassembled his revolver. "You mentioned Kiowas earlier. Any trouble with them?"

Shaking his mop of gray hair, Zeb replied without taking his eyes off the skillet. "None I heard of. Kicking Bird's trying to keep his hotbloods under his thumb right hard. Big Tree's pumping them up to fight. Why? Run into some?"

"Back west," Slade replied, shoving cartridges into the cylinder and then sliding the .44 back into its holster. He went on to tell Zeb about the couple he had befriended.

The older man shook his head. "They be asking for trouble out there. Wouldn't surprise me none that some young hotblood's already dangling two fresh scalps from his belt."

"Hope you're wrong about that," Slade said with a grunt. "They seemed like good people—at least, she did. Right nice-looking too."

Zeb looked up from the skillet into Slade's face as if trying to read his young friend's meaning. He arched a knowing eyebrow and turned back to the fire. "Good people get kilt too." He forked the slab of venison onto a tin plate and filled a tin mug with steaming coffee. "Here you go," he said, setting them in front of Slade. He nodded to a loaf-shaped object under a towel on the table. "Cut yourself a chunk of bread." He poured himself a cup of coffee and sat across the table. "Now, let me tell you what I found out about your little sis."

While Slade dug into the venison and coffee, Zeb filled him in on what he had learned from a Mexican peon who had fancied himself a pistolero until the unfortunate man ran up against Zeb Walker.

"One of the Comancheros you're looking for could be called Vado. According to this pistolero, he stays down in Mexico except when him and his band of vermin raid across the Staked Plains. About a month back, they run into a bunch of them cavalry boys out of Fort Richardson under a Cap'n McClellan."

A frown knitted Slade's forehead. "Never heard of him."

Zeb grunted. "He's been around a spell. He's the one who's been trying to convince the Kiowa to stay close to the reservation at Fort Sill. Anyways, he'd been out on patrol, and he run across them Comancheros and captured this Vado feller."

"Where'd he take the Mex?"

"Fort Sill."

"Why there? You said McClellan was out of Richardson."

"Sill was closer, I reckon."

Slade eyed his old friend. Zeb Walker was two inches shorter than Slade's six feet, but he was a thickly muscled man with a wild thatch of gray hair and a beard to match. His blue eyes still glittered with the fierce intensity with which they first surveyed the virgin Rocky Mountains.

Slade asked. "What makes you figure this Vado is one of them?"

The older man touched his gnarled finger to the bridge of his nose. "Don't know that he is, but the pistolero said the Mex's nose was messed up."

Slade suddenly became more interested. "Blowed away?"

"All he said was 'messed up.'"

The younger man grimaced. "This could be another wild goose chase."

Zeb shrugged. "Might. Might not. Never know 'til you see."

Slade blew out through his lips. "I know." He couldn't take the chance that this Vado was not one of the three Comancheros for whom he had been searching. Images of their leering faces had seared painful scars into his brain. He would never forget that night.

He had been eight years old. He watched helplessly as his mother was raped and murdered and his little sister thrown into a wagon. The last thing he remembered was the big Comanchero with the bad nose shooting him. He sipped his coffee. "Maybe it is him." He polished off his venison and washed it down with the last of his coffee. He pushed back from the table. "Reckon I'd better get on out there."

"I'd light a shuck were I you. Word is they sent him to the hoosegow in Fort Sill to stretch his neck good and tight." He reached across the table for Slade's plate and cup. "Wait 'til morning, and I'll ride with you. What with them young Kiowa hotbloods running an' maybe a chance of a stray lawman around, an extra gun won't hurt. Besides, ain't nothing pressing around here right now."

A crooked grin curled Slade's thin lips. From the first time they had met in 1863 when the young half-breed joined up with Nathan Bedford Forrest, and later under Joe Wheeler and then J.E.B. Stuart, the older man had taken Slade under his wing. He was thirty years Slade's senior in years, but fifty in the ways of the white man. "Still trying to look after me, huh?"

Zeb grinned broadly, revealing a set of worn yellow teeth. "Hell, son. Somebody's got to. Don't reckon you done growed any more brains than that day you latched onto that green outlaw in Forrest's remuda."

Slade's own smile broadened as he remembered those days in Forrest's brigade. "I don't reckon I have."

The old man shook his head. "Yore old Pa would have busted a stitch seeing that."

A tightness constricted Slade's throat. He had never known his father, and the unlikely meeting with Zeb Walker smack in the middle of the War of Secession seemed nothing short of a miracle to the young half-breed, for the older man had met Slade's pa at one of the trappers' rendezvous in the late twenties. "I wish I'd known him," he replied wistfully.

"He wuz an old bear, despite his fancy name, 'Jacob Resolution Slade, Jr.' Reckon that makes you a 'third.' I heard onct or twice that he come from a monied family back east."

Slade grinned. "That's one horse that don't plan on being rode."

"Who knows? It might be true."

"Don't bet good money on it."

Zeb laughed. "You even sound like yore pa." He paused. His forehead wrinkled in concentration as his memory dropped the years from his shoulders. "I guess I was eight or ten when I went to a rendezvous with my old man. Him and yore Pa had partnered up from time to time afore then. The last time I saw him was when Pap and me paid him and yore ma a visit on the way to the mountains, but I'd hear about him from year to year—him and that purty ma of yours."

Mention of Slade's mother brought back dark memories. Zeb had told the story before. Slade didn't want to hear it again. He rose from his chair and glanced around the room. "That's all in the years past. Where do I bed down? Same place?"

Zeb arched an eyebrow. "Same place. I'll wake you early."

Slade grunted and looped his gun belt over the back of a straight-backed chair. He stepped from his moccasins and rolled out his blanket in front of the fireplace.

Sleep came slowly. Zeb's mention of his family brought back troubled memories, shadowy bits and pieces of his life before his eighth birthday. Years earlier,

Zeb had been able to fill in a few more slivers of Slade's childhood, but that was all. The Apaches who had saved his life knew nothing. Usually, he was able to push the painful memories from his mind, but not tonight.

He remembered his little sister. Her Christian name was Laura Ann, but he always had called her Butterfly, the Indian name given by their mother. And he remembered his mother and her stories of his grandfather and his uncles, great leaders of a tribe far to the north.

His mother had been a Nez Percé princess, daughter of old Chief Joseph, who reluctantly permitted her to marry the white man from the mountains. Her older brother, Slade's uncle, was given the tribal name Thunder Rolling in the Mountain, but upon his baptism, took the Christian name of Joseph and later became Chief of the Nez Percé. Slade had another uncle, the younger brother of Joseph. His name was Ollikut, the Frog.

A great sadness filled his heart for the blood family he had never known. He had often promised himself that when he did find his sister, he would take her to visit their mother's people.

He rolled onto his side and stared at the dying fire. Finally sleep released him from the pain of his memories, and in his dreams, he saw Catheryn Dubuisson.

Zeb awakened instantly. The moon cast a white square on the floor by the side of his bed. He sat up and strained his ears against the silence. The stockade-walled house slumbered. Only a faint hiss from the dying fire in the next room broke the silence. But something had awakened him. He reached for his ancient navy .36 and slipped into the shadows next to the wall.

Outside, an owl hooted. Zeb gripped his revolver

tighter. He listened intently. A second owl joined in. Zeb relaxed. Two horned owls, male and female, singing together. He eased across the room and pulled back the blanket that served as a drape in the doorway.

A few coals blinked in the darkness. Zeb made out the bare floor in front of the hearth. He stepped into the room and looked around. Jake Slade had disappeared.

"Damn that boy," Zeb muttered, laying the .36 on the table and lighting the coal-oil lamp. He knew what had happened. There was no need to be in a hurry now. He stirred up the banked coals in the hearth and laid some kindling over them before mixing up a fresh pot of coffee.

While it brewed, Zeb Walker looked in the barn even though he knew what he would find. The buckskin's stall was empty. Back outside, he glanced at the Big Dipper. The handle pointed west. That made it about 4 A.M.

He shook his head. "Good luck, son," he mumbled to the night breeze that had sprung up. "Maybe you'll find her this time."

FOUR

Far south of the ranch, Slade was making good time, four to six miles an hour. Instead of cutting southeast directly to the Fort Sill Trace where Catheryn Dubuisson had said they were to meet their partner, he headed due south. With a greenhorn couple like the Dubuissons, a jasper couldn't guess where they would intersect the river.

He planned to hit the Red miles west of the Trace. Then he could follow the meandering shoreline eastward to the Fort Sill trail.

He insisted to himself that since he was going to the fort anyway, a quick check on how they were doing would not be out of his way. He was simply concerned about Phillip and Catheryn Dubuisson, but deep down, he knew his concern was more for her than for her drunken husband. The feeling he was experiencing was a strange emotion, one he had never encountered in his twenty-two years, not even with the little White Mountain Apache girl. The feeling nagged at his conscience. For some reason, he felt guilty.

The moon lit the prairie like day. Just before sunrise,

he pulled up at the red sandstone bluffs overlooking the north fork of the Red River. He gazed out over the river to the southeast. There, five or six days beyond the horizon, lay Fort Sill.

A strange excitement filled his wiry body. He tried to tell himself that it was the anticipation of confronting the man he had sought for so many years, of finding his sister. That was part of the excitement, but in truth, the expectation of a second meeting with Catheryn Dubuisson was part of it also.

He studied the Red, a broad, sandy riverbed half a mile wide. Red sandstone bluffs pocked with caves overlooked the north bank of the river. Willow brakes lined both shorelines. In dry weather, a thin trickle of water twisted and curled downriver. Seldom wider than ten feet, the narrow stream moved back and forth across the bed, one day meandering down the middle of the riverbed, the next down the south side along the willows, and the next under the imposing sandstone bluffs on the north. Even in wet weather, the stream rarely approached a quarter of the full breadth of the bed, except during flash floods.

With each move of the narrow stream, water seeped through the sand, collecting in the deep pits of sandstone beneath the riverbed, forming deadly pools of watery quicksand that sucked unwary travelers and animals into their depths.

Slade remembered the first stories Gokhlayeh had told him after he had been found and nursed back to health by the Apache. The tales were of this river, and of the Spanish aristocrats who forced the Apache to bear heavy loads of gold to these very caves.

A shudder of fear raced through him as he eyed the

innocent-appearing but deadly belt of sand that twisted from horizon to horizon. He shook his head and spoke to the buckskin. "Those greeners probably don't even know what quicksand is."

The portent of bad weather, a red glow filled the eastern sky as the sun burst over the horizon. The wind shifted to the southwest. Slade frowned and pressed his knee into the buckskin's ribs and turned the animal into the rising sun.

Best he could figure, the Trace was a two-day ride to the east. He pulled the brim of his slouch hat over his eyes against the glare of the sun and set his jaw. He hoped Phillip Dubuisson was a smarter hombre than he appeared, that he would have the sense to ride out the coming storm in one of the numerous caves along the base of the bluffs.

Bad weather would send a wall of water roaring down the Red, destroying everything before it. Slade had seen it happen when he came to this river with the Apache to move the gold. That one time was enough. He kicked the buckskin into a trot, a dangerous gait on the uneven sandstone, but there was no time to waste.

The clouds thickened throughout the day. The wind continued to shift slowly to the west. Slade usually halted at noon for coffee and a chew of beef jerky. The stop broke up the day and gave both him and his pony a rest, but today, he kept moving.

Once or twice, the buckskin slowed. Slade grunted. "Not today, horse. There's a powerful lot of weather coming our way later on. We need to make as much ground as we can."

He continued his search. The wind intensified, picking up loose sand and hurling it through the air. The sky darkened in the west. Late afternoon, Slade pulled up and squinted downriver, his hat pulled low over his eyes and his neckerchief a mask over his face against the stinging sand. The wind came in gusts now, carrying with it splatters of rain.

Between gusts, Slade made out a wagon in the middle of the riverbed about two miles downriver. Tied to the wagon were four animals. Too short at the shoulders to be mules, they had to be oxen. "Damn that man," he muttered, angered by Phillip Dubuisson's inexperience.

He quickly searched along the bluffs for a trail down to the river. By the time he reached the bed, the clouds had thickened, turning the afternoon to dusk. He had no time to waste. Only a fool wandered across the Red at night.

Staying between the willow brakes and the bluffs, Slade hurried downriver. His race to the wagon was not with the Indians now, but with the darkness.

Slade pulled up when he ran across the wagon tracks leading out onto the riverbed. He peered into the encroaching darkness. A shiver ran down his spine. The wagon's undercarriage appeared broken. The two foolhardy souls were sitting inside with the pucker ropes drawn against the night, content and unconcerned just as if they were serving tea in their parlor back in Philadelphia or wherever they came from.

He glanced around, noting a dark opening in the side of one of the sandstone bluffs behind the willow brakes. Caves. Shelter for the night. A splatter of rain raced across the riverbed to disappear in the darkness on the far side.

Taking care to keep the buckskin between the wheel ruts, Slade hurried to the wagon. He drew up when a rifle barrel poked through the pucker hole. At least they were watchful, Slade told himself.

"Don't get spooked," he called out. "It's me, Slade."

A white face appeared from the darkness of the wagon, and then another. "Come on in, but come slow." The voice was Phillip Dubuisson's.

When Phillip recognized Slade, he lowered the rifle and loosened the pucker ropes and stepped outside. "Mr. Slade. You've again found us in distress. I—"

Slade interrupted, glaring angrily at Phillip. "We don't have time for fancy jawing right now. I don't know whether you noticed it or not, but we got some dangerous weather heading our way. Come morning, you'll have an ocean of water around you. And if the water don't get you, the Kiowas will," he added, his gray eyes cold as steel.

Catheryn Dubuisson pressed her hand against her lips. She looked up at Phillip and then back to Slade. "What are we going to do?"

"We'll be fine, Catheryn," Phillip said, glaring at the young half-breed. "The main part of the river's over behind us."

"Come morning, Mr. Dubuisson, this river will see water from bank to bank." Slade's words were taut with suppressed anger at the tenderfoot's ignorance. He pointed to the sandstone bluffs. "There are caves over there where you'll be safe."

"And just how do you figure we'll get over there?" Phillip retorted, jutting his weak chin defiantly. "In case you haven't noticed, my wagon is broken."

Now that Slade had found them, and they were unharmed, his patience grew thin. "Busted or not, come morning, you won't have nothing left of it. You neither, unless you get yourself out of here."

As they spoke, Catheryn Dubuisson lit a lantern. A pale yellow glow filled the interior of the wagon. She gestured to their belongings. "I can't leave these, Mr. Slade. They're all I've got in the world." She paused and smiled at him. "Can't you repair the wagon?"

He eyed her a moment, his face impassive. "Please," she whispered.

He stuck out his weathered hand. "Give me the lantern."

Minutes later, he reappeared. "The reach is broke, and the back axle snapped right in the middle." He looked at Phillip. "You got an axe, I'll chop the axle off, and then we can drag the bed back into the willows. Come morning, I'll rig you up a cart that'll get you into Fort Sill."

Phillip started to protest, but Catheryn laid her hand on his arm, a gesture not missed by Slade. "We'd be most grateful, Mr. Slade."

He nodded. "Mr. Dubuisson, you hook up the oxen. I'll take care of the axle." Inside the wagon, Slade chopped out the bolster and bed around the U-bolts and then went back outside to help Phillip complete the harnessing of the oxen.

Throwing a loop around the yoke and fastening the other end to his saddle horn, Slade turned the wagon back toward the cave. Phillip and Catheryn started to climb into the wagon, but Slade stopped them. "We'll walk in. It's going to be tough enough on the animals with the bed dragging."

Holding the lantern and leading the buckskin, Slade

headed to the shore, taking care to stay within the ruts.

"Why not cut straight across?" Phillip asked testily. "You're going at an angle this way."

A wry grin twisted Slade's lips. "Quicksand."

A startled gasp escaped Catheryn's lips.

The young man nodded. "This whole river is filled with pits. As long as we stay between these ruts you made, we're safe." He paused, then added, "You folks were damned lucky when you cut across the river. You managed to miss every quicksand pit along the way."

The rain gusts became more frequent. The wind began to moan with that long, drawn-out whine that never ends and is as much a part of the prairie as the sage itself.

Slade found a cave a few feet above the river that was large enough for them and all their gear. In one corner, he rigged a rope corral for the animals. Soon a cheery fire warmed the room while a pot of coffee boiled, giving off a full, rich aroma.

He explained how they would modify the wagon into a two-wheeled cart to carry them and some of their belongings to Fort Sill.

"No," said Phillip. "We'll go on downriver with you, but I'm staying at the Trace until our partner shows up." He hooked a thumb at the sandstone wall. "There's gold stashed here somewhere, and I'm going to get my share."

The howling wind whipped around the corner of the cave, fanning the coals. Slade's anger flared. "All you're going to do is get yourself killed. If—"

Catheryn Dubuisson deftly smoothed the waters.

"What Phillip means, Mr. Slade, is that we have provisions enough to allow us to remain until our partner arrives. After all," she added, a sly tone in her voice, "what's wrong with wanting to find gold? You probably know where a lot of it is, being part Indian, I mean." She hesitated. A distraught look crossed her face. "I'm sorry. I didn't mean to just blurt that out. I hope I didn't hurt your feelings."

Slade recognized the shrewd gleam in her eye. He had seen that same look in hundreds of Apache eyes. The Apache admired trickery more than bravery, but if a man was going to practice deception, he had to prevent his own face from giving him away. He leaned back against the sandstone wall and eyed the two of them carefully. "Yes . . . and no."

Catheryn frowned.

"What I mean is that yes, I know where much gold is, and no, you didn't hurt my feelings. I lived seven, almost eight years with the Apache—the Mimbres and then the Chiricahuas. The Mimbres first. Magnas Coloradas was their chief. I reckon you've heard the name."

"No," Catheryn replied. "Have you, Phillip?"

Her husband shook his head. "Only Apaches I heard of is those murdering savages, Cochise and Geronimo."

Slade continued to stare at them, his face revealing nothing. The young half-breed knew both Cochise and Geronimo. Back when Slade first came to the tribe, Geronimo's name was Gokhlayeh, the One-Who-Yawns. He was a magnificent storyteller, and he lived with the Mimbres until Cochise organized the Apache tribes into an attack on the Mexican village of Arizpe.

During the battle, Gokhlayeh fought as a demon defying the gods, and as a result, he gained the name Geronimo. After the battle, he placed himself under the leadership of the Chiricahua chieftain, Cochise.

Catheryn's voice dropped lower. "You say you know where there is gold. Around here?"

"No," he replied, lying with the casual aplomb of the Apache. "I know of none around here, but," he added when Phillip frowned at him, "I have heard the stories of this Spanish gold you seek. Believe me, the stories are only rumors. Now, if you were back in my country in Arizona, you could walk out of your tipi and come back with a handful of nuggets."

Phillip's lips curled in disbelief. He cut his eyes to Catheryn. An unspoken signal passed between them. He glanced at Slade and then said to his wife. "You can listen to this nonsense if you want. I'm going to get some sleep."

The sullen man leaned against the wall and folded his arms over his chest. When he closed his eyes, Catheryn moved closer to Slade. The perfume she wore enveloped the two of them. He glanced at Phillip, wishing that the man had retreated farther into the cave.

Outside, the rain beat down, whipping into the open mouth of the cave.

"I've heard stories like that, of gold nuggets just lying on the ground. Is that really true? Are there really places like that?" Her voice was soft and throaty.

Slade looked into her eyes. Yellow flecks of firelight danced in the deep blue of her irises. He felt a tightness in his throat. He swallowed. The sudden urge to impress her overpowered him. He said, "Where I come from in Arizona Territory, there's a valley with a chimney of solid gold that rises two hundred feet up the side of the canyon."

Catheryn caught her breath. She had heard claims like this, but she had never before met anyone who had firsthand knowledge of the location of such a bonanza. She laid her hand on his arm. It burned his flesh like a branding iron. "Tell me about it," she whispered, her voice courting him.

Phillip snored lightly.

Her fingers tightened on his muscular forearm. "Please."

His eyes held hers for several long seconds. What was this strange fascination she held over him?

"Please," she implored again.

"Why? It'll do you no good to know. It's far away, and if you did go there, the Apache would stop you. And if they didn't, the curse would."

His words puzzled her. "What curse?"

"The curse that goes with the canyon—the curse of the chimney of gold."

She laid her fingers on his forearm. "Please. Tell me."

Her pleading flattered Slade. He consented. "In the days when the Earth was being made, the Coyote was given the task of making all of the gold for the Great Spirit. The Raven was white then, like the dove, and his task was to carry the gold around the world and drop it so man could find it and make a good life for himself. But the Raven and Coyote decided to make a better life for themselves, so for each nugget the Raven dropped for man, he placed two in a great hole for him and the Coyote.

"Work did not progress as the Great Spirit wished. When He questioned them, the Raven and Coyote lied that there had been many unforeseen problems. Work continued slow. The Great Spirit asked the Apache for help. When the Apache discovered the truth, he went to the Great Spirit as he had been commanded.

"When the Great Spirit learned of the treachery, he cursed the Raven and Coyote as outcasts, as liars and thieves. He turned the Raven's feathers black as a symbol of death and cast the Coyote into the wilderness to be scorned as a scavenger. He then created great upheavals in the earth. The great hole was split down the middle. Nuggets were strewn over the earth, but many fell in the valley.

"From that time on, each outsider who picked up one of the nuggets died and was turned into another nugget. Only the Apache who is the obedient child of the Great Spirit can claim the gold without becoming a nugget."

He hesitated, shrugged, then added, "That is how the chimney of gold came into being. At least, that is what the Apaches believe. Only the Apache can approach the chimney. The curse slays all others."

"I don't believe in curses," Catheryn replied defiantly. "That's for fools."

Slade shrugged. "Who can say? I am part white, and I understand your words, but I have also seen many strange things in my life. I do not laugh at curses."

Her face clouded. She pouted her lips. "Why do they want it all? From what I hear, Indians are savages. They're too ignorant to understand just what gold can buy for them."

Anger burned Slade's cheeks. "If ignorance is being happy and content, then the Apache is truly ignorant, for he does not lie to himself that gold will make him happy as does the white man. The Apache is content with his land, and he is jealous of it. He will never permit the white man to intrude onto his land without fighting."

"The white man could bring the Indian many miracles of civilization," she replied. "Why—"

Slade interrupted. "When the white man finds gold, he builds towns and brings in civilization. With your civilization, there comes strange illnesses, killings, whiskey—many bad things." Slade paused. The frown wrinkling her forehead told him that she did not understand his words.

"I don't know about that sort of thing," she replied, smiling sadly. She glanced at her snoring husband whose mouth gaped open. "All I know is that if I had the money, I wouldn't be around here."

A gust of wind snapped around the mouth of the cave. The flames flared and sparks filled the air.

Catheryn ignored the wind and rain. She glanced at Phillip. "You've no idea what it's like to be shackled to someone who doesn't know how to take care of you, or of himself." She looked into Slade's eyes. Her fingers tightened around his forearm. She ran her tongue over her full lips, wetting them until they shone in the firelight.

She smiled. Her eyes danced. "Just suppose that you and I . . ." She hesitated. "It's silly, I know, but suppose you and I decided to go back to . . . say, Philadelphia with all of the money we wanted. What would you buy?"

He shook his head. The game she was playing was a

childish game, but strangely enough, he enjoyed it—almost wished it.

Slade studied her sensuous face.

"Well? What would you do with it?"

He shrugged. "I figure you could probably find a way to spend it for us," he replied, emphasizing the word *us*.

Catheryn laughed softly. Tiny lines radiated from the edges of her eyes. She squeezed his forearm. "You would love what I would buy for us. Fine clothes, travel—I've read about the nights at sea. Your—our own room, the fresh smell of salt air. Take a last walk around the decks before retiring to our boudoir. . . ."

Her voice trailed off. She looked deep into his eyes. She said no more, but the words unsaid throbbed in Slade's head.

He returned her look.

At that moment, Catheryn Dubuisson decided that she wanted to learn more from this man, that she and her husband would accompany Slade to Fort Sill, but she was shrewd enough to know that now was not the time to announce her intentions. She put her slender fingers over her lips to stifle a yawn. "I guess that means it's time for bed," she said, rising and reaching for her blanket.

Slade nodded silently and watched as she spread her blanket by her husband. She lay down. Under lowered eyelashes, her eyes caught his. A faint smile curled her lips. Her eyes never leaving Slade's, she smoothed the blanket by her side as a woman would do for her lover.

A lump caught in Slade's throat. He touched his tongue to his dry lips.

Finally, Catheryn Dubuisson pulled the blanket over her. "Goodnight," she whispered.

"Goodnight," he croaked.

* * *

It was still dark when Slade awakened. He looked to the mouth of the cave. A few stars twinkled through the clouds. He lay still, his ears tuned to the sounds of the night. Then he heard again the sound that had awakened him, a dull roar like distant thunder that vibrated the walls of the cave.

The fire had died. He rose silently in the dark and made his way to the mouth of the cave. The storm had passed, dragging after it a sky filled with broken clouds through which the moon struggled to shine.

He stood in the gaping mouth of the cave. Behind him, he heard a stirring. Tiny footsteps padded across the cave. "Is something wrong?" Catheryn stopped by his side, her hand on his arm.

"No. Just watching. Soon, you'll see why we had to get off the riverbed."

The roaring grew louder.

She clutched his arm. "What is it?" she asked, alarmed.

"You'll see."

Patches of white moonlight raced across the riverbed like a herd of Indian ponies, skimming over the ever-growing stream of water cutting through the sandy bottom.

"There," Slade exclaimed, pointing upriver. "That's what I warned you about last night."

She gasped and clutched his arm, pressing her body against his in an instinctive act of self-preservation against unknown danger.

To the west, a wall of water stretching from bank to bank raced toward them like a giant wave. The moonlight gleamed off the white foam churned up by the roiling waters. The roaring intensified. Darker objects, great trees uprooted by the water, twisted and swirled as the raging flood swept them away like pieces of straw.

"What the hell . . . ?"

Slade didn't look around. He had heard Phillip stumble from his blankets.

Phillip stopped behind Catheryn. "What the hell?"

Catheryn remained pressed against Slade, his arm between her breasts. "You've already said that once, Phillip." Slade's arm burned from the heat of her soft flesh.

The crest of the flood swept by, smashing its angry waters into the willow brakes and up the side of the sandstone bluffs. The willows bent. With a sudden lurch, several ripped from their roots and were caught up in the swirling maelstrom.

Just as quickly as the giant wave passed, so did the waters begin to recede, rushing back into the riverbed, pulling debris and small stones with them. Far downriver, the moonlight gleamed white on the churning heads of foam until they disappeared into the night.

Slade released his breath, now acutely aware of how closely Catheryn pressed against him. Was it a deliberate ploy? Or was she so stricken by the awesome forces of nature she had just witnessed? He could feel the warmth of her body searing his arm.

Phillip broke the silence. "It's a damn good thing we didn't stay on the river."

"Yeah," Slade replied, turning back into the cave. His eyes swept over Catheryn's face, but her gaze remained fastened on the turbulent waters rushing past the mouth of the cave.

He stirred the fire and slid a pot of coffee into the coals. "While the coffee is brewing, I'll get the wagon ready to work on. With the Kiowa around, we best be lighting a shuck out of here as soon as the river's down."

Phillip started to protest, but Catheryn stopped him. "We've reconsidered your offer, Mr. Slade. If you don't mind, we would like to accompany you to Fort Sill. As you say, it is foolish for just the two of us to stay out here with the Kiowas stirring up trouble. Our partner, Mr. Butler, will just have to wait."

Slade glanced at each of them and nodded. "Now you're making sense."

When Slade turned back to the fire, Catheryn shot her husband a warning look.

A sly smile played over Phillip's face. Under his breath, he remarked, "He doesn't strike me as the kind you can twist around your finger like the others, dearest."

She laughed. "Trust me, dearest. Have I ever let you down before?"

He shook his head. "No, but there's always a first time."

"Maybe so," she replied, laughing. "But this isn't it."

FIVE

Before they pushed out that morning, Slade cut a Moses' stick for Phillip. The six-foot staff was used to drive oxen. "You walk beside them, Mr. Dubuisson. Use the staff to direct them, not a whip."

Phillip glared at Slade, but Catheryn caught his eye. He fumed but said nothing.

A few miles from the cave, the river angled northeast, a half-mile-wide sandy band between imposing cliffs of dark red sandstone. Slade led the way along the side of the sandy bed, constantly alert and cautious. More than once, they pulled into willow brakes or hid in a cave.

On the fourth day, Slade spied a thin slash in the blood-colored bluffs on the south side of the river. He tugged on the reins. "Hold up," he called over his shoulder.

Phillip halted the oxen. After days of following such a cautious man, Phillip Dubuisson had to bite his lips to hold back his anger. He was sick and tired of constantly stopping, of concealing himself in the brakes, of hiding from shadows. "Now what is it?" Sarcasm weighted his words.

Slade ignored the derision. He nodded downriver. "Yonder. The road to Fort Sill."

Catheryn shot a warning glance at her husband. She forced a cheerful mood into her voice although she, too, had grown frustrated, but for a different reason. The unexpected rigors of the last few days had given her no time to use her charms to ferret the location of the gold from the young half-breed. "How much farther now, Mr. Slade?" She attempted to brush off some of the grime that had embedded itself in her cotton dress.

He touched his heels to the buckskin's flanks. "Four, maybe five days, depending on the Kiowas." He dismounted and waved them forward. "Let's get ourselves across the river during the daylight. Quicksand's easier to spot."

Without replying, Phillip, as Slade had earlier instructed, turned the oxen onto the tracks of the buckskin. "Don't stray to either side," Slade warned. "Those iron rims'll sink in the watery sand before you can catch your breath."

"I know, I know," Phillip muttered.

Slowly Slade led the way, his gray eyes studying the sandy bed at their feet, searching for the watery sheen that marked a quicksand pit. An hour later, they had zigzagged across the river to the Trace.

To the west, a red sun hung just above the horizon. Shadows fell into the narrow cut that twisted through the bluffs. The trail led through a natural path in the sandstone, one begun centuries earlier by runoff from heavy rains.

Travelers naturally followed the easier path. Hooves and iron wheels quickly cut through the soft sandstone until now the road lay twenty feet beneath the original bed. Sheer walls of bloodred sandstone rose above the Trace, which was no more than fifteen feet at its greatest width.

"Get your Winchester and wait here," Slade whispered, halting them at the mouth of the trail. He pulled the close-coupled buckskin around.

"What are you going to do?" Catheryn was concerned.

He glanced back at her. "Just scout ahead apiece. In case you hadn't noticed," he added, "this is a good spot for an ambush."

At his words, both Phillip and Catheryn looked around in alarm. Instantly they saw what he meant. The narrow trace, clothed in the shadows of the setting sun, snaked through the sandstone with more curves than a prairie sidewinder. Each bend could hide Kiowas.

Before either could reply, Slade heeled the buckskin and pulled his .44. The heavily muscled animal pranced forward, its hooves bouncing hollow echoes off the soft stone walls. Despite the coolness of the shadows, sweat rolled down Slade's back. His gaze swept the road ahead, searching for the slightest sign of danger.

Back in the cart, Phillip turned to his wife. His tone was sarcastic. "Well, have you learned anything from our lord and master, dearest?"

Her eyes blazed. "When the right opportunity presents itself, dearest. Just don't you worry."

Phillip snorted.

At that moment, Slade emerged from the stone canyon onto the sage and short-grass prairie that rolled away to the eastern horizon. For long minutes, he sat motionless in his saddle, his eyes studying the skyline. A breath of warm air brushed his leathery cheeks. Behind him, the sun slid slowly below the western horizon.

Satisfied that they were safe, Slade called over his shoulder, "Come ahead." But he kept the .44 leveled. Often, as a young boy, he had accompanied the Apache war parties, and he knew just how expertly an Indian made use of even the least cover. And the bunches of sage thickly dotting the prairie before him offered excellent hiding places.

"When are we stopping?" Phillip Dubuisson whined when they pulled up beside Slade.

The wiry young half-breed kept his eyes on the prairie before them. "Later." He nudged the buckskin, and the animal trotted stiffly forward. Slade pointed with his revolver to the east. "A couple miles, and then we'll camp."

Dubuisson shook his head. "I don't see anything wrong with right here."

Slade reined up. He glanced from Dubuisson to his wife. The frail, arrogant man had no idea just how lucky he was to have his wife accompanying him. Slade's patience was wearing thin as Durham paper. At that moment, he would have liked nothing better than to leave that wet-eared sonofabitch sitting in the middle of the damned prairie as a ready meal for the first passing band of Kiowas to feast on. But there was the woman.

Patiently, Slade explained, "Kiowas use the Trace to Sill regular. When they're not using it, they're usually watching it." We'll move off to the side of the road a couple miles and then keep it in sight on to the fort. That way, if any of Big Tree's braves are roaming around, we should spot them before they lay an eye on us." Slade paused, one eyebrow arched in question. "Well?"

Dubuisson glanced at his wife. Catheryn nodded. "Do as he says, Phillip. Mr. Slade has experience in these matters."

Stars sparkled overhead when Slade pulled up for the night. "This'll do. We'll camp cold until we reach the fort. No sense in telling Big Tree where we are."

"Cold camp? What can a small fire hurt?" It was Dubuisson again.

Slade dismounted and quickly removed his saddle. "Take a look at the horizon. What do you see?"

"Nothing except a bunch of stars. It's too dark," replied Phillip.

"Exactly. On a night like this, even a match could be seen for miles. If there was a moon, we could try a small fire, but not tonight." Without any further explanation, Slade turned to his horse and removed the saddle blanket and quickly rubbed down the buckskin.

Grudgingly, Catheryn and Phillip Dubuisson did as he said. As they pulled their blankets over their shoulders, Slade's voice came from the other side of the buckskin. "We'll rise early and get packed. At sunup, we'll build a small fire. Hot coffee and flour cakes. Soon as we're finished, we'll pull out."

"So fast?"

"Just in case some unwanted eyes see the smoke. By the time they reach us, we'll be gone."

Catheryn heard the scrape of his footsteps in the sand for a few feet until they faded away. In her mind's eye, she saw him spreading his blanket several feet from the wagon.

"No sense in all of us being in one spot," he explained from the darkness.

Phillip began snoring almost instantly. Catheryn considered paying Slade a late-night visit, but while she was making her plans, the day's strenuous travel caught up with her, and she fell asleep.

SIX

They rose early, ate a hasty breakfast, and hit the trail before the sun peeked over the horizon. The remainder of the day was the same as the first—long hours of steady travel in the hot sun, a brief noon break, and a cold camp at nightfall. As he had the night before, Slade spread his blanket away from the wagon.

And again Catheryn fell asleep as soon as her head touched her pillow.

Slade rose several times to kneel quietly beside a sage, tuning his ears to the sounds of the night. Nothing out of the ordinary.

The next day began as the previous. Shale and granite began to appear in the sandy soil.

The strain of the rigorous journey showed on all three. Catheryn's blue cotton dress was grimy and stained with perspiration. Her hair was windblown and tangled. Phillip had removed his tie and wore his jacket unbuttoned. His lacy shirt was limp and dirty. He scratched constantly at the irritation of an unaccustomed beard. Slade's clothes showed the least wear, just another thick coat of dust.

The cart rattled and groaned as the wheels bounced over sagebrush and dropped into shallow runoff races cut by infrequent rains. Slade maintained their course just below the crest of a gentle rise. On the other side of the rise, the prairie fell away to the Trace two miles below. Beyond, the terrain continued dropping into a great basin before ascending to another rise on the distant horizon.

From the saddle, Slade could see over the crest, yet his body and that of his animal offered no silhouette for unfriendly eyes.

Catheryn spoke up. "I don't suppose there's a water hole anywhere ahead? I'm dirty and tired."

"Yeah," Phillip chimed in. "We haven't seen anything except a lot of sun and sand the last couple days. I say we take a break. Camp early and have a hot meal."

Suddenly, Slade wheeled the buckskin and kicked the animal toward them.

Catheryn threw up her hand in alarm. "What the—," Phillip exclaimed as Slade slid the buckskin to a halt in a cloud of dust and grabbed the reins.

"Duck," he whispered hoarsely, wheeling and pulling the oxen after him down into a shallow arroyo not quite shoulder deep.

Once in the arroyo, he leaped from the saddle and shot a look in their direction. Phillip stood up and looked around for the cause of the alarm. "Dammit, I said duck," Slade spat out, ripping his slouch hat from his head and in the same motion flinging it to the ground. Without waiting for a reply, he slithered over the edge of the arroyo on his belly and quickly crawled to the top of the ridge, where he dropped to the ground at the base of a sagebrush.

Both Phillip and Catheryn rolled from the wagon seat and threw themselves against the side of the arroyo. They peered through the sagebrush, seeing nothing except sand and sage and Slade staring through the gray bushes down into the basin.

Phillip hissed through his teeth, "What is it?"

Slade kept his eyes forward. He waved behind his back for silence.

Across the basin, heading directly toward them, a small column of mounted Indians had topped the far rise and now trotted for the Trace. Squinting his eyes, Slade studied them. They were too distant to recognize the markings of the tribe. The party was too small to be on the warpath. Still, no squaws followed, and only two or three young boys tended a small remuda of no more than half a dozen horses.

The party moved at a rapid, but not urgent pace. Whatever their purpose, they were in no hurry, Slade surmised, although their steady gait indicated they did have a definite destination.

Slade counted. There were six, plus three young boys. He frowned. The sun beat down on his bare head. The taut skin over his cheekbones burned from its blistering rays.

His face showed no expression as his steel-gray eyes remained fastened on the column. If he had been a superstitious person, he would have made a sign for luck, hoping the column would turn onto the Trace. But he had no belief in anything beyond himself.

With the stoic fatalism of the Apache, he simply waited and watched. If the Indians continued toward him, that was the way it was. If they turned, that also was the way it was. Such uncomplicated beliefs made a hard life simple.

Within minutes, the Indians crossed the Trace without altering their direction. By the time they were halfway up the hill, he had identified them, but not by sight as much as sound. The jingling of bells. Kwahadi Comanches. Chief Quanah Parker's people. The daring chief, as a show of disdain for his enemy, tied small bells to his saddle, a practice his warriors quickly copied.

Although Slade hated the Comanches with the intense passion generated by his Apache upbringing, the white man's blood in Slade permitted him to admire the audacity of Quanah Parker, and the statement that the jingling bells flung in the face of the chief's enemies.

The young half-breed considered the Comanches' presence in this part of the state. The Kwahadis lived in the Palo Duro Canyons. What were they doing so far to the east? And with such a small party? Unless . . . His forehead knitted in a frown.

The column continued up the slope toward him. If the band did not change its course, within minutes he would have himself a lapful of Comanches. A rush of anticipation filled his body. Excitement coursed through his veins as his blood grew hot in anticipation of battle. He glanced over his shoulder at the Dubuissons. But not here, he told himself.

Quickly he returned to the cart. He picked up his hat and, in a few clipped words, explained the situation.

"You stay hidden. I'll draw them away." He studied the prairie around them. If the Kwahadis crossed over their back trail, they would discover the wheel ruts in the sand, which would lead them straight to Phillip and Catheryn.

He glanced to the southeast, toward the fort. "I'll lead them to due south. When we disappear over that far rise," he said, pointing to a sand hill some two miles distant, "you take off for the fort. The Trace is on the other side of this hill. Stay off the road, but keep it in sight. If you travel all night, you should reach the fort by morning."

Phillip smirked but said nothing. Slade knew what the thin man was wishing, the thoughts going through his mind. "But what if they capture you?" Catheryn asked.

Slade heard the concern in her voice, but he could tell from the fear in her eyes that her concern was not for him. He permitted himself a faint grin. "The Comanches are dogs. They capture only the blind or sick—or the white man," he added, looking deliberately at Phillip and slapping a sneer on his own lips. "I'll catch up with you before you reach the fort."

Suddenly frightened, Phillip drew the back of his hand across his dry lips. His eyes darted about with a wild look. "Maybe you shouldn't go. What if your plan doesn't work? What if the Indians don't follow after you? From what you've said, they'd come right across us."

Slade choked back the sharp retort that formed in his throat at Phillip's whining. He glanced at Catheryn. Fear was in her eyes, too, but she handled hers. He forced a smile. "I know the Comanches. A small band like that doesn't plan on much fighting. The extra horses are probably gifts, which means they're heading for a parley somewhere."

Catheryn's tiny voice was frail in the fragile stillness of the vast prairie. "But where?"

"Beats me." Slade shrugged. "But the bottom line is that they'll light out after me when I show myself."

Phillip snorted. "Says you. Suppose they don't? Suppose they keep coming straight? Suppose they—"

Slade's patience snapped. His eyes narrowed, and his broad jaw hardened. "Suppose you just throw a rein on your damned whining. We got work to do here, man. There's no time for crying, not"—Slade nodded to Catheryn Dubuisson, whose eyes were wide with fear— "not if you plan on taking care of your woman."

The younger man's caustic reply slapped Phillip across the cheek. His face grew livid, but Catheryn's hand on his arm held his tongue. He glared at Slade.

For several moments, the men stared into each other's eyes. Black humor curled one edge of Slade's lips faintly. If looks could kill, he thought. But that was probably the only way Phillip Dubuisson could kill, he told himself with disgust at the older man's obvious cowardice.

Slade nodded to the revolver on Phillip's hip and looked at Catheryn. When he spoke, it was to her. "Your husband's got a couple revolvers and the Winchester. You got plenty ammunition. If the Comanches don't come after me, I'll be back." He turned his eyes back to Phillip. "All you got to do is watch. When we disappear over that hill yonder, light a shuck out of here."

Phillip nodded. Hatred burned in his eyes.

Slade tugged his hat on his head and at the same time swept his gaze over his own gear. He withdrew his own

Winchester and chambered a cartridge before slipping it back into its deerskin boot. He checked the laces of the case that held his elmwood bow with two dozen iron-tipped arrows in their own deerskin case. He felt the .44 on one hip and the war club on the other. He was ready for the Comanches.

For a fleeting moment the years dropped away, and Slade remembered his own vision as a fourteen-year-old boy among the Apache, a vision of the black cougar.

After relating his vision to the venerable chief, Magnas Coloradas, Slade listened intently as the elder Indian whom he had grown to love as a grandfather explained the meaning of the dream. The words of the ferocious man still rumbled in his head. "The spirits have been kind to you. You have been given both great inner and physical bravery. Not even Gokhlayeh or Cochise has spoken of the black cougar. Use your gift well. The cougar will always be waiting for your call."

A few months later in the small town of Pinos Altos, Union soldiers murdered and decapitated Mangas Coloradas. When word reached the *rancheria,* Cochise called for patience and asked the tribe for time to consider the ramifications of the deed.

Slade refused to give Cochise the time, instead joining the Confederacy to fight the Federal troops and begin his search for his lost sister. He did his best to kill as many Union soldiers as possible, each time whispering a short prayer to the old chieftain.

And now, he felt the strength and daring of the black cougar coursing through his veins. With the grace of a mountain lion, he leaped into the saddle. He fixed his eyes on Phillip Dubuisson. "Remember what I said.

Keep the wagon down in this arroyo, out of sight. Soon as we top the rise, get the hell out of here."

Without replying, Phillip helped Catheryn climb into the cart.

"Be careful," she said.

Slade glanced around. Catheryn smiled at him. He nodded.

He guided the buckskin through the sage to the top of the rise. There, he would permit the Comanches to see him before he broke to the south.

His plan worked just as he hoped.

No sooner had the first Comanche spotted Slade than their blood-curdling war cries echoed across the prairie. Digging his heels into the buckskin's tender flanks, Slade drove the wiry animal into a blistering gallop. He raced south along the crest of the rise.

The entire party of screaming Comanches pounded after him, their tough, slender bodies leaning over the straining animals as if they were an appendage to the galloping horse. Slade didn't lie to himself. Next to the Kiowa, the Comanches' prowess with horses was unequaled. But Slade was not without skill.

Before the Comancheros murdered his mother, he had lived on horseback, small game hunting, hauling in venison, packing in pelts, and a hundred other tasks that demanded expert horsemanship, especially for one so young.

Now, with the brash confidence of the Apache, he figured there were very few Comanches who could outride him. But if one of them happened to be among the six in pursuit, that particular warrior had damned well better be able to fight like a wildcat.

Slade leaned over the buckskin's neck, his sinewy body fully in rhythm with the racing animal. Holding the reins in his left hand, he used his right to caress the buckskin's neck. He felt the power of the animal flowing into his own muscles, filling him with great strength.

A wave of giddiness swept over him as he envisioned the upcoming battle, but just as quickly, his common sense told him that now was not the time to die. That he could turn upon the pursuing six and slay most of them, he had no doubt, but for himself to survive would demand luck.

Luck was one chance he did not want to depend on. There was too much at stake. And luck was like a feather in the wind.

Not only did he have to get the Dubuissons to Fort Sill safely, but also at the fort, he reminded himself, was the Comanchero who could lead him to his sister. No, to stand and fight was foolish. Jake Slade could not afford to be foolish today.

The buckskin breathed well, his large nostrils channeling fresh oxygen into his lungs. Slade tightened the reins imperceptibly. The strong animal responded immediately. The pursuing Comanches were less than a mile behind now. The remuda was half that distance behind the riders.

He spied a shallow arroyo ahead. That's where he would make his cut to the east. Less than a mile ahead was the sand hill he had pointed out to Phillip and Catheryn.

What terrain lay on the far side of the rise, he had no idea. More of the same, he supposed. That meant that he could expect another hill. And that's where he would turn and attack.

Slade slowed even more. By the time he reached the top of the first hill, the screaming Comanches had closed the gap to less than a quarter of a mile. He slid the buckskin to a halt and stared back at the Comanches. He resisted the urge to potshot one of them. "Not yet," he muttered, swinging the buckskin around and digging his heels into the animal's flanks.

Sure enough, less than a mile ahead, another sand hill rose from the short-grass and sage prairie. Slade tightened his legs against the buckskin. The animal bunched its thickly muscled hindquarters and leaped forward. The wind whipped Slade's face, stinging it with grains of sand hurled from the horse's pounding hoofs.

Behind, six wild-riding Comanches raced down the sand hill in frenzied pursuit. A single white man was a great prize.

When Catheryn saw the last horse disappear over the rise, she said, "Let's go, Phillip."

Without replying, Phillip backed the cart out of the arroyo and pointed the oxen toward the Trace. He ignored Slade's instructions to walk beside the oxen, instead climbing up on the seat beside Catheryn. Gathering the loose ends of the reins, he stood and beat the plodding oxen in a futile effort to gain speed.

Catheryn grabbed his arm. "Stop it, Phillip. This is as fast as they can go."

Phillip plopped down on the seat. "Damn these beasts. What I wouldn't give for a horse."

The cart crawled toward the fort.

SEVEN

The wind stung Slade's sun-darkened skin as the buckskin flew across the sandstone and shale flat. At the crest of the next rise, Slade pulled up. Through narrowed eyes, he studied his pursuers. The Comanches were only seconds behind. Blood pounded in his ears. He jerked the buckskin around and raced to the base of the hill, where he spun and waited for the first Comanche to top the rise.

As if by magic, the elmwood bow appeared in his hand, an iron-tipped arrow nocked. His lips tightened into a thin, almost cruel line as he waited. The buckskin stood without moving. Now we will see how brave the Comanche truly is, Slade said to himself.

The lead Comanche burst over the crest of the hill, a wild scream on his lips. In the next instant, the surprised warrior threw out his arms and screamed as the arrow drove through his neck, ripping his jugular. The sudden impact somersaulted him over the rump of his warhorse. Blood spurted into the air.

The braves behind could not stop in time. They collided with the first. His blood sprayed them. They milled about in momentary confusion.

Slade had wasted no time. He fitted another arrow, and let it fly. A third followed in the next second. Without waiting to see the results, he turned and drove his heels into the buckskin's flanks.

Two stunned Comanches cried out. Each grabbed at the arrow suddenly appearing in his chest. They tumbled from their saddles. By the time the remaining three collected their shattered senses, Slade had gained several seconds. He was already two hundred yards away, leaning low over his horse's neck.

With a cry of rage, the Comanches drove their mustangs down the hill and set out in pursuit once again, their blind fury driving aside all reasoning. They did not stop to consider the skill with a bow of the man they were pursuing, that very few white men, if any, possessed such skill. Their only thought was to kill the white man.

The sparse-leafed sagebrush blurred as the galloping buckskin tore across the prairie. Slade's lips curled into a savage smile when he glanced over his shoulder. They were still pursuing. Gokhlayeh's words rang in his ears. The Comanches had the brains of the snake. One Apache was worth ten Comanches. Slade believed him.

A savage joy filled his body, expanding his muscles, swelling his veins with excitement. Ahead was another small rise. He tensed his muscles. Now was the time to finish it all. At the top of the hill, he leaped from his horse, yanked the Winchester from its scabbard, and pulled the buckskin to the ground as a breastwork.

Even as he brought the Winchester up and sighted

61

along the barrel, his mind raced with the oblique reasoning of the Apache. Should he kill the one at the rear first and work forward? He could kill them all in such a manner, for those in front would assume the bullet had missed.

Or should he kill the first one? Let the others see their own fate. A cruel grin twisted his lips. There was no choice. He blew the first one out of his saddle.

Two more shots rang out before the echo of the first reached the ears of Phillip and Catheryn Dubuisson.

Several hundred yards distant, at the base of the first rise where he had killed the first three Comanches, the three young Comanche boys watched with uncertainty. The small remuda had stampeded.

Slade mounted the buckskin as it lay, kicked it to its feet, and drove it toward the three boys. Instantly they wheeled about, ran into each other in their confusion, and finally untangled themselves and raced back in the direction they had come. Slade smiled grimly and pulled up. He didn't want to kill the young ones. Not if he could avoid it.

A whinny caught his attention. One of the mustangs had halted a short distance away. Slade frowned when he spied the beaded belt draped over the withers. A chill raced through him, cooling the blood boiling in his veins. He nudged the buckskin forward. He hoped the belt wasn't what it appeared to be.

Within the half hour, Slade caught up with Phillip and Catheryn and tied the Indian mustang to the rear of the cart. The sun seemed to pause on the horizon, bathing the western sky with a reddish orange glow. Catheryn glanced over his shoulder in the direction from which Slade had come. "Did you . . . I mean, are they . . ."

"They won't bother us now," he said.

, He glanced at Phillip, who stared at Slade with open resentment on his face. The slender man was like all weak men, gloating when stronger men fell, resenting stronger men's success.

"Dead?" Catheryn whispered in disbelief.

Slade nodded. He tossed the beaded belt to Phillip, who made an awkward grab for it. "A peace belt. Looks like they were headed for a parley with another tribe. Maybe even the Kiowas. He glanced at the setting sun. "Can't figure what Quanah would want to side up with the Kiowas about—unless it was because the government tried to put the Comanches and Kiowas on reservations at Fort Sill last year. Even the greenest shavetail should know that's like trying to grab water with your fingers. They were at each other's throats from the first day. But now, if they side up . . ."

Catheryn sensed the apprehension in Slade's words. "Trouble, do you think?"

Phillip snorted. "Just his imagination." He held up the belt in the last rays of the setting sun. "From all I hear, Kiowas and Comanches are mortal enemies. They're never going to side up against nobody." His words were a deliberate challenge hurled at Slade, who grinned crookedly and shrugged his broad shoulders.

"Think what you want, but we're riding tonight. We'll reach the fort tomorrow morning."

He pulled the buckskin around and continued southeast.

The night passed slowly. From time to time, Slade

glanced over his left shoulder at the Big Dipper. At midnight, the dying moon rose, illumining the prairie with a pale glow.

Phillip eyed the waning moon. He leaned toward Catheryn. "What happened to your plan with our hero there?" His voice carried an amused sneer.

Her eyes remained fixed on the trail ahead. "I'll figure something out, don't worry. You should know. Whenever I want something, I get it."

Slade called a halt. "We'll stretch ourselves for a few minutes," he said, pouring water from the canteen into his cupped hand and holding it under the buckskin's nose. Then he watered the oxen and the mustang.

Catheryn disappeared into the night. Phillip relieved himself next to the cart. "How far now?" he asked.

Slade shrugged. "Not far. Eight, maybe ten hours."

"You figure I'll be able to outfit us at the fort? Most forts have sutlers, don't they?"

"Yeah, there's a sutler there, but no need to outfit yourself," Slade replied. "The stage runs through there. It'll connect you with Dodge City." He nodded to the pony tied to the cart. "Sell the mustang if you want. You can get a few coins for him."

"Not yet," Phillip replied tersely. "We haven't finished what we came out to do."

Slade shook his head wearily and climbed into the saddle. Some people would never learn. Even after their close calls, they were still mule-headed. Bound to search out the gold. "Let's get us to the fort first," he said, clicking his tongue. "Then you can do what you want." The buckskin fell into a comfortable trot.

At sunrise, they paused for coffee and flour cakes in the foothills of the Wichita Mountains. The Wichitas are an oblong block of rough granite protruding several hundred feet above the scrubby plains. An oppressive stillness lay over the mountain range.

Just before ten, after four hours of following the rising and falling of the tortuous trail across the serrated ridges and sheer promontories of the Wichitas, they spotted lazy curls of smoke on the horizon. "Look!" Phillip shouted.

Catheryn looked at Slade hopefully. "Is that the fort?"

He nodded. "That's it. We'll be there in about an hour."

The mountain terrain was deceptive, its clear air appearing to lessen the distance between two objects.

Phillip laughed and whispered softly to Catheryn, too softly for even Slade's keen ears to pick up. Slade ignored the slender man. With satisfaction, he reminded himself that once they reached the fort, not only would he be rid of the couple, but he could also come face-to-face with one of the men responsible for the kidnapping of his sister fourteen years earlier. Right now, he was closer to finding her than he ever had been.

"Hell. Anyone can put up with this for another hour," he muttered under his breath.

While the woman, Catheryn Dubuisson, was attractive, and Slade felt himself drawn to her, he sensed also that she was trouble. Part of him did not want to leave her, while the other part, however reluctantly, was glad to be rid of her.

Just before noon, they reached the fort, if such could be called a fort. Built the year before by General Phillip Sheridan, Fort Sill was a ragtag, ill-constructed assortment of rectangular buildings arranged in a large square facing a parade field with a flagpole in the very center.

The post headquarters and the local church sat on the north side of the square. Across the square was a collection of small buildings, officers' quarters and enlisted men's barracks of weathered clapboard. The post exchange, livery, hay barn, and blacksmith bordered the east side of the parade field. On the fourth side was the mess hall, the brig, and the gallows. Beyond the brig, outside the fort proper, was the local watering hole, Bishop's Saloon.

Slade's eyes sought out the brig as soon as he entered the fort. He hoped Zeb's pistolero had been right, that this Mexican was the Comanchero with the chunk missing from the bridge of his nose, that this was the bastard who had raped and murdered his mother before shooting him and leaving him for dead. He glanced to his left.

Formalities first, he reminded himself, reining the buckskin toward the post headquarters. He was not too concerned about the Wanteds around here. The cavalry, as a rule, left civilian law enforcement to the local marshal.

A young enlisted man stepped from a doorway in the headquarters building and watched as the small party approached. His eyes swept past Phillip and Slade to settle on Catheryn Dubuisson, still attractive despite several days of dust and sweat.

Slade nodded. "Howdy."

The private returned the greeting, his eyes remaining on Catheryn. A lieutenant stepped onto the porch.

"Good morning. I'm Lieutenant Dobbins." He paused, waiting for a response.

A grin slid over Slade's face. Smart. Make the other party carry the conversation. Might be a shavetail, but he was learning the right way. Slade made the introductions. "Your commanding officer around?"

Lieutenant Dobbins tore his gaze from Catheryn. "Yes, sir. Captain Sheridan."

Slade arched his eyebrows.

The lieutenant laughed. "No, sir. No kin to the General." He gestured to the open door. "He's right inside here."

As the lieutenant spoke, Phillip climbed down and helped Catheryn to the ground. Slade dismounted, and the three of them stepped onto the porch.

Slade glanced around the quadrangle. Suddenly he froze. A cold fist clutched his heart. "Damn." Both Catheryn and Phillip spun at his exclamation. Catheryn gasped. She pressed her fingers to her lips.

On the gallows across the parade ground, a slowly revolving body dangled at the end of a rope. A detail of soldiers stood near a cart watching, waiting for the command to cut the dead man down.

Lieutenant Dobbins explained, "A renegade Comanchero." He hesitated, noticing the frustration scribbled across Slade's face. "Are you all right, sir?"

"Huh?" Slade blew through his lips. He removed his hat and ran his fingers through his short-cut hair. "I hoped I'd get here before you strung him up," he said as he stepped off the porch and headed across the quadrangle. He slapped his slouch hat against his leg and crushed it back on his head.

The lieutenant called after him, "Fifteen minutes earlier, and you would have made it." As he spoke, the detail backed the cart up under the gallows and cut the rope. The limp body bounced when it struck the wagon bed. One soldier threw a blanket over the dead man.

EIGHT

Catheryn watched Slade cross the parade ground to the gallows. To ask why the younger man was journeying to Fort Sill had never entered her head. Even now, his actions only aroused an idle curiosity in her.

The sun beat down on Slade's shoulder, but he didn't feel the heat. A terrible fear filled his heart, fear that the only man who could lead him to his sister was dead.

The corporal in charge of the detail looked around as Slade approached. He stepped in front of the cart, his eyes taking in the lithe, muscular man approaching. A sneer curled his lips when he saw that the man was a half-breed. He glanced past Slade to the post headquarters. Lieutenant Dobbins stood on the porch, and Captain Sheridan had stepped off the porch and was coming in his direction.

Slade nodded. "Corporal."

The beefy man's sneer broadened. "Yeah. Whatta you want, breed?"

The grin on Slade's lips remained fixed, but his gray eyes turned into slivers of ice. Without taking his eyes off the corporal, he replied coldly, "A look at the Comanchero."

Briefly, the corporal toyed with the idea of stomping the hell out of the breed and then running him off the post, but decided against it since that damned shavetail, Dobbins, and Captain Sheridan were looking on. He stepped aside. "Have a look. Maybe he's one of your own," he added, his voice heavy with sarcasm. "Too bad you missed our little hoedown. It was some necktie party."

Slade ignored the man. He pulled the issue blanket back from the Comanchero's face, expecting to see a swarthy face with part of the nose missing.

A surge of excitement raced through him, but his expression did not change. The dead man was not the one he sought. That meant his man was still alive. Slade looked to the west, disappointed because of the fruitless trip he had endured, but pleased because his man was still out there somewhere.

Without a word, he pulled the blanket back over the man's still features and turned back to the post headquarters.

"You know him?"

Slade halted abruptly, face-to-face with another officer. He saw the captain's bars. "You must be Sheridan." He extended his hand. "Name's Slade. And no, I don't know him."

Catheryn and Phillip Dubuisson were shown to their quarters, but Slade turned down the captain's offer to bunk in the dog house.

They sat in the captain's office. "That Mexican out there. His name Vado?"

Sheridan shook his head. "Montoya. Luis Montoya. At least that's the name he gave us."

"Any other prisoners?"

"Nope. Montoya was the only one left alive after Captain Anderson attacked their band near the Adobe Walls."

"Anderson? I though McClellan was the one who captured the Comancheros."

Sheridan shook his head. "Captain McClellan is out of Fort Richardson. Word is that he captured some Comancheros in another encounter, but he's taking them to Fort Richardson. Anderson got this one."

A frown darkened Slade's face. So there were two bands of Comancheros. At the first opportunity, he needed to telegraph Richardson.

"I'd like to see Captain Anderson if you don't mind."

"He's on patrol, but you're welcome to hang around. It'll be a couple days before he returns. There's not much for a civilian to do around here except for the church or the bar, whichever you might be partial to. Like I said, I can have Private Loomis show you to the dog house. Nothing elaborate about army barracks, but they're dry."

"Thanks anyway, Captain," Slade replied. "If it's all the same to you, I'd just as soon camp outside the post."

Fourteen years of sleeping under the stars except for a few nights in tents during the War of the Secession was a difficult habit to break. Besides, there was no telling when some of those old Wanteds might show up, or someone come along who recognized him.

"Let me know if you change your mind."

"What about the Comancheros McClellan's patrol captured? Any names? Anything at all?"

"No." Sheridan frowned at the question.

"If you could accommodate me, Captain, I'd like to send a telegraph to Fort Richardson."

Sheridan arched an eyebrow.

"I'd sure like to find out if any of McClellan's prisoners has a chunk missing from the bridge of the nose."

Sheridan hesitated.

Slade knew that the army wires were not intended for civilian use. "It's important, damned important."

The captain studied the younger man, then nodded. "We can handle that for you." He called his aide into his office and gave him the message.

"The bridge of the nose is missing. Like it was shot away," said Slade. "That's the one I'm looking for. His name might be Vado."

The aide scribbled words onto a pad and departed.

Sheridan said, "This might take only a few minutes or several hours, Mr. Slade. You be around here?"

"I'll be here."

"You sure you won't take my offer about the bunk?"

"No, thanks."

"Suit yourself," Captain Sheridan replied, taking a longer look at the younger man. Younger, yes, Sheridan thought, but a hell of a lot more dangerous than anyone he had ever known. "You look familiar, Mr. Slade. Do we know each other?"

The hair on the back of Slade's neck bristled. Open questions spooked him. Thoughts of the gunfight and the dead Texan down in East Texas came rushing back. He looked at the captain warily. "Doubt it."

Sheridan leaned back in his chair and grinned warmly. "I'd swear we've run across each other. You from around this part of Texas?"

The captain's questions seemed innocent enough, just friendly banter. "Nope." Slade thumbed over his shoulder. "Arizona. Out to California once or twice, but mostly around Tucson and down south."

"Never been out there myself." He rocked forward and reached for a cigar. He offered Slade one. "You known the Dubuisson couple long?"

Slade bit off the end of the cigar and spat it on the floor. "Ran across them north of the Red," he answered, striking a match with his thumbnail and touching the flame to the cigar. He drew in deeply and blew a fragrant plume of smoke into the air.

"How did the three of you end up here?"

Dropping into a chair with his back to the wall, Slade told Sheridan the story.

"They really believe there's gold along the Red?" The captain was amused.

"Don't ask me why. Maybe because of the caves, and the old Spanish Mexicans' liking for hiding gold in caves."

Sheridan studied the cigar between his fingers. "Damned shame the government can't stop fools like them. They're both green as grass about the West. It isn't like back north in Boston or wherever. Out here, you got to be on your toes even going to the latrine." He turned and stared at Slade. "You got any influence, send 'em back east."

Slade grinned. "I got no influence on anybody." His face grew somber. "But I did run across something out there I figure you best know."

Captain Sheridan leaned forward as Slade told him of the encounter with the Comanches and the peace belt. When Slade finished his story, Sheridan shook his head.

"There's something in what you say, all right. There's been unusual unrest on the reservation lately. We been trying to get a handle on it."

"Just wanted you to know," Slade said. He rose to his feet and waved the stub of the cigar at the captain. "Thanks for the smoke. If—"

A knock at the door interrupted him. The captain's aide entered briskly, handed the captain a dispatch, and left the office.

Sheridan's face reflected his growing disgust as he read the message. "Damn," he muttered, handing it to Slade. "Here's the answer to your inquiry. It isn't what you were looking for."

The younger man arched an eyebrow at the captain's change in demeanor. He read the message and understood the reason for Sheridan's profanity. The prisoners had escaped when a band of Comanches attacked the patrol. But no one remembered seeing a Mexican of Slade's description.

He crumpled the paper into a ball and tossed it in the trash. He stared out the window at the stark mountains around them. A sense of frustration washed over him, filling him with despair. Another dead end. Was the Mexican with the bad nose even alive? After all these years, he could be dead. Maybe Slade was only chasing a ghost.

"Dammit," he said between clenched teeth. He wasn't going to quit now. The man still lived. And Slade would find him, somewhere, sometime.

Captain Sheridan studied the younger man. He broke the awkward silence. "Sorry about the bad news. The offer still goes for that bunk."

Slade looked around as if he were seeing the captain

for the first time. The hardness faded from his face, and he forced a crooked grin. "It isn't the first time I've been disappointed. I don't reckon it'll be the last. Thanks again, but if you don't mind, I'll see to my animal and then find me a big steak to put myself around."

Captain Sheridan grinned and walked out onto the porch with Slade. The young breed was a friendly sort, wary, but that was to be expected. Still, he looked mighty familiar. Sheridan drew deeply on his cigar as Jake Slade climbed into his saddle and turned the buckskin toward the livery. He sure as hell rode well, almost military. Sheridan scratched his head. He was damned well certain he knew the young man from somewhere. Releasing a deep sigh, he returned to his desk. Never mind. Sooner or later, he would remember where he had seen Jake Slade.

NINE

The buckskin whinnied as Slade rubbed his damp hide with a handful of straw. The animal turned its head to watch the man by his side. The animal was still a biter, Slade figured, but it had learned painfully not to nip at him.

A wry grin played over Slade's lips when, from the corner of eyes, he saw the buckskin staring at him. The puzzled animal had no idea what was happening when it tried to bite him.

The young half-breed had broken the buckskin quickly from the habit, using a trick he had learned early in his cavalry career from Zeb Walker.

He sharpened a small branch and stood beside the animal. He held the pointed stick on his hip where the buckskin had first nipped him. Every time the animal reached around to bite, the horse jammed its nose on the sharp point. The buckskin was a smart horse. After a few efforts to nip Slade, the animal realized that there was something about this particular human that caused pain—but only when the animal tried to bite.

Slade finished the rubdown and dumped a measure of

oats into the trough. "There you go, boy." He slapped the buckskin on the rump.

The livery doors swung open, spilling a patch of yellow sunlight onto the dirt and straw floor. Slade stiffened. His hand rested on the handle of his .44 as he squinted against the sudden light in an effort to discern the features of the approaching man. He relaxed. It was only Phillip Dubuisson.

His stiffly erect carriage gave him away. "Ah, Mr. Slade. I was hoping to find you." Phillip stopped at the end of the stall.

"Well, you found me. What can I do for you?" With a final smack on the horse's rump, he stepped outside the stall and fastened the rope gate.

Phillip hesitated. He tilted his chin slightly. "Mrs. Dubuisson and I . . . well, we talked it over and decided we would like to hire you to lead us back to the Red River to meet our partner. We have more than sufficient funds for outfitting. Your responsibility would be to—"

Slade shook his head and started for the door. "Not interested."

"But—" Phillip hurried after him. "At least listen to our offer."

"No need." The younger man continued walking. "I got other things to do."

Phillip grabbed Slade's arm and jerked him around. "Dammit. Now you listen to me, you heathen half-breed. I said that—" The words stuck in his throat and his eyes bulged at the wicked-looking knife that had magically leaped into Slade's hand, the point pressed into the flesh under Phillip's chin.

Phillip glanced into the younger man's eyes, and his

blood ran cold. Jaw set, eyes narrowed, Slade's face was a mask of hatred and fury.

Slade hissed. "Don't . . . ever touch me again." He fought to control the sudden fury that had exploded within his body. His brain understood what had happened, but instinct had taken over. In his daily element, such reactions were essential for survival, but in the more civilized environment of the fort, they caused nothing but trouble.

Here, they were in Phillip's world. Out there, in the willow brakes, on the sage prairie where the wind blew clean and free, they were in Slade's. The muscles in his jaw twitched as he realized just how close he had come to killing Phillip Dubuisson. Slade sheathed his knife, but the fear remained in Phillip's eyes. The frightened man took a step back, then stepped around Slade and hurried from the livery.

Slade took a pint of rotgut Indian whiskey from his saddlebags and then threw them over his shoulder. He downed several gulps and jammed the bottle in his pocket. At least, he had not hurt Phillip Dubuisson.

By the time Slade reached the post exchange, absorbed two more slugs of whiskey, and watched as a thick steak surrounded with mounds of fried potatoes was placed in front of him, he had pushed the incident with Phillip aside. Quickly he dispatched the steak and potatoes and downed two cups of steaming coffee, the second while he smoked a cigar.

Later, his belly full, Slade stood on the porch of the exchange as the sun dropped below the horizon. Across the parade ground, beyond the gallows, the lights of Bishop's Saloon beckoned from the darkness.

He sauntered through the deepening shadows to the saloon.

Inside, he sat at a rear table nursing a tumbler of Bishop's watered-down, molasses-treated whiskey, to all appearances oblivious to the ebb and flow of the laughter and shouting and profanity from the boisterous soldiers milling about the saloon. But his eyes missed nothing. He couldn't afford to miss anything.

The batwing doors swung open and a large soldier, obviously drunk, staggered in, his voice the bellow of a bull. It was the big corporal who had jeered Slade at the gallows. "Hey, Bishop. Lemme have 'nuther bottle. A live one. That last one's already dead." He laughed loudly.

Slade watched warily, hoping the corporal would take his bottle and return to wherever he had come from.

The corporal didn't oblige. He spied Slade, and a cruel grin turned his thick lips inside out. He staggered across the room. "Look here who we got. The breed." He jerked to a halt and glared down at Slade with his bloodshot pig-eyes. "What the hell you think you're doing in here, drinking with white people?" He swayed on his feet.

The smoke-filled room grew silent. Bishop hurried from around the bar to head off any trouble. "Come on, Sam. The kid's not hurtin' no one." He tugged on the corporal's arm. "Come on back to the bar. Let me buy you a drink."

"Go to hell," the bulky man bellowed, jerking his massive arm from the bar owner's grasp. "I don't drink with no Injuns, and I sure ain't goin' to drink with no breed."

Slade slid his chair back slowly and stood up to face

79

the larger man. He was being deliberately provoked. He wanted no trouble that would call attention to himself. He still had a few days to await Captain Anderson's return. That he could take the corporal, he had no doubt. The man's muscle had gone to flab, and Slade was wiry as green willow and tough as the iron tips on his arrows. "That being your feelings," he replied, "I reckon I'll mosey on." He hoped the corporal did not press the matter.

The sneer on the corporal's face grew larger. "I figured you was a coward. Get one of you damned redskins alone and your backbone turns to mush."

Slade had his answer. The corporal refused to let him back away from the fight. For whatever reason, the whisky or just his hatred for the Indian, the larger man wanted a scrap. Slade shook his head. Damned hardheaded man anyway. "Look, Corporal. You're pushing for trouble. I don't want any. Just step aside, and I'll walk out of here."

The big man did not move. The other soldiers pulled in around the two men. Bishop was still trying to get the corporal to back off.

Glancing at the expressions on the other soldiers' faces, Slade knew without a doubt that he would be forced to fight. He had to make it fast. To string it out would only encourage some of the other soldiers to join in once their own kind started taking a beating.

Slade's arms hung relaxed at his side.

The corporal leered at him. "You ain't walking away nowhere, breed. I'm gonna bust you into pieces and sweep you out with the rest of the manure."

Without warning, Slade kicked the table into the corporal's knees, causing the big man to fall forward. As he did, Slade swung from the floor, smashing his balled fist into the big man's throat. He felt cartilage give.

The corporal's eyes bulged, and he fell to the floor, clutching his throat and struggling to suck in gulps of air. Quickly, Slade knelt by his side and felt his throat. It was not permanently damaged, but it would be damned sore for several days, and he sure as hell wouldn't feel like bellowing at anybody else.

Slade glanced up into the ring of surprised faces. "Get him to his bunk, and get one of your medics to tend him. He'll live." He rose and started for the door. Surprised soldiers stepped aside, clearing a path for the young man.

Once outside, Slade hurried to the livery. A figure stepped from the shadows as he approached. It was Catheryn Dubuisson.

"Hello, Jake." Her voice was throaty and inviting.

He nodded, a warm feeling flowing through him. "Mrs. Dubuisson."

She laid her hand on his arm and stepped closer. "Call me Catheryn. We know each other well enough for that, don't you think?"

Her hand burned his arm. "All right—Catheryn." He glanced around for her husband. "What are you doing out here? Even if it is a fort, you're not safe out at night by yourself. Where's Mr. Dubuisson?"

She laughed bitterly. "Back in our room, drunk. Anyway, don't fool yourself. I can take care of myself. Besides, I was waiting for you." She tugged him toward the livery. "Let's go in here where we can be alone."

Slade pulled back. This was asking for trouble. A white woman and a half-breed on an army post. Still, thoughts of her warm and soft body tempted him. But why here? Why now? The Apache upbringing prickled his skin. "What's got into you, Catheryn?"

"What do you mean?"

"Why me?"

"You're you," she said.

"You mean different?"

"Partly, but the main reason is that you're a man, a real man. Phillip . . ." She hesitated. "Well, Phillip is sweet and gentle to me, but he's a weakling. I don't like weaklings. I like men who are strong, who know what they want, and who stop at nothing to take what they want. Besides," she added seductively. "How many white women have you been with?"

"Enough."

His answer surprised and confused her. "Oh, I . . ."

He laughed now. "Others have felt as you, Mrs. Dubuisson. And to be honest, I'd be lying if I said your suggestion wasn't downright tempting. You're a right beautiful woman." He paused to gesture to the buildings around them. "But this is not the time or place."

Her demeanor changed. "Well, if that's how you feel, you can go in the stable and sleep with your horse. Besides, I was just seeing what you would say. I wouldn't dream of doing anything with an Indian," she added caustically. She spun on her heel and stormed away.

As she disappeared into the shadows of the post headquarters, Phillip rose to meet her. "What went wrong?" he asked in a whisper so soft she had to lean forward to hear it.

"Nothing."

"Something must have," he replied, his voice containing a trace of sarcasm. "I thought you had the perfect blackmail scheme."

"Oh, shut up," she retorted, tossing her blond hair and brushing past her husband.

In the livery, Slade wasted no time in saddling the buckskin. He tied his warbag behind the cantle. Catheryn Dubuisson's behavior puzzled him, but he knew for sure that hanging around the fort now would be asking for trouble. Once some of the corporal's drunken friends had time to think about what had transpired, they would become indignant and want to redress the humiliation the corporal had brought on himself.

He wound his way up into the mountains surrounding the fort, finding a suitable camp beneath a granite overhang hidden behind a clump of mountain cedar. To the south, lightning flashed. The wind freshened against his face.

Throwing his tarp on the ground under the overhang, he spread his blankets on one half of the tarp. The other half, he pulled over him as a cover against the rain.

Slade lay on his back, his hands behind his head, staring into the fast moving clouds overhead. He waited for sleep, but it was long in coming. And he never could figure out exactly what Catheryn Dubuisson had been up to, but he had the uncomfortable feeling that she had more on her mind than bedding him.

TEN

Slade remained in the desolate wilds of the Wichitas for the next two days, preferring the solitude of his camp to the daily hubbub and bustle of the post. He drank from a tiny spring of sweet water that rose from the mountainside rugged with faults and folds into a small pool. Between him and his buckskin, there was little water to spare.

The first day, he waited three motionless hours to snare a rabbit. After checking its belly, he roasted it, providing himself with the only solid meal during his stay in the mountains. This country, he decided, was as sterile and unproductive as a gelded pony. No wonder the government decided to make it a reservation for the Comanches and Kiowas. And no wonder the Indians resisted.

While he awaited the return of Captain Anderson, Slade busied himself with the repair and maintenance of his gear, tedious tasks for which there was little or no time during his travels.

From his vantage spot high in the jagged mountains, he had a perfect view of the post below. Occasionally,

Catheryn Dubuisson left her quarters and went into the post exchange. While the distance to the post was too great to discern individual features, her blond hair made her easily identifiable as she accompanied Phillip to the livery and then to the blacksmith with disturbing regularity.

The young half-breed rubbed his jaw as he speculated on what they were up to. He had an idea, and he hoped he was wrong.

Late afternoon of the third day in camp, Slade spied Captain Anderson's patrol coming through the pass. Exhausted troopers slumped on weary horses that plodded down the dusty trail winding through the granite slabs in a circuitous course to the fort.

Wasting no time, Slade broke camp.

When the patrol entered the fort, the young half-breed was waiting, leaning against the hitching rail in front of the livery, his slouch hat pulled low over his eyes against the sun. His arms were folded over his chest.

Patiently he waited as the captain reported to the post headquarters. Later, both Captains Anderson and Sheridan stepped onto the porch. Sheridan pointed out Slade. Anderson headed toward the livery, leading his horse.

Just before he reached Slade, the livery door swung open and the large corporal Slade had put down in Bishop's Saloon stepped outside. He saluted Anderson. The captain returned his salute. "Take care of my horse for me, Corporal." He handed him the reins.

The big man took the reins and turned to lead the animal into the livery. He stiffened visibly when he saw Slade, but continued inside, his pig-eyes glaring at the younger man. Slade ignored him.

Anderson introduced himself. "Captain Sheridan tells me you've been waiting around for a few days to see me."

"That's right, Captain. It's about that Comanchero that was hanged a few days back. Sheridan says it was your patrol that caught him."

"Yeah." Anderson paused and pointed to the saloon. "I don't know about you, Mr. Slade, but I've been on water and rations for a week now. Officially, I'm off duty, and I'd like a drink. How about it?"

Slade returned the captain's grin. "Sounds good to me," he replied, taking an instant liking to the older man. He unhitched the buckskin and fell into step with the captain.

The saloon was dark and cool, and the whiskey burned as it went down. Anderson poured another. Slade declined a second. "Word came back to us when we were camped north of Palo Duro that the Comancheros were running between Fort Bascom and Adobe Walls. Well, sir, when I heard that, there was nothing on God's green earth that was going to stop me from breaking up that renegade band of murdering bastards. You can understand that."

"Yeah. I can," Slade replied. He hesitated. The big corporal pushed through the batwing doors and headed for the bar. Slade continued. "But what puzzles me is what they were doing so far north. This is the first time I ever heard of them operating around that part of the state. Especially with the cavalry running all about trying to keep the Kiowas and Comanches on the reservation."

Anderson shrugged. "No telling. I figure it was a

onetime sweep to see what they could pick up. Hoping, like you say, that the cavalry was too busy with other matters." He laughed. "They sure got the hell surprised out of them."

He then moved the bottle and glasses about on the table to illustrate his tactics. "We waited behind these two sand hills. Over here, a few hundred yards beyond the hills was an arroyo. I stationed men on both hills and in the arroyo. After the bastards passed the hills, we opened up, drove them straight to the arroyo." He drained the last of his whiskey. "We whipped their asses good." And he slammed the glass down on the table as if to punctuate the finality of his words.

"You captured everyone?"

"Either captured or killed."

"Any more Mexicans?"

Anderson nodded. "Three Mexicans and four Indians—Comanche, I guess."

"Or Papago."

The captain arched an eyebrow.

Slade nodded. "More Papagoes ride with the Comancheros than Comanches. Any of the Mexicans have part of his nose shot off?" Slade touched his finger to the bridge of his nose.

"Nope. Young boys for the most part, but none like you describe. He the one you're looking for?"

"That's the one."

Captain Anderson drained his glass. "Wish I could have been more help."

Slade grimaced. "Me too, Captain, me too."

"Anyway, the Comancheros will probably stay in their own backyard now."

Slade grinned. "Don't kid yourself. Those Comancheros know how busy the Comanches and Kiowas are keeping you bluecoats. They'll be back."

Anderson laughed. "I wish they would. They'll be in for a big surprise if they do."

"How's that?"

The captain lowered his voice. "A colonel by the name of Mackenzie is coming with reinforcements for Fort Richardson, Griffin, and Concho to make sure the Comanches and Kiowas stay on the reservation. That frees the rest of us to take care of those murdering Comancheros." He grinned broadly. "I can't wait for him to get here."

Slade considered the new information. "Well," he drawled. "I wish you good luck."

Anderson studied Slade carefully. The laughter faded from his face. "You really believe we'll need it, don't you?"

"Captain, when I was a boy growing up with the Apache, I had a friend who wanted to prove just how brave he was. He kept saying, like you, that he couldn't wait—he couldn't wait for a chance to prove himself. One time a band of Papagoes was passing through. He planned to steal some of their horses. It would be a fine coup. That night he slipped into the camp." He paused.

"Well?" asked Sheridan, leaning forward.

He replied without emotion. "They killed him." Slade pushed back from the table and rose to leave. "Appreciate the drink, Captain. But I need to be moving on."

Anderson reflected on Slade's story, then rose to his feet. "I'll walk out with you," a more somber Anderson said. Slade nodded, but said nothing.

"Where you heading now?"

"This lead's dried up. McClellan had some prisoners, but they escaped. I don't think my man was with them, but I'm not sure. Anyway, they're probably all down in Sonora soaking up tequila by now. So, I reckon I'll ride up to Fort Bascom, then back home."

"Arizona?"

"Tucson—just outside there."

Anderson stopped just outside the batwing doors. Slade turned to him. "Look, Mr. Slade. If you're not in an all-fired hurry, hold off leaving tonight. We got to deliver supplies to Fort Bascom. We need a scout. Pay's good; grub's not fancy, but solid. It'll give you a small grubstake for wherever your search for the Mexican takes you next."

Slade eyed the captain curiously. "Who said I was going to keep looking for him?"

Anderson grinned like a redbone hound eyeing a chicken egg. "Hell, man. Nobody hangs around an army post for pure pleasure. Something mighty powerful held you around here, I figure. Not that it's any of my business, you understand."

"No big secret," Slade said, stepping off the porch and unhitching the buckskin. "Comancheros stole my sister. I'm still trying to find her."

The grin on Anderson's face faded. "I'd reckoned on something, but not that. Anyway, good luck to you. Now, what about that scouting job?"

Slade swung into the saddle. He was surprised at the hospitality shown him. And the scouting job would buy some grub. Living off the land wasn't the best way to pack on winter fat. He nodded to the Kiowas leaning against the hitching rail in front of the livery. "You got scouts."

"We'd like you to scout for us."

"Why?" He stared down into the open face of Captain Anderson.

"Two reasons. First, the Kiowas and Comanches are running wild through the Panhandle." He arched an eyebrow. "Off the record, I can't say as I blame them. We took them off their Panhandle reservation in '68 and brought them here." He gestured to the weather-beaten mountains. "How would you like to be forced to live around here? Hell, the land's as barren as old Cooty's mare and useless as hind tits on a boar hog. I want somebody ahead of me who knows Indians, and who won't back down from a fight."

The younger man considered Anderson's words. "How do you know I won't?"

"That's the second reason. I remember you from Topotomoy Creek."

Slade arched an eyebrow. "You were there?"

"Yep. Six or eight of us on this post was there." A rueful grin spread over his face. " 'Course, we were on the other side."

Narrowing his gray eyes, Slade studied the captain. "It was a good fight, wasn't it?"

Anderson grinned. "For you Rebs, but not for us."

Slade returned the captain's grin. "What time you pulling out?"

Anderson nodded. "Sunrise, day after tomorrow. You can draw your pay at Bascom."

"See you then." Slade pulled the buckskin around and headed out of the post.

As he rode off, the large corporal pushed through the batwing doors and stopped at Captain Anderson's side.

"I wish I could get that sonofabitch alone for five minutes," he muttered, his voice a hoarse croak.

Remembering Slade's story about the fate of his boyhood chum, Anderson said, "Don't wish too hard, Corporal. You might get your wish."

"That's okay with me."

"Don't be too sure, Corporal."

"How's that, Captain?"

"Back in 1863, that young man there was with that bunch of Johnny Rebs that whipped our asses at Topotomoy Creek. You haven't forgotten Topotomoy Creek, have you, Corporal? You were there."

The large corporal frowned at the captain. "What are you talking about, sir?"

Anderson watched Slade ride off the post grounds. He replied, "Captain Sheridan finally remembered where he had seen the man before. Mr. Slade was just a kid then, probably no more than fourteen or fifteen, but he was good enough to ride with J.E.B. Stuart when they rode around McClellan's Army of the Potomac, cutting our supply lines and fooling the general into believing he was outnumbered two to one when it was really the other way around. That was the same ragtag and bobtail band of Confederate cavalry that General Lee's son and nephew rode with."

"Damn," the corporal muttered. He sure as hell remembered Topotomoy Creek. He would never forget June 12, and how the Union's 56th Cavalry outnumbered Jeb Stuart's band six to one. But those damned Confederate boys went right ahead and routed the hell out of the 56th, sending them scattering through the briars like scared rabbits. "I wonder if Colonel Cooke ever spoke to Stuart again?" he said of the 56th's commanding officer.

Anderson laughed. "Hell, Corporal. What would you do if your son-in-law scattered your command like a possum loose in the henhouse?"

ELEVEN

Two mornings later, Anderson rose before sunup. He glanced at the clock on the stand by his bunk. Four o'-clock. He dressed quickly, ready for his eye-opening mug of steaming coffee over at the mess hall. He strapped on his army-issue revolver and grabbed his hat. The captain opened his door and halted abruptly. He grabbed for his sidearm, then relaxed.

Slumped astride his buckskin at the hitching rack, Slade nodded. "Been waiting for you, Captain. You boys sleep late around here."

Anderson laughed. "You scared the hell out of me." He gestured to the mess hall. "Let's get some coffee first."

Over coffee, hot biscuits, red-eye gravy, and fried meat, Anderson briefed Slade. "Twelve days is what I figure it'll take us."

Slade frowned. "Twelve? Hell, Captain, what's the Army having us do, pick up buffalo chips along the way? The Apache can make a trip like that on foot in four days. Even with wagons, we should make it in eight days, nine at the most."

93

A wry grin ticked up the edges of Captain Anderson's lips. "Not when you got civilian passengers."

Slade suppressed a surge of excitement. He had been right in his speculations. In a flat voice, he said, "The Dubuissons talked Sheridan into letting them go, huh?"

"How'd you know?" Anderson asked around a mouthful of gravy and biscuits.

"Figured they would. They've got their minds set on gold. Dubuisson tried to hire me, but I turned him down." He sipped his coffee. The Dubuissons' decision was poorly made, but at the same time, Slade felt an increasing excitement knowing that he again would be traveling with Catheryn Dubuisson.

Briefly he told Anderson of his meeting with the Dubuissons and the subsequent journey to the fort, although he omitted the nocturnal visit Catheryn paid him outside the livery. "I was hoping they'd pack up and head back to Philadelphia. I even left them an Indian pony if they was strapped for cash."

"Well, they sure as hell aren't going back to Philadelphia. I got my orders to take them with us as far as the Red River."

Draining his coffee, Slade rocked back in his chair and said in a matter-of-fact tone, "They'll get themselves killed out there."

"That's what Sheridan told them," Anderson said, mopping up the last of the gravy with a chunk of biscuit. "But that's their own lookout. We're just servants of the population. If we refuse, they remind us their taxes pay our salaries, little as they are," he added, a trace of bitterness in his words.

Slade permitted himself a small grin. He knew what the captain meant. Civilians didn't give a damn about the army except when they needed its protection. They treated it just like they treated half-breeds, as poor relatives who embarrassed and shamed them. "That's something that'll never change, Captain. A hundred years from now, the army will still be treated the same, like bastard stepchildren."

Anderson pushed back from the table and put on his campaign hat. "Until they need us," he added, a cynical gleam in his eye.

"Until they need you," Slade replied.

Two hours later, the detachment departed the fort, four supply wagons, eight troopers, and a freshly stocked Conestoga wagon pulled by six well-fed draft horses.

Slade fell in alongside the wagon and nodded to the couple. Catheryn, wearing a new bonnet and a pink-and-white cotton dress, tilted her chin and stared into the cloudless sky. Phillip grinned as if he knew a secret.

Clearing his throat, Slade said, "I had hoped you folks wouldn't be making the trip back to the Red." There was much more he wanted to say, but he had said his piece before, and they had not listened.

Phillip looked at him with unconcealed dislike. "We're not quitters, Mr. Slade. There's gold stashed in one of those caves, and we're going to find it."

"That how you feel, Mrs. Dubuisson?" He knew what her answer would be, but he wanted to hear it from her lips, if for nothing else than to ease his conscience.

She gave him an icy glare. "Some of us strive to better ourselves, Mr. Slade. But that's something you wouldn't understand." She scooted around on the bench seat and turned her back to him.

Slade removed his hat and ran his fingers through his

short-clipped hair. No sense in talking to a stump, he figured. And that's just about the caliber brains it took to deliberately go back to the Red.

The journey settled into an uneventful, boring routine, a fact that pleased Slade immensely. He spent much of his time away from the detail, ranging far and wide across the prairie, hoping to spot trouble before it found them.

Day after day dragged, even slower than the tedious progress of the train. Slade stayed busy, too busy to think about Catheryn. But the nights were different. More than once, Slade remembered Catheryn's throaty invitation, and more than once, he mentally kicked himself for turning her down. At the time, however, the decision was the right one. Had there been trouble over a white woman at the fort, a half-breed would have been strung up by the short hairs.

That was one facet of the white man's world that had puzzled Slade after he left the Apache. The relationship between man and woman in the Apache world was natural, unassuming, outgoing. Honest words were spoken, honest feelings revealed.

If a brave took another's woman, he sent the husband a calumet. If the injured husband smoked the pipe, all was well. If not, then the offending brave understood the husband would seek revenge.

But the white man's world was filled with shadows and hiding places. Words spoken after dusk were denied in the morning. Feelings expressed in the darkness were refuted in the glare of sunlight. Emotions revealed under blankets were never revealed in the open.

Even after more than seven years, Slade still didn't completely understand the white man's world, but he had learned how the game was played. And he was becoming a very adept player.

On the seventh day, Captain Anderson rode out to meet Slade as the younger man returned from his patrol to the Red River.

"River's still down, Captain," Slade reported, reining up by the waiting officer. "We'll hit it tomorrow, around noon." He turned a knowing eye to the sky. "No rain about, so we'll have a dry crossing."

Anderson nodded and glanced over his shoulder at the approaching column. "Dubuisson's brains must be scrambled by the sun if he goes ahead and pulls out at the river."

Slade grunted. "He'll pull out, Captain. You can go to the bank on that."

Opening his canteen, Captain Anderson took a long drink. "Can't you make them see just how dangerous it is?"

"Not me. Nobody else either. You stack gold in front of some people, they'll tear each other apart to grab what they can."

"Maybe so. I wish I could leave a detail with them, but I've no such orders." He shook his head. "They'll sure be needing help, I'm figuring." He hesitated, then added, "Sure wish I could do something."

The young half-breed's eyes narrowed at the prodding tone in Anderson's voice. "What're you driving at, Captain?"

Captain Anderson grinned sheepishly. "I can't leave any of my men to look after them, Mr. Slade. You're the only one that'll be free once we reach Bascom. You suppose—"

Although he had mixed feelings concerning Anderson's unfinished request, Slade cut the older man off. "I got other plans, Captain. I aim to prowl around Bascom and on up to Adobe Walls to see if I can run down anyone who knows anything about those Mexicans you took care of."

"Certainly, I understand, but maybe when you finish your inquiry up there, you might look in on the Dubuissons on your way back to Arizona. I know it's some out of your way, but it would make me feel better. She's too fine-looking to end up as a side dish for the coyotes and vultures."

Slade started to refuse. Messing around with Catheryn Dubuisson was like juggling nitroglycerin; one mistake and they would be picking up the pieces. Still, her husky invitation that night outside the livery continued burning in his brain. "We'll see, Captain. We'll see."

Anderson grinned. "Thanks . . . Jake."

No word passed between Slade and the Dubuissons until the eighth day. At noon, the detachment crossed the Red River.

On the north shore, the Dubuissons broke off from the supply train. Slade pulled up beside them. "Sure you won't change your mind?"

Phillip patted the new Winchester propped against the seat. "We can take care of ourselves." Catheryn Dubuisson kept her eyes straight ahead, staring out over the vast sage prairie.

"Need any help with the belongings you left in the cave?"

Catheryn answered for them. "No."

An unfamiliar sense of disappointment washed over Slade. All he could do was nod and wheel around to rejoin the slowly moving supply train.

A sand tortoise moved faster than the remainder of the journey to Fort Bascom. The route of the supply train dropped off the prairie down into a labyrinth of vast canyons cut out by runoff from the flash floods that frequented the Texas Panhandle. Miles in breadth, the canyon snapped axles, knocked rims from wheels, and sapped the strength of the straining mules as they struggled against their harnesses.

Rattlesnakes abounded, and more than one trooper tasted gravel when his spooked mount crowhopped off the trail. The evening the detachment finally topped out of the canyon, the detail's greasy belly, a creative cook, whipped up a tasty meal of hot biscuits, succulent rattlesnake stew, and a dessert of berry cobbler.

Slade ate well that night, for over half the detail opted for jerky instead of the stew. Anderson sat by Slade's side, watching with amusement as his scout mopped up the last of his stew with a plump biscuit. "Hot rocks and gravy hit the spot, don't they?"

"Best I've had in quite a spell."

Anderson rolled a cigarette and took a deep drag. "You figure we'll get there tomorrow?" He offered Slade the Durham.

The young man declined the smoke with a shake of his head as he replied, "About noon."

"What are your plans then?"

Slade sensed a purpose behind the question. "Like I said before, prowl around some, ask a few questions. I don't figure to learn anything, but you can't tell. Might get lucky."

Captain Anderson flipped his cigarette into the fire. "I hope so." He paused, cleared his throat. "What about the Dubuissons? You figure to look in on them?"

Slade nodded. "Yep, but I need a favor from you." Anderson arched an eyebrow. Slade continued, "You've never seen me if anyone should ask about me."

Anderson studied him a moment. "Don't worry."

Fort Bascom was even less of a fort than Sill, but a government designation made any collection of tottering, ramshackle buildings a fort. As with Fort Sill, Bascom's buildings were arranged in a square facing a central parade ground.

After collecting his pay and learning that the only law in Bascom was military, Slade nosed around the fort until he was satisfied that no one could provide any new information concerning the Comancheros.

At the local sutler, he stocked up his own larder with coffee, flour, and cartridges. He headed northeast across the empty plains for Adobe Walls, a once-abandoned trader's post on the Canadian River.

He rode wary, the sutler's final warning in his ears: "I'd be mighty careful, was I you. Them Kiowa and Comanche are thicker'n maggots on a dead mule out thataway."

TWELVE

Slade paid attention to the sutler's words. He rode wary, his eyes constantly sweeping the vast prairie around him, his ears tuned to the ever-present moaning of the wind blowing through the sage. He spotted a few small war parties but managed to drop out of sight before they laid an eye on him.

Despite his caution, he ate well. His meals consisted of small game taken with his slingshot, sage hens, rabbit, and dove. While the plains abounded with herds of buffaloes and white-rumped antelope, the larger animals were too much for one person, and there was no time to dry the meat.

On the fourth day, he spotted another band of Indians astride warhorses. He dismounted and prodded at the buckskin's shanks with his toe. The horse dropped to its knees.

He watched the Indians warily. Kiowas, he figured, for he was in their country. After they disappeared, he continued his journey.

Later that day, he guided the buckskin into a thicket

of cedar on a bluff overlooking the Canadian. Below and for about a mile upriver, several thin columns of smoke drifted lazily into the still air. More Kiowas.

For several minutes, he remained motionless, his gray eyes studying the countryside around him, noting, cataloging, considering, discarding. The column he had spied earlier in the day must have come from around here. "Which means I'm right smack dab in the middle of them," he muttered to the buckskin.

With a shrug, he dismounted. Nothing to do now but wait for dark. He glanced around the thicket. There was browse for the buckskin. After dark he would push east. Adobe Walls could not be too distant.

He hobbled the buckskin and removed the bit. For insurance he tied a latigo around his ankle and fastened the other end to the hobbles.

After chewing on some jerky and washing it down with a swallow of water, Slade lay back and immediately fell asleep.

Slade's eyes popped open abruptly. Clouds had rolled in, obscuring the stars. The night was as dark as the inside of a buffalo. He sat up, his ears straining for the alien sound that had awakened him. Other than the soft munching of the buckskin browsing and the occasional cry of a night bird, all seemed normal. Yet something had awakened him.

Living with the Apache, he learned to trust his instincts. Now was no exception. He moved fast. Silently he rose and deftly slipped the bit between the buckskin's teeth, tightened the cinch, and untied the hobbles.

In the next instant, he swung astride the animal and dug his heels into its flanks. The wiry horse shot forward out of the thicket, bowling over an unseen figure just as it burst from the cedars.

A half-uttered scream died in the brave's throat.

Slade leaned over the buckskin's neck. They sped across the vast plains, Slade trusting to the instincts of the buckskin to avoid prairie dog holes. From time to time, Slade glanced behind, but the darkness was so complete that had there been any pursuit, he could not have seen it.

After a few miles, he slowed the pace. The clouds thinned. Occasional starlight filtered through, allowing him to discern shades of black. Another few miles, he pulled into another thicket to await the new day.

At the break of false dawn, Slade moved out. He glanced over his shoulder. Whoever had been prowling around his cold camp the night before had not given pursuit. Probably a young brave trying to count coup, he told himself, remembering some of the wild and crazy chances he and his own boyhood friends had taken with travelers in their own country.

He reached the edge of the Canadian River valley while the river was still covered in darkness. Downriver several miles, a faint yellow light broke the darkness. Adobe Walls.

The sun filtered through the cottonwoods lining the river, splashing the hard-packed ground around the trading post with thousands of sun-spiders dancing in the gentle breeze swaying the tall trees.

Slade reined to a halt. He hallooed the fort when he saw muzzles poke through the rifle ports in the log walls of the trading post.

"Looking for some coffee and grub to put myself

around," he called back after a voice asked him what he wanted.

The door creaked open and a bearded man in greasy buckskins stepped outside. Just skin and bones, the man was all angles from his knobby knuckles to the prominent cheekbones protruding over cavernous cheeks. His alert eyes belied his initial appearance. He was a man who knew what he was about.

Glancing over Slade's back trail, he grunted, "Come on in, stranger. Coffee's hot. Bring your pony. Put him out back." His eyes settled on the war club at the younger man's side.

Pausing to loosen the cinch on the buckskin, Slade followed. Three other hunters were inside, all wearing buckskins, all dirty and greasy as the first.

A fourth man, the owner, stepped forward and introduced himself. "Nubbin Buckalew," he said, holding up his left hand, which sported only a single forefinger. "Cheyennes know all kinds of ways to make a man spew out his guts," he said, laughing. "Who might you be, mister?"

Slade eyed the curious hunters, instinctively feeling that he could trust them. Over a breakfast of coffee and buffalo steak, he told them of his search.

"Goddamned Comancheros," one of the hunters exclaimed. "Oughta dee-ball ever' damned one of them heathens."

Buckalew shook his grizzled head. "Shore wish I could help, son, but we ain't seen nothing around here. 'Course," he added, glancing at the others, "of late, we don't git out too far what with the Comanch' and Kiowa thicker'n fleas on a dog."

"One thing's for sure," another one added. "When

you leave here, you damned well better be ready to fight. That's what puzzled us about you in the first place. Just how in the name of Aunt Sally did you git this far to begin with?"

Slade grinned for the first time since arriving. "It wasn't easy."

They laughed, but Slade could tell the first hunter had something on his mind. "You seem to have something weighing heavy on you, mister," Slade said.

All attention turned to the lank, angular hunter. He shook his head. "I don't like to douse water on no-body's campfire, but if you find your sister after all these years, you ain't gonna like what you get. Them Comancheros hard use the women theyselves and then sell 'em to whatever heathen tribe of savages they run acrost." He paused, then added, "After that, it's all downhill for the females."

Slade studied the older man, appreciating the man's candor. "I've done thought a spell on that before I started all this. You take a greenback and wad it up and pour grease on it and then tear it in half, you still don't throw it away. It's still got value." He paused. "But I'm obliged you being honest. However, I reckon I'll keep on looking." Slade rose from the table and reached for money with which to pay for the meal.

Nubbin Buckalew waved away Slade's offer to pay for the breakfast. "Can't tell when four bits might come in handy."

Slade nodded to the trader. "A favor, if you got a mind."

"Shoot."

"I'd take it kindly if no one has seen me should you be asked."

The hunters had enough experience on both sides of the law to understand his request. They glanced at each other knowingly. "We ain't," one replied, winking at the younger man.

"Thanks," Slade replied.

Twenty minutes later, he topped out on the bluff overlooking the Canadian River valley. To the south lay the Red. With no problems, he should reach the river tomorrow. He set his jaw, hoping to find Catheryn and Phillip Dubuisson alive and well.

What he would do then, Slade had not decided, but he could feel his pulse racing when he thought about the soft, blond woman with the throaty voice.

THIRTEEN

Sweltering under the summer sun, the prairie sprawled before Slade, broad, desolate, silent. Rising heat waves distorted the rolling hills, creating shimmering images that made the sage appear disjointed.

The buckskin's mile-eating gait carried them over the undulating sand hills and shallow basins that rolled to the Red. Midafternoon, Slade halted in a patch of shin-oak, tough, wiry trees no more than head high and wrist thick.

After watering the buckskin from his canteen, he leaned back in the shade and chewed on a strip of jerky, his slate gray eyes studying the prairie around him. He had deliberately selected this patch of oak for it perched on the crest of a broad hill that dropped away into a shallow basin several miles wide. With luck, he would make it across the valley before dark.

Rising to his feet, he dusted off his denims and swung into the saddle. For a moment, he sat motionless, soaking up the complete and utter silence of the sand hill prairie. A cricket chirruped.

As an Indian, Slade drew strength from the vastness

of the sage and short-grass prairie, which spread as far as the eye could see.

After several minutes, he pressed his legs against the buckskin's side and the wiry animal broke into a easy lope.

Dropping down into the broad valley, Slade kept the game little horse in an easy gait the remainder of the afternoon. Several hours later, he reined up. The valley lay behind, but ahead was another broad valley. To the west, the sun paused before rolling off the horizon.

Below and to his right, a twisting arroyo made a sweeping curve into the bottom of the valley. Half a mile from where Slade sat on the buckskin, several more arroyos joined into the first.

While the arroyos provided ample cover for a small fire, they were no place to spend the night. The shallow gullies were natural roads for coyotes, wolves, and rattlesnakes as well as travelers of all colors who wanted to stay out of sight. After his coffee, he poured the grounds over the small fire in the hole he had dug and covered it with sand, over which he sprinkled pieces of dead branches.

Leading the buckskin out of the arroyo, he staked the animal in a patch of sage at the base of a sand hill. In the darkness, the shadows of the animal and bushes blended. Silently he made his way to the crest of the hill and spread his blanket under a pile of sagebrush he had uprooted. Now, he could see anyone approaching from any direction. Overhead, the cold blue stars shone down on him with an eerie light. He fell asleep quickly.

He awakened suddenly. He rolled onto his stomach and gazed into the darkness, his muscles bunched, ready to spring. He saw nothing. But something was out there. He looked across the valley he had traveled earlier. Still nothing. He stared to the south. A flicker of firelight reflecting off a sagebrush caught his attention. There it was again. On the edge of an arroyo, near the one in which he had prepared his evening meal.

He reached for his revolver, wondering who had laid the fire. Rising into a crouch, he glided through the sage to the buckskin where he tightened the cinch and slipped the bit between the animal's teeth.

Leaving the buckskin ground reined, Slade slithered through the silvery blue bushes to the edge of the arroyo several yards from where the firelight faintly flickered. Peering through the sparse branches of a sage, he saw half a dozen Kiowa braves squatting around the small fire.

Strips of meat were spitted on slender, pointed sticks driven into the sand. The spatter and crackle of the cooking meat reached his ears, but the subdued conversation around the fire was unintelligible.

Backing away from the arroyo, the young half-breed circled around until he was close enough make out their words. Although the Kiowas spoke a language different from the Apache, there were enough similarities that Slade picked up scattered words.

He pieced together enough of the discussion to realize that the Comanche and Kiowa chiefs, Quanah Parker and Kicking Bird, had agreed to a parley. This party of Kiowa braves was riding to meet with the Comanches to set up a time and place for the meeting.

Slade shivered. The only reason more white blood had not been shed in the Texas Panhandle was that the Kiowas and Comanches had spent the last few years fighting each other. But, if they should decide to make peace . . . He didn't like to think about it.

He listened intently as the Kiowas whispered of the upcoming meeting. He stiffened as if struck by a jolt of lightning. The Kiowas were to meet the Comanche at the Tower on the Red River!

The Tower? He'd never heard of a Tower. Quickly, but carefully, he pushed back from the arroyo and rose into a crouch as he zigzagged through the sage to the buckskin. He led the animal several hundred yards before mounting.

Slade walked the animal for several minutes before digging his heels into the animal's flanks. The wind whipped the brim of his slouch hat and the sand stung his face. He knew he could reach the Red ahead of the Kiowas, but what if the Comanches were already there—at the Tower, wherever it was located?

He had to get the Dubuissons to safety—if they were still alive, if the Comanches had not already captured them, and if he could find the couple. He shook his head. A hell of a lot of ifs.

With the rising sun, Slade pulled up on the edge of the Red. Turning east, he rode along the sandstone cliffs until he found a narrow trail leading down the face of the bluffs to the willow brakes lining the river. Leaning back in his saddle, Slade let the trailwise horse gingerly pick its way down the winding trail.

At the base of the sandstone bluffs, Slade paused to rest his horse and chew a mouthful of jerky. Minutes later, he tightened the cinch and mounted, ready to begin his search for the Eastern couple.

He ranged up and down the Red for miles, constantly

alert for hostiles. Late in the afternoon, he spied a dark object lying in the sandy bed on the far side of the river. There he discovered a man's hat, a bowler, at the edge of a pit of quicksand. From his saddle, he studied the wide-spaced tracks with deep heel prints leading up to the pit. He understood immediately what had happened. Whoever the man was, he had been running from something, and that something was either Comanche or Kiowa, the latter probably.

Slade concluded that the man must have been the one Phillip and Catheryn were meeting. Phillip had been wearing a wide-brimmed hat when they departed the train. That he switched to a bowler was unlikely. The young half-breed leaned from his saddle and scooped up the bowler and stuck it in the parfleche bag tied behind the cantle. He stared across the river, his keen eyes scanning the shore and the tumbles of boulders for any sign of Phillip or Catheryn Dubuisson.

A wisp of a breeze cooled his sweaty cheeks momentarily, then gave way once again to the suffocating heat. Slade decided to follow the man's back trail and hope to stumble onto Phillip or Catheryn, or at least some clue to their whereabouts.

The trail ended in the rocks along the base of the bluffs on the far side of the river. Stymied, Slade slouched on the buckskin and looked upriver. The possibility existed that the man at the bottom of the quicksand pit had nothing to do with Phillip or Catheryn. He might not have been the one they were planning to meet. Yet, another stranger on the Red was too much to ask of chance. But what if by some chance that were true? The Dubuissons had departed the supply train some twenty miles to the west. They could be as many as sixty to eighty miles downriver by now. "Or within shouting distance," he reminded himself.

All he could do now was continue the search.

Riding easily, Slade permitted the buckskin to pick its way among the rocks and boulders as he made his way downriver. Suddenly he stopped. On the ground before him was Indian sign, unshod ponies crossing the riverbed. He could not tell if they were Comanches or Kiowas, but either meant trouble.

Glancing over his shoulder at the sun, Slade realized he had only a couple of hours to find them before dark. He figured to search down one side for an hour and back up the other the second hour.

Caves were plentiful and, with the hostiles ranging the countryside, an ideal place for him to spend the night. A boom of thunder rumbled through the air. To the west, a heavy bank of clouds rolled down the river. Jagged streaks of lightning lanced from the dark clouds to the sprawling prairie.

The last few streams of daylight faded quickly. A few splatters of rain pelted the packed sand at his feet. Suddenly, Slade jerked the buckskin to a halt. He sniffed the air, trying to pick up the vagrant breeze that had curled a familiar aroma around his head. It was gone. All he could smell was horse and sweat.

A gust of cool air rushed down the river. Then the smell was there again, stronger. Just as suddenly, it faded. But Slade recognized it this time. Perfume! The unmistakable aroma of lilac. And the only person he knew who wore the perfume was Catheryn Dubuisson.

The storm exploded without further warning, dropping torrents of rain, soaking Slade instantly. Calming his spooked horse, Slade headed the animal into the willow brakes lining the river. He stopped in front of a small cave. Dismounting, he peered inside. The dust on the soft stone floor was undisturbed.

He pushed upriver as the rain slackened. The next cave was much larger. Slade grinned when he spied the wagon sign outside the cave, the rainwater quickly filling the tracks. He glanced into the cave. Water pooled just inside the mouth of the cave. A wet path led across the cave to the wagon, which was parked against one wall. The team of draft horses stood hipshot inside a rope corral.

Revolver in hand, Slade eased inside. The Dubuissons might be here. Or they might be dead. Kiowas could be holed up inside. He moved silently, his feet whispers on the stone floor. The horses perked their ears when they saw the newcomer. One pranced nervously. Another whinnied.

The wagon creaked.

Slade froze. His eyes fastened on the wagon as if the intensity of his stare could penetrate the oak sides. A faint groan cut through the silence. Slade moved to the rear of the wagon and peered inside.

Thunder cracked and lightning flashed simultaneously. Catheryn jerked upright, a scream forming on her lips. Then she recognized Slade. Tears erupted from her eyes, and she threw herself at him. "Oh, Jake. Thank God, it's you."

Awkwardly, the younger man attempted to soothe her. His cheeks burned as he felt her soft breasts pressing against his chest. Her aroma filled his nostrils. After a few minutes, her sobs faded, and her body ceased trembling.

Holstering his revolver, Slade helped her from the wagon. "Where's your husband?" Her face was hidden by the shadows, but he saw her shake her head. Outside, lightning cracked, illuminating the interior of the cave with a bluish glow. Catheryn's wet clothes clung to her body, and her hair hung in tangled ropes on her shoulders. Slade saw the strain and worry on her face.

"He's been gone since yesterday. He and Sam Butler left to search for a cave that's filled with gold bullion. I was out looking for them when the storm hit." Lightning flashed again. Her face twisted with fear. She shivered. Her teeth chattered. "C-Can you find them?"

"Don't worry. I'll find them. Right now, we need to take care of you." Striking a match, Slade found a blanket in the wagon bed and pulled it around Catheryn. The cave was damp even during the heat of the day, and the night rain added a penetrating chill. "Come on," he said, lighting a lantern and throwing several blankets over his shoulder. He led her to the rear of the cave. Catheryn was too frightened to protest.

She needed a fire and dry clothes. But any size fire in the mouth of the cave would draw every stray Comanche or Kiowa for miles around.

The Red River stretched for hundreds of miles. The chance that the Kiowas were meeting the Comanches nearby was unlikely, but that was one chance Slade could not take. "Back this way," he said.

Fifty yards inside, the cave angled sharply to the right and then broke into three separate, smaller caves. Pausing at the juncture, Slade held the lantern so the yellow glow poured down the first several yards of each tunnel, dispelling the darkness. He held to the right. A few yards farther and the ceiling arched sharply upward.

Suddenly something struck his shoulder. Catheryn screamed and jerked away from him, flailing wildly at her blond tresses. Slade spun and a ten-inch black-and-red centipede dropped to the floor. He crushed it with his heel. Catheryn screamed again. A giant centipede had tangled itself in her hair.

FOURTEEN

Whipping his hat from his head, Slade slapped at the squirming, twisting centipede, knocking it to the floor, where he crushed it. Catheryn continued screaming hysterically. Slade shook her roughly, jerking her head like a rag doll's. "They're dead. You're okay. You hear me? You're okay."

She stiffened, stared up at him with terror-filled eyes. Fear twisted her face. Slowly, his words soaked through the panic seizing her body. She frowned. He nodded assurance. Catheryn swallowed hard and shivered.

Slade draped a blanket over her head and shoulders and led her deeper into the cave until they entered a large room. He turned the lantern to inspect the ceiling for more centipedes. Satisfied, he spread the blankets next to the wall and set the lantern by her side. He turned to leave.

"Wait!"

"Don't worry. I'm just going for firewood," he said brightly. "A cup of hot coffee and a bowl of stew will fix you up." He tried to look beneath her drawn features for some indication of that night outside the livery back at the fort. All he saw was fear.

He made his way back to the front room of the cave. Flashes of bluish light flared against the walls as the lightning crashed. Phillip had left a small supply of firewood in the cave. Gathering it in his arms, Slade returned to the back room.

Soon a cheery fire blazed, filling the room with its warmth. Catheryn gave him a wan look.

"Coffee's almost ready."

Catheryn didn't reply, but her eyes remained locked on him warily, almost as if she were frightened that he might suddenly disappear, leaving her alone once again.

Rising to his feet, he said, "I'll be back."

"Where . . ." She took a tentative step toward him.

He grinned. "I'm just going to the wagon."

Taking the lantern, he returned to the wagon, where he rummaged through the trunks and found her a gingham dress.

Back at the fire, he tossed Catheryn her dry clothes. "Get out of those wet things. I'll wait by the wagon."

Catheryn pressed the dress against her breasts and watched Slade start to leave the room. "Wait."

He paused and glanced back. When he saw the fear on her face, he grinned. "I'm not going anywhere. I'll be right out here. Just shout when you've changed."

Five minutes later, she called him. He stopped when he came back in. She had spread her wet garments on the boulder behind her. Slade glanced at the floor, his cheeks flushing. Except for those of the few fast women he had known, he had never seen ladies' undergarments. Ears burning, he busied himself with the meal. Fifteen

117

minutes later, they sipped hot coffee and delighted in the thick aroma of boiling venison jerky.

Catheryn looked up from her coffee. "Do—Do you think Phillip is safe?"

He coughed. "Yeah. Probably holed up in a cave just like us." He hesitated. She smiled. Slade cursed himself for lying to her. Yet, he reminded himself, Phillip could be doing that very thing.

But he could not convince himself of his own lie.

After two steaming cups of bouillon, Catheryn relaxed and told Slade all that had happened since she and her husband had departed the supply train. "After meeting Sam Butler, we camped in this cave. Phillip and Mister Butler left two days ago."

Slade said nothing.

She paused. Noticing his silence, she said, "You think we're just foolish people, don't you?"

He shrugged, surprised that she seemed concerned about his opinion of her. "Not for me to say. I just figure there's a hell of a lot more to life than gold. All that yellow metal does is get folks killed."

Catheryn did not reply.

"We're going to need more wood," he said, rising and turning toward the front of the cave. "I'll bring in some so it can be drying. Come early morning, we'll be needin' it. You be okay while I'm gone?"

Catheryn nodded, her pale cheeks flushed with the heat now. She smiled. "I'll be fine."

Slade was soaked by the time he had brought in several loads of driftwood. Catheryn rose and tossed him a blanket. "It's your turn now. Give me your wet clothes. We'll put them beside mine to dry."

He took a step back and shook his head. "Don't fuss about it. They'll dry on me just as well."

"Don't argue," she said, a mischievous smile playing over her lips as she tossed him a blanket. "Besides, if you get sick, I've no one to take care of me." She stuck out her hand. "Now, your clothes."

He went into the darkness of the cave to change. She was a different woman than the one who left Fort Sill. That one had been distant and cool, but this one was warm and coy.

When he returned, his wet clothes and gun belt over his arm and the blanket draped around him, she tossed him some of Phillip's apparel, corduroy pants and a silk shirt with ruffles. "I dug these out while you were getting out of yours."

Embarrassed, Slade retreated back into the cave and returned moments later wearing Phillip's clothes.

Catheryn giggled.

Slade grinned wryly and, pinching one of the ruffles between his thumb and forefinger, waved it at her. "Feel purty funny, so I reckon I look funny too."

She shook her head as she shook out his wet clothes. "You look just fine," she said as he laid his gun belt on the stack of firewood. Catheryn spread his clothes on the boulder, next to hers.

Slade glanced at the garments, feeling a warm glow when he saw how his denims almost touched her petticoat. An unsettling sense of intimacy came over him.

They had another cup of coffee against the chill of the rainy night as they stared wordlessly into the small fire. Steam rose from the damp wood with a tiny hiss.

The soaking warmth of the fire and a full stomach

made her drowsy. Slade grinned when Catheryn's head jerked in a nod. She looked up at him in surprise. He laughed. "Why don't you get some sleep. I'll stay up a while longer."

Catheryn didn't argue. She pulled the blanket over her shoulders as she curled next to the fire. Moments later, her breathing grew regular and soft.

Slade carried his unfinished coffee back to the mouth of the cave. He stood in the darkness, silhouetted by the flashes of lightning, watching as the rain lashed the willows, bending the slender trees to the ground. One good thing about the storm, he told himself. Even Comanches and Kiowas were holed up against it.

He glanced over his shoulder. Catheryn had made no mention nor acted in any manner to suggest that night back at the livery. The young man shrugged. He'd met many a camp follower during the war, and he had never ceased to be amazed at just how wanton they were between the sheets and how prim the next day on the sidewalks. He wasn't really sure if he intended his thought as a reflection of Catheryn or not. In fact, he told himself, the smartest thing for him to do would be to leave her alone; to not get tangled up with her. *Still* . . . He said no more, but he wondered how her arms around him would feel, imagined what their children would be like, visualized where they would live.

The lightning crashed, casting an eerie blue glow over the riverbed. Slade squatted against the wall of the cave, remembering the times he and his Apache brothers, Nana and Paleto, sat out fierce storms in the snug warmth of caves, a great adventure for nine-year-old boys, Indian or half-white.

The howling of the storm outside faded as Slade relived those days. He remembered the Comanchero with the missing nose shooting him, then awakening in the wickiup of the Apache, Santos, follower of Cochise; husband of Big Calf, who nursed him back to health; and father of Nana and Paleto, his new brothers.

Adventure filled the life of Apache boys. Slade and his brothers roamed the Dragoon Mountains, playing at being warriors, always extending their excursions a little beyond the limits given them by Santos. One evening, a violent storm caught them miles from the rancheria. The boys took refuge in a rocky cave where they roasted a rabbit and whiled the night away fabricating tales of the great deeds they would achieve in their lifetimes.

A crash of lightning brought Slade back to the present. He looked over his shoulder into the darkness where Catheryn lay. With resignation, he knew that Catheryn Dubuisson could never accept this life that was his. He tossed the remainder of his coffee into the rain and returned to his own blankets.

In the early morning hours when the fire was out and the darkness complete, a hand touched his shoulder. Instantly he awakened, his hand clutching his revolver.

It was Catheryn. "I'm cold," she whispered, pressing against his back. Before Slade could reply, she slipped under his blankets and pressed her body against his, a soft purr in her throat.

For a moment, Slade remained motionless, his common sense battling the emotions surging through his veins; then he rolled out of the blankets. "I'll build the fire."

Catheryn stifled a protest. Angrily, she jerked the blanket to her neck and turned her back on him.

After the fire had warmed the cave, Slade leaned back against the wall and drew his knees up to his chin. Folding his arms over his knees, he laid his chin on his forearm and studied the motionless figure lying under the blanket. He cursed himself, not understanding just why he had refused her offer, wondering if he would ever understand why he had, then knowing that he probably would never understand. Soon, the young half-breed fell asleep, his back against the wall of the cave.

Slade awakened early, stirred the banked coals, and fed kindling to the small fire. Taking the coffeepot, he went back to the wagon for water. When he returned, Catheryn was standing by the fire, fully dressed. He nodded. "Morning."

She looked at him coolly. "Good morning, Mr. Slade," she replied, brushing past him for her morning toilet, her chin tilted. She deliberately slighted him.

He arched an eyebrow. What else could he expect after last night? She was an odd woman. No question about it. She and that husband of hers sure as hell deserved each other.

Anxious to remove himself from the suddenly unfriendly environment, Slade gulped down his coffee and swallowed the flour cakes whole. "I'll look to the west for Mr. Dubuisson. You stay in here." He told of the meeting between the Comanches and Kiowas and gestured to the Winchester he had taken from the wagon. "It's loaded. All you do is pull back the hammer and squeeze the trigger."

Catheryn nodded, her blue eyes looking through him.

He led the buckskin outside the cave and swung into the saddle. He stared at Catheryn, who had come to the front of the cave. Her blouse buttoned high around her neck, she returned his look, a haughty curl to her lips. She pivoted on her heel and disappeared into the darkness of the cave.

Hours later, he found Phillip Dubuisson lying beneath a patch of sage far out on the prairie south of the Red. Had it not been for the circling buzzards, he would have ridden past the unconscious man. An ugly wound creased Phillip's temple. The blood had dried. Slade bathed the wound and poured some water between Phillip's parched lips.

Remembering the Indian sign he had stumbled across the day before, Slade draped Dubuisson over the saddle and swung up behind him. He slapped the reins against the buckskin's neck. "Let's go, boy. This is no place for us."

As he made his way back to the river, he managed to piece together what had happened. After the Indians jumped them, the two men separated. For whatever reason, the Indians had ignored Phillip, probably because the other man was a much easier target. But who knew for sure? No one. Not even the Indians themselves. Especially the Indians. For the most part, they simply reacted to a situation.

Darkness crawled across the sky, and Slade was still an hour out from the cave, which meant he had to either camp out tonight or cross the Red in the dark.

"No choice there," he muttered, glancing down at the unconscious figure still draped across his saddle. He was worried. Phillip should have come around. Maybe it was one of those coma things he'd heard a medical orderly talking about during the war, or maybe just lying out in the weather all day and night had done something. Slade was no doctor. He had to chance crossing the Red.

At the edge of the river, he dismounted, and leading the buckskin, he started across the broad riverbed. His moccasins allowed his feet to sense any give in the bed in time to back away from quicksand.

Finally, after backtracking several times to pick out a new route, Slade reached the far shore.

Catheryn gave a squeal of joy when she saw Phillip. Her happiness turned to dismay when Slade carried the still unconscious man into the rear room and related just how long he had been unconscious.

"Where's Mr. Butler?"

As they made Phillip comfortable, Slade told her about the bowler, the Indian sign, and how he figured it all tied in with her husband. "If your friend's not at the bottom of a quicksand bog, then he's lying dead out on the prairie somewhere."

Catheryn tended her husband gently, bathing his burning forehead with a damp cloth and dressing his wound with Cuticura plaster as Slade checked him over for any other injuries. "Only the crease alongside his head," he announced, sitting back on his heels. "He'll be all right."

Fearfully, she looked up into his eyes. "But he's been unconscious so long."

Slade hid his own concern. "I've seen it before. Sometimes a couple days. Sometimes less. Then they snap right out."

"We've got some stomach bitters in the wagon."

Slade grunted. "A shot of whiskey would do just as good."

A soft moan from Phillip caused both of them to look down at the unconscious man. "He's waking up," she said excitedly, leaning over and caressing his cheek with her hand.

Slade poured bouillon in a cup and handed it to her. "Here. See if you can get any of this down him. It'll be better for him than the bitters." He sat back and watched thoughtfully as she gently pleaded and prodded at Phillip to sip the broth, like a mother with an ill child. She was a tough woman to figure out.

Later, Phillip slid into a restful slumber. Slade stared across the fire at Catheryn, whose eyes remained on her husband. Her face was lined with worry. "You two are set on striking it rich, huh?"

She looked up at him, not comprehending his question. Then its meaning registered on her. She shook her head. "We were, but now . . ." She looked back at Phillip. "Now, I don't know. I don't think so. If anything should happen to Phillip . . ."

He studied her for long minutes. They were a strange couple, but one thing for sure, they didn't belong out here. Unfortunately, they were too damned stubborn to understand that simple fact. And sooner or later, that stubbornness would get them killed.

He could help them. He could save their lives. But should he? Other than their word, what guarantee would he have that they would return to the East and remain there? One certain fact, he couldn't hang around the next ten years playing nursemaid to hardheaded tenderfoots set on getting themselves scalped.

"You two stay in this part of the country, and next time, you might not be so lucky." He eyed her coolly.

"I know that now." She looked straight into his eyes, her face innocent of deceit. "If we can get back to Fort Sill, somehow we'll earn enough money to take us back where we belong. I might have to wait tables, but we'll do it." She nodded past Slade to the broad riverbed and the vast, empty prairie beyond. Her eyes grew hard. "This is a savage land. Only savages can survive out here."

He grinned. She was right, even if she did include him in her assessment of the West. "Soon as your husband is able to travel, I'll take you back to the fort."

Catheryn Dubuisson's eyes glistened in gratitude. "Thank you, Mr. Slade. I'll always be grateful. For everything," she added.

Slade studied her a moment, wondering at the implication of her last remark. "My privilege, ma'am." He nodded and rose to go stand in the mouth of the cave. She'd mentioned a Sam Butler. Whoever that jasper was, he had been right about the gold along the Red. But even if he hadn't gotten himself swallowed up in a quicksand pit, he still would never found it.

But Slade could. The landmarks were indelibly printed in his brain because that night outside the cave long years past would always live in his memory. That was the night he heard the story of how Geronimo got his name in the battle with the Mexicans.

To a young, impressionable boy, the story throbbed of danger, resonated with excitement, pulsated with bravery. He and his brother, Nana, were present because they had been given the much sought-after honor among Apache boys to tend the warriors' horses.

The story told how Gokhlayeh, torn by grief over the death of his wife and children, screamed like the cougar and fought like the badger while killing many Mexicans until one soldier, running for his life, cried out the words, "Geronimo, Geronimo."

Slade remembered staring up in awe at Geronimo who stood in the entrance to the cave after the Apache party had transferred the gold from one cave to another. They would never touch the yellow metal for personal gain, but they did not want any of the descendants of the Spanish noblemen to lay their hands on it either. Above Geronimo's head, a ledge of sandstone shaped like an arrowhead pointed east. That had been almost ten years earlier, but Slade remembered. That was one night he could never forget.

Telling Catheryn he was going for game, Slade trekked downriver to the gold. He argued with himself as he rode. He was violating an Apache trust. Why? To help the Dubuissons, he told himself. But deep inside, he knew that the real reason was to impress Catheryn Dubuisson, and no excuse he could give would change that reason. With the stoic fatalism of the Apache, he accepted what he was doing.

Quickly he loaded two bars in his saddlebags, resealed the cave, and headed back. He would wait until they reached the fort before giving them the gold.

FIFTEEN

When Slade returned, Phillip was awake, his head propped on pillows. He smiled weakly at his rescuer. "Thank you, Mister Slade," he whispered. "Catheryn says I owe you my life."

The younger man shrugged. "Thank the buzzards. I just followed them."

Phillip started to say more, but Catheryn gently stilled him with her hand. "Hush now. You need rest." She tipped a cup of bouillon to his lips. "Drink this and then try to sleep."

Later, she turned to Slade. "Do you think he can travel tomorrow?"

"I don't see any reason why not. We'll make him a pallet in the wagon bed. Pushing it, we can reach Sill in five or six days."

They moved out before the sun rose the next morning. Luck rode with them. For the next several days, they rolled across the vast prairie without sighting a single person. They camped late and cold, taking no chance on a fire that would shine like a beacon in the darkness.

The last day, Phillip was well enough to ride at Catheryn's side. They reached the Wichita Mountains at dusk, and Slade led them to a granite overhang that offered shelter.

"Can't we have a fire tonight?" Catheryn asked. "I've forgotten what hot coffee tastes like, and Phillip could use some hot food."

"Can't chance it. Too many Kiowas and Comanches coming and going from the reservation."

"Then let's stop wasting time and get on to the fort." Her words were taut with frustration.

"Too dangerous. The trail through the mountains is rough. I don't want to risk busting a wheel."

She glared at him, her eyes blazing. "Then let's build a fire. No one's going to see it back in these rocks. "We're not wild savages like your Indian friends."

Phillip laid his hand on her arm. "Hush, Catheryn. He's right. Any Indians out there, they'll smell the fire as well as the coffee. Mr. Slade's got us this far. Another night won't kill us."

The fire died from her eyes and a tiny frown knit her forehead. "Phillip's right, Mr. Slade. I apologize. It's just that I'm so tired and dirty and hungry."

"I know. Tomorrow, all of this will be over." He paused, thinking of the gold in his saddlebags. "Believe me, one more night without a fire will be well worth it."

The moon rose with the setting sun. A full moon, it bathed the mountainside in a cool white glow. The three of them sat on Slade's tarp, chewing tough jerky and washing it down with warm water that had turned flat.

Unbidden, Phillip told Slade of their futile travels in order to find quick riches. "But that episode back at the river taught me a lesson I'll never forget. When I saw those murdering Indians coming after us, I figured I was a goner. Now, thanks to you, I've got another chance. Once I get us back to Philadelphia, I'll never go west of Broad Street again."

"It's a shame, though," Catheryn said. "You'd think with all the gold out there, we could have found some."

Slade grinned. "It's there all right, but most people are better off not finding it."

Phillip agreed. "We've seen it happen, men killing others over it. You're right, Mr. Slade. People are better off without it. Take us. We've probably spent a small fortune just outfitting all of the trips we've taken, but no more." He paused and turned a curious face to the younger man. "Still, the stories a person hears are intriguing. Are the tales we've heard about Apache gold really true?"

"They're true."

"But, if they are, why haven't you taken some? You could lead a life of comfort."

Slade leaned back on the tarp, propping his torso with his elbows. "Maybe so. There's gold. Plenty of it. But no white man will ever get it, and no Indian wants it."

Catheryn leaned forward. "You once said there was a place where gold nuggets lie on the ground just for the taking. Is that really true?"

Slade knew he should remain silent, but the urge to satisfy her curiosity was too impelling. "When I was about twelve, Cochise made a trip to a place called Black Mountain, a peak in the Catalina Mountains. He took half a dozen or so warriors with him. Two of us boys went along as jinglers to look after the horses. We stopped in a small canyon with a solid vein of gold as wide as an axe handle running across the floor of the valley and up the far wall like a chimney. About halfway up, the vein fanned out wide, wider than your wagon is long, all the way to the top of the canyon."

"Is that the one you told me about, the one with the curse? Raven and Coyote?"

"Curse? What curse?" asked Phillip.

"Yes," said Slade. "That's the one."

"What's this about a curse?" Phillip insisted.

"I'll tell you later," she said. Then to Slade, "And there are really nuggets lying all over the ground?"

"Like grass in a meadow," Slade replied.

Catheryn and Phillip leaned forward in rapt attention. The moon was on their backs and their faces were shadows, but Slade knew that greed shone in their eyes. They were just human, and he knew the thoughts racing through their heads. He added a warning. "The Apache guard the valley. A few gold-seekers have tried to enter."

"What happened to them?" asked Catheryn.

"They were killed."

She shivered. "What about you?"

Slade cut his eyes to Catheryn. "They would kill me if I attempted to remove gold without permission. Besides," he added, rising and brushing the dust from his denims, "what use would I have for it?" He went to his saddle and reached into the saddlebags.

"We could find a use for it," Phillip said, laughing.

"But you would die. And that would be a waste." Slade turned back to the couple. He extended his arms. "Here. This will provide the money you need to start a new business back East."

Simultaneously, the Dubuissons sucked in their breath as their eyes fastened on the rough bars in

Slade's hands. The moonlight glimmered softly on the shiny metal.

He pushed the bars at them. "Take them. They will help."

Phillip looked up at him, the moonlight bathing his slender face. "But, why? Why would you do this for us?"

Out of the corner of his eyes, Slade saw Catheryn stiffen. "I want a promise from you."

Catheryn relaxed noticeably.

"A promise?"

Slade nodded. "These bars will bring you much money, not enough to live on for the remainder of your life, but more than enough to start a business and see you through the first two or three years. Promise that you will do that, and they are yours."

Without replying, Phillip rose and held one of the bars up to the moonlight. He licked his lips nervously as he inspected the bar. It was rough and out of square, but it was solid gold. He looked at Slade. "I still don't understand."

Catheryn spoke up quickly. "Thank you, Mr. Slade, thank you very much."

"You must promise."

"We do," she replied. "Oh, we do. I don't know how we can ever thank you. We—"

"As long as you keep your promise. That will be thanks enough." He handed Catheryn the second bar. His eyes fastened on hers. Was she telling him the truth? He told himself that she was. Now all he had to do was make himself believe it. Slade said, "Now, we must sleep. We will reach the fort at midmorning. There I leave you. You can make connections out of there to Dodge City."

Phillip cut his eyes from Slade to his wife and then to the bar of gold in his hand. With a wry grin, he shoved the gold bar under the blankets in the bed of the wagon.

The next morning, Slade left them when they came within sight of the fort, eliciting once more their promise to return to Philadelphia.

As Slade rode away, Phillip stared after him with a cunning glitter in his eyes. "Butler was right. There is gold on the Red River."

Her own eyes fixed on the back of the young half-breed, Catheryn replied, "Yes, but Black Mountain will be easier to find."

SIXTEEN

Back in Tucson, Slade returned to his old job of riding shotgun with his old friend Alexander Bent, better known as Three-Fingers Bent due to the loss of his thumb and forefinger in a game of chance between him and a band of White Mountain Apache at a drunken party on the banks of the Gila River. Bent was a distant relative of the Bent brothers, William and George, who had established Bent's Fort near the confluence of the Arkansas and Purgatory rivers thirty-five years earlier.

The stage ran between Tucson and Fort Yuma on that part of the Oxbow Route winding along the border between Arizona and California. This stretch of desolate country was most favored by Comancheros coming and going to Mexico. Slade had traveled the route so regularly that wranglers at each swing station knew him and of his search for his sister. Any information they received, they either passed on to him when he arrived or sent by the first stage if he were not riding shotgun.

After the rolling prairies of the Texas Panhandle and the sobering vastness of the Staked Plains, the granite monoliths of the Catalina Mountains and the blistering desert of southern Arizona were a welcome respite. Even the sidewinders and scorpions seemed like old friends, as did the rocking, swaying motion of the Concord coach on its leather thoroughbraces as it sped across a desert populated with sharp-spined cholla cactus and the majestic saguaro.

The first two weeks were uneventful despite the fact that Cochise was on the rampage. The stage pulled out of Tucson on Tuesdays and Fridays at 1:30 P.M. for the 141-mile trip through the Cimarrons and Saucedas to the Gila River, a journey of 31 hours. The next leg was 135 miles through the foothills of the Mohawk Mountains to Fort Yuma, where Slade and Three-Fingers laid over for a few days and then headed back on the return trip.

The third week, as a favor for their boss, they took the run from Fort Yuma on into Los Angeles, another 254 miles. There, Three-Fingers successfully managed to stir up drunken brawls in half the cantinas in the city while Slade spent several lazy days luxuriating in the conviviality and hospitality of Alberto Munoz, an old wartime friend who was a member of a prominent Spanish family in old California.

Slade's last night in Los Angeles, his host ordered his servants to prepare an exquisite dinner for his old friend. The meal began with bean-and-cheese appetizers called *totopos*; cool gazpacho, a delightful tomato soup; followed by platters of *bacalao veracruzana* and *mochomos*. Slade preferred the latter, for minced pork was more to his taste than codfish in tomato sauce. Side dishes of *colache, ensalada de aguacate y maiz,* and *salsa cruda* completed the repast.

Later, the two friends retired to the red-tiled patio to

indulge themselves with an after-dinner cigar and glass of Anaheim wine and luxuriate in the sweet per fume of orange blossoms. After several minutes of pro found silence, Alberto asked Slade of his search for hi sister.

"Still running into dead ends." Slade paused an gazed into the warm night. For a moment, a wave of de pression seized him, but he forced it aside. "But soone or later, I'll find her."

Alberto shook his head. "How old is she now, m friend?"

"Eighteen," Slade replied without hesitation.

"The same age as the young one at the mission," A berto said. "She, too, as you, has no family."

Slade grunted. "I don't even like to think about th number of children without family. At least this girl o yours at the mission got the chance to be raised by th priests, by decent people. My sister probably can't eve read or write."

Alberto leaned forward and laid his hand on Slade shoulder. "You can always teach her to read and write That will be no problem. The problem is finding he no?"

A wry grin replaced the frown on Slade's face. "S That is the problem. But it is one that I will handle."

Alberto nodded. There was no doubt in his mind tha Slade spoke the truth.

Two weeks later, Slade and Bent pulled out of the sma village of Point of Rocks on the last leg of the run bac to Tucson. The six horses fell into a comfortable strid The Concord rocked lazily on its leather straps.

"Only seventeen miles to go," Slade said, cradling the Winchester in the crook of his arm.

"Heard some news out of Tucson back there," Three-Fingers said, and then squirted a stream of tobacco juice over his shoulder.

Slade stiffened. "Comancheros?"

"Nope. Prospectors. Large party." He eyed Slade. "Armed to the teeth."

The young man frowned. "So? There's a lot of those fools out there."

"Yep, but this bunch asked questions about the Catalina Mountains, and there was a blond-haired woman doing the asking."

Slade sat back with a jolt as if he had been struck between the eyes with a singletree. So the Dubuissons had lied to him. He cursed himself. He should have known even though he had wanted to believe her. "How'd you hear?"

The wiry driver turned loose with another stream of tobacco juice over his shoulder and cracked his whip over the lead horses. "Back at the Western Union office, Ollie said word had come in over the wires five, maybe six days past."

They rode in silence for several minutes. Then Bent spoke. "Them the ones you told me about?"

"Yeah." The young man nodded, his gray eyes blazing like pitch torches. "I figured they'd had their bellies full of hard times. Greenhorns like that don't understand what kind of short deck they're up against out here."

"What they doing up in the Catalinas?" Three-Fingers asked the question, but from his tone, it was obvious he already knew the answer.

137

Slade shot him a blistering look. "Why in the hell do you ask when you already know the answer? Black Mountain."

The crusty driver spat again. "Just wanted to hear you say it."

"Well, you heard me. And yeah, I told 'em about the vein of gold." He went on to fill Bent in on that last night in the Wichitas. "They sure suckered me," he added. "I figured for sure they'd light out for Philadelphia."

Bent laughed and cracked the whip. "You still got a mite to learn about the white man, son. He's pure, plumb greedy when it comes to gold. Ain't nothin' going to stop him . . . or her." He slid the lumbering Concord around a sharp curve. Muttered curses exploded from inside the coach. Bent laughed again. "What do you reckon on doin'?"

Slade had cooled off. "Not much I can do. First thought I had was to go in and drag them out of there, but armed like you say they are, they probably wouldn't come too easy. Talking won't help. It didn't back on the Red. Looks to me like their minds are set on looking for gold."

"It appears that way. 'Course you know that the only thing they're goin' to find in the Catalinas is trouble, especially with Cochise running wild."

"I reckon you're right," Slade said, shrugging his broad shoulders. He saw Catheryn in his mind's eye. "Damned shame too." He lapsed into silence.

Slade tried to push Catheryn and Phillip from his thoughts, but that night in the cave with Catheryn Dubuisson refused to be shunted aside. Maybe he should try to talk them out of their foolhardy expedition once more.

The Santa Cruz River loomed ahead. Beyond lay the small village of Tucson, its flat-roofed adobes basking lazily in the sun. The stationmaster hailed Slade as Bent lent a hand helping the hostler to unhitch the team.

Hooking his thumb south to the Mexican border, the stationmaster told Slade that a mescal-soaked Apache had offered information about a Comanchero with a messed-up nose. "Vado's the name he goes by, according to the Apache."

Vado again! Despite his many disappointments, adrenaline coursed through Slade's veins. This could be the payoff. "Where's this Vado supposed to be?"

"With a bunch of Comancheros at a temporary camp a few miles across the border. You know, where the Santa Cruz cuts back to the east."

"How temporary?"

"Who knows? The Apache says they've been there less than a week. My guess is another week, two weeks."

Undecided, Slade stared through the shimmering heat waves toward the Mexican border. He shook his head in frustration.

If he went after Vado, Cochise would probably kill the prospecting party before Slade could return. But, if he helped the Dubuissons, Vado could drop out of sight, perhaps for years once again.

He glanced over his shoulder at the looming peaks of the Santa Catalinas. Beyond them lay Black Mountain. He quickly calculated the time. He could reach the Black within a day, try to talk sense to the Dubuissons, and return the next day.

That was only two days. Maybe he would then still have time to find Vado. Usually when Comancheros staked out a camp, they stayed put for a few weeks. And across the border, they were safe from U.S. pursuit.

Slade saddled the buckskin. The animal was well rested and full of vinegar as they headed north. Once or twice, the high-stepping animal crowhopped just out of sheer pleasure. Slade grinned. The animal wanted to run. Why not? He drove his heels into the buckskin's flanks. Within a half-dozen steps, the buckskin was at a full gallop. The Nez Percé in the young man grinned broadly for the sheer joy of riding such a magnificent animal.

Once he reached the Catalinas, Slade had no trouble following the trail of the prospecting party. The few Apache he met were well aware of the intrusion of the party of white-eyes. The last Apache, a toothless old woman gathering roots, grinned when she told him that Cochise, at that very moment, was heading for Black Mountain.

Kicking the buckskin back into a gallop, Slade raced deeper into the Catalinas. Beyond the Catalinas, the foreboding peak of Black Mountain rose on the horizon.

Long before he reached the party, the popping of gunfire echoed down the mountain valleys and across the granite ridges. Suddenly, two Apache braves materialized on the trail ahead of Slade. He drew up and held up his hand, recognizing both men, who were about his own age. "Ito. Paleto. It is I, Busca." With his other hand, Slade removed his hat.

The two braves approached cautiously, their dark eyes taking in his appearance. Suddenly, Ito broke into a broad grin. "It is you, Busca. It is good you are home."

Paleto stopped by the buckskin's shoulder and stared

up at Slade. He offered his hand. "My brother, my heart is happy that the One-Who-Seeks has returned."

Slade slipped from the saddle and took Paleto's hand. The two Apache braves barely came to his chin. He grinned down at them. As boys, Slade and Paleto had lived as brothers in the same wickiup, but the three had run together. "It does my heart good also, little brother. Nana would be happy for you."

"I would like to see my other brother."

The Apache brave pointed to the south. "He is with the Nednis."

"Perhaps later," Slade said.

Paleto stepped back and looked Slade over, comparing his brother's broad shoulders and towering height to the wiry suppleness and thinness of his Apache friend. "You have grown much since you left, Busca."

"But you could still best me at swing-kicking."

Both braves smiled at Slade's humility toward the game at which he excelled. He had not forgotten the ways of the Apache.

The sound of distant gunfire interrupted them. Slade looked around. "Who is that?"

A sneer curled Ito's thin lips. "Greedy white-eyes. The same thing. They believe they can come into our home and take whatever they wish just because their skin is white."

"I understand," the young half-breed replied. "Tell me, my brother. Is a woman with them?"

The two braves glanced at each other. Ito replied, "How did you know?"

"It is my fault they are here. Like a foolish boy, I spoke of the gold. Who leads our people?"

141

Paleto's chest expanded. "Who else? Cochise."

Slade swung back into the saddle. "I would see him."

Momentarily, their eyes grew wary. Ito nodded. "If you say you must."

"Will you return to the rancheria with us after the white ones are slain?" Paleto asked.

"Not today. Another time. Now I must see Cochise."

Cochise was not difficult to find. He stood out in any group. Taller and more muscular than the average Apache, he exuded a majesty in every move he made. He nodded when Slade approached. He remembered well the One-Who-Seeks, for he had given the young man his blessing when Slade left the tribe to fight the bluecoats and to seek out his sister if she still lived.

Quickly Slade told Cochise the reason for his visit. "If we permit the white eyes to leave, we will stand tall in the eyes of the bluecoats. The Comanches and the Kiowas have much trouble now on the Staked Plains. The army is planning to send Colonel MacKenzie to Texas, where he will set up patrols at many of the forts to force the tribes to the reservation. Richardson, Griffin, and Concho, those forts I know with certainty. If we can end this with no killing, it will be the best for the Apaches."

The solemn chief stared levelly into Slade's eyes. He understood the meaning of the young man's words. Once the bluecoats forced the Comanches and Kiowas to the reservation, they would turn on the Apache. Meager rations of tainted pork and wormy cornmeal did not appeal to Cochise. But even rotten food was preferable to permitting the white man to steal from the Apache's sacred valley.

"Whatever the gods say must be." He nodded to the puffs of smoke coming from behind the boulders at the mouth of a small canyon. "The white man must be punished."

Slade tried again. "If you were to grant their lives, I guarantee that the people and soldiers in Tucson will hear of your generosity. And word will spread to the bluecoats in Texas."

Cochise considered the young man's request. He had always held Busca in high esteem and had managed to always know how the young man was progressing. He knew Busca was respected by the white people, that there were many who would listen to the young man's words. Perhaps he was right. Perhaps a show of mercy would still the current unrest among the whites.

Cochise nodded to the fighting. "What if some of the white-eyes should refuse?"

Slade shrugged. "Always, there are foolish ones. I will take out those who wish to take advantage of your generosity. They also will speak not only of your good-will but also of the foolishness of the others."

The chief nodded. Cupping his hand to his lips, he gave the strident, broken cry of an eagle. The firing ceased on the Apache side. Moments later, the firing near the mouth of the canyon died out.

Slade called out. "Hold your fire. It's me, Jake Slade. I'm coming up."

A man's voice replied, "Don't stick yore stinkin' Injun hide out if you don't want yore head blown clean off. Ain't nobody comin' up here."

An abrupt undercurrent of voices drifted down from the canyon. A familiar voice called out, "Slade. This is Phillip Dubuisson. Is that really you?"

"It's me."

"Step out where I can see you."

Slade saw amusement in Cochise's eyes. He grinned ruefully. "I'll step out. Just don't any of you fellers get itchy fingers, especially if you want to get out of this scrape with a whole hide."

Taking a deep breath, Slade stepped into the open, his muscles bunched, ready to leap aside at the slightest sign of treachery. Phillip Dubuisson rose from behind the boulders and waved Slade forward.

Thirteen men and one woman made up the party. Catheryn looked up at him hopefully. Her hair was tangled and matted. Her grimy cheeks were streaked with tears.

Phillip stepped forward. "Am I glad to see you. I—"

"You're a damned fool!" He glared at Phillip, and at each man in the group. "Every damned one of you is a fool. This is Apache country. This is their home. They will no sooner let you steal from their home than you would let someone steal from your own."

"Bullshit," spat out one of the prospectors, a burly man with a bushy red beard and a mop of red hair sticking out from under a beaver-skin cap. "This is wide-open country. Belongs to all of us. Ain't no Injun lover goin' to tell me what to do."

Slade's fingers slowly eased the rawhide loop from the hammer of his .44 as he replied, "I'm not arguing with you, mister. I'm not talking about what's right, or what's wrong. All I'm telling you is if you want to live, then Cochise will let you walk out of here right now. If you stay and fight . . ." He looked directly into Catheryn Dubuisson's frightened eyes. "If you stay and fight, you'll die."

He turned back to the redheaded man. "The only reason that red hair of yours won't be dangling from an Apache lance is that the Apache don't take scalps, but you'll be just as dead."

The man glared murderously at Slade. Slowly he raised the muzzle of his Sharps. "You'd like to be the one to do that, wouldn't you, Injun lover?"

"Not me, mister." He hooked his thumb over his shoulder. "Those men out there. They'll take care of the job, don't worry." Shaking his head, Slade glanced at the others. The men stared at each other. He read their thoughts. They were wondering if this was a trick to get them into the open. His eyes narrowed. To hell with them. He turned to Phillip. "Well?"

Catheryn cried out, "Slade! Behind you."

Instantly he dropped to his knee, his .44 leaping into his hand. The booming thunder of the Sharps deafened him. He felt the concussion as the slug exploded against the boulder at his back. Slivers of granite stabbed into his flesh. In the same instant, the .44 barked twice.

Two dark holes appeared in the redheaded man's shirt. The man's eyes grew wide as he stared with disbelief at the two pools of blood spreading over his chest. His knees folded. He crumpled to the ground.

The remainder of the party stared in stunned surprise. A barrage of gunfire from below brought them back to their senses. They threw themselves behind the boulders and returned fire.

Slade cursed under his breath. The whole plan had blown up in his face. All he could do now was try to save Phillip and Catheryn. But how? Where would they go? He looked around the small canyon behind them.

SEVENTEEN

Slade ignored the slugs whining over his head and ricocheting off the rock wall as he crouched against the granite boulder. Phillip huddled by his side. Across the small clearing, Catheryn hunkered down in a shallow crevice, her face buried in her hands, her shoulders shaking with fear.

Quickly Slade studied the canyon behind him, sifting back through years of memories. The sheer granite walls of the box canyon towered over them, giving the impression of a solid, unbroken escarpment. Lining one side of the canyon, a thicket of cedar struggled out of the rocky soil. Beyond the cedar, in the corner of the canyon, was a patch of creosote bushes.

If they were in the canyon where Slade believed them to be, then there was a narrow crevice in the granite wall behind the creosote. But not only did it lead to safety, it also led to the canyon of gold!

Nothing he could do about that now. He hoped he remembered correctly. Once they broke from the protection of the boulders, there was no turning back. If he was right, he could lead the couple to safety. If not . . . He shrugged with Apache fatality. If not, then where they died really made little difference. Death was as final one place as another.

Acrid gun smoke stung his nostrils. If they were going to make a move, now was the time. He shouted above the gunfire to Phillip. "Now!" He burst from his crouch and dashed across the clearing to Catheryn. Slugs exploded against the granite above his head. I hope to hell she don't crowhop on me, he said to himself as he raced to the cowering woman.

Her eyes were wide with fear as Slade grabbed her wrist and yanked her after him. He didn't look back, but he knew Phillip was following for the thin man was gulping air like a laboring horse. Slugs smashed into the rock walls above their heads and knocked out chunks of granite at their feet.

They zigzagged around the boulders and dodged through the spindly cedar along the base of the canyon wall. The gunfire slowly faded behind them.

Slade led them into the patch of creosote at the rear of the canyon. Behind the thicket, a narrow seam split the granite wall. "In here," he whispered, pulling Catheryn into the fissure behind him. Phillip crowded in on their heels.

The crevice grew narrow, forcing them to turn sideways. A frightened whimper escaped Catheryn's lips. Slade assured her. "We're going to make it. Just don't quit on me now."

The darkness surrounding them was complete and suffocating. Slade's knees brushed against the wall as the crevice narrowed to less than eighteen inches.

Phillip groaned. "We'll get stuck in here."

The young man ignored Dubuisson. "Not long now," he said. "A few more feet."

Catheryn pulled against him. "No. Let's go back. We'll get lost in here."

Slade held her wrist in an iron grip and jerked her after him. They rounded a bend, and a light at the end of the narrow crevice greeted them.

"Look," shouted Phillip. "Daylight."

"Not that way," said Slade, abruptly leading them into another dark tunnel.

Phillip hurried down the first cave to the daylight. He jerked to a halt just inside the fissure. His eyes bulged. Across the canyon, the sun reflected off a fan-shaped vein of gold that stretched from the base of the sheer wall to the rim. The valley was about ten acres in size, and nuggets of pure gold lay strewn about the valley floor.

He started to step into the valley, but three Apache braves came into sight on the canyon rim. Phillip jerked back into the darkness, then hurried after Catheryn and Slade.

No more than thirty seconds had passed, but Slade had stopped. He was calling softly in the darkness. "Phillip! Dammit, where are you?"

"Here," he whispered. "I— I fell and hit my head. Must have stunned me for a moment."

Slade grunted.

Catheryn asked, "You all right?"

"Yeah. Fine. Let's go. I hate caves."

Five minutes later, the three emerged from the cave overlooking a broad valley filled with huge boulders rounded by the weather.

"Wait here. I'll see what's out there," said Slade, disappearing among the boulders.

He returned moments later. "Let's go. If we hurry, we can be off Black Mountain before sundown. Then we'll be safe."

Slade led the way. Phillip walked beside Catheryn. He tilted his head to her. "I saw it."

"Saw what?" she replied.

"Shhh. Not so loud." He glanced at Slade, who continued down the rocky path. "He'll hear."

Catheryn nodded. She hesitated upon seeing the blaze of excitement in his eyes. "Hear what?"

"Back in the cave. Remember seeing the daylight before we turned down that other tunnel?"

"What about it?"

"That's it," he said, unable to keep the excitement from his voice. "That's the canyon with all of the gold!"

She jerked to a halt and stared at him in disbelief. He pulled her after him. "Come on. Don't let on that we know. But that's it. That's the canyon. That's the one with the gold Slade told us about."

Slade glanced over his shoulder. The Dubuissons had dropped behind. "Hurry up," he whispered. "We've got to get off the mountain."

The Dubuissons' eyes met. Catheryn nodded. She and Phillip hurried after Slade.

They camped at dusk in the foothills of a nearby peak. Slade built a small fire with flint and tinder. Later, when Phillip had gone to relieve himself, Catheryn told Slade that she had been forced to go with her husband, that he was the one who insisted on cashing in the gold Slade had given them and using the cash to outfit this last expedition.

Before Slade could reply, a six-gun bellowed from the dark. Phillip screamed. Leaping to his feet, Slade raced into the darkness outside the fire. A crushing blow struck him in the side of the head, smashing him to the rocky ground. Instinctively he rolled when he hit the ground, lashing out with his feet. Suddenly the ground disappeared beneath him, and he felt himself falling.

Desperately he grabbed at the granite wall. Sharp slivers slashed his fingers, but he felt no pain. His fingers seized a straggly bush growing from the side of the bluff. His momentum was too much for his grasp, ripping his grip loose, but his fall was broken.

He hit the ground in the next instant. His knees buckled, and he collapsed in a heap at the base of the bluff as a dark wave of unconsciousness swept over him.

Overhead, dark figures stared into the night. With a grunt, they moved away.

The next morning, Slade rose slowly, testing his stiff body for broken bones. His head throbbed. Gingerly, he laid a finger on the lump on the back of his head. He winced as he touched the raw flesh.

He looked up and saw the small bush that had broken his fall. Lucky. The cliff from which he had fallen was over thirty feet high.

Clambering up a slope of talus, Slade found the camp empty. He studied the sign. He discovered a deep heel print in a crevice filled with sand. He shook his head. No Apache made that track. It was Comancheros. That's who was responsible.

Outside of the camp, Slade discovered Phillip unconscious, a bullet wound in his chest.

Packing the wound with spider webs, Slade rigged a travois and dragged Phillip down the mountain to the winding road where he hailed a freight wagon and hitched a ride to Tucson.

He reached the small village after dark. Leaving the wounded man with Doc Burk, Slade headed back to the small hut he shared with Three-Fingers Bent.

A soft whistle halted him. Palming his revolver, he stepped into the shadows alongside an adobe. The soft thud of hooves sounded in the night air as a shadowy figure on horseback moved toward him.

He relaxed and holstered his .44. It was Paleto with the buckskin. The lithe Apache slid from the saddle and handed Slade the reins. "Thanks," said the young half-breed.

Paleto grinned, his teeth bright in the moonlight. "Thank Cochise. I would have kept the buckskin. He is a fine animal." His tone was teasing.

Slade returned the Apache's grin. With mock dismay, he said, "But, my brother, he is my animal. Would you have treated me so? I would not do you as such."

The Apache's grin broadened. "Nor I, Busca, my brother. Nor I. We learned of the ambush only today." He paused, the smile fading from his face. "Cochise is much relieved that you are without injury. He had taken the animal with him when you did not return."

Slade nodded. "He is a good friend, and you are a good brother."

Paleto grinned. "The man, he is alive?"

"Barely. What about the woman? Do you know who the Comancheros are?"

"Their leader is called Diaz, but he did not lead the ambush."

"Then who?"

"It was the one called Vado. He follows Diaz—who is one the gods would gladly see dead."

Slade grunted with grim satisfaction. Vado again. The Comanchero had come up from his camp on the Santa Cruz. "That is good."

The Apache frowned. "I do not understand, Busca."

"I believe Vado is one of those who also killed my mother and stole my sister. Find him, and we save the woman and capture the man I have searched years to find."

Paleto grunted. "You are certain he is the one?"

Slade shrugged. "Nothing is certain. Has he returned to his rancheria?"

"Yes." Paleto nodded to the south. "A few miles beyond the border."

"With the woman?"

"That I do not know. I do know he will not harm her for himself. Vado prefers the *degrados, Indio* or *Mexicano.* The white ones, if untouched, he and Diaz sell for much money."

His eyes narrowing, Slade asked, "Is Chief Juh still buying white women?"

Paleto laughed softly. "Is Chief Juh still alive?"

That was Slade's answer. "So he is?"

"Yes."

The young half-breed swung into the saddle. "Can you take me to Vado?" he asked, looking down at his brother.

152

"I know the place well," he replied, breaking into a fast trot down the dirt road that led out of town.

"But first to my home," the broad-shouldered man said.

EIGHTEEN

Paleto waited in the shadows cast by the small adobe as a cool breeze swept across the prairie. Moments later, Slade came out of his adobe and dropped a pouch of nuggets into his saddlebags. "Gold. For the Comanchero."

Paleto held up his double-edged knife. "This is what the Comanchero needs."

"Later. If this doesn't work," he replied, laying his hand on the saddlebags.

The Apache nodded and cut between the adobes to the desert. Slade fell in behind, not even considering offering his brother a ride. He knew what the answer would be. Paleto would sneer at his offer with the boast that an Apache can run the legs off any horse. And, Slade knew from experience, he could.

False dawn found them at the border. By the time the sun peeked over the horizon, they had secreted themselves in a small cave on a bluff overlooking the Comanchero camp. Slade watched the camp as Paleto slept. The morning passed slowly.

He studied the camp in an effort to spot Diaz and

GET
4 FREE BOOKS!

You can have the best Westerns delivered to your door for less than what you'd pay in a bookstore or online. Sign up for one of our book clubs today, and we'll send you **4 FREE* BOOKS**, worth $23.96, just for trying it out...**with no obligation to buy, ever!**

———◆•◆———

Authors include classic writers such as
LOUIS L'AMOUR, MAX BRAND, ZANE GREY
and more; PLUS new authors such as
COTTON SMITH, TIM CHAMPLIN, JOHNNY D. BOGGS
and others.

———◆•◆———

As a book club member you also receive the following special benefits:
- **30% OFF all orders through our website & telecenter!**
- **Exclusive access to special discounts!**
- **Convenient home delivery and 10 days to return any books you don't want to keep.**

There is no minimum number of books to buy,
and you may cancel membership at any time.
See back to sign up!

*Please include $2.00 for shipping and handling.

YES! ☐

Sign me up for the Leisure Western Book Club and send my FOUR FREE BOOKS! If I choose to stay in the club, I will pay only $13.44* each month, a savings of $10.52!

NAME: _____

ADDRESS: _____

_____

TELEPHONE: _____

E-MAIL: _____

☐ **I WANT TO PAY BY CREDIT CARD.**

☐ VISA ☐ MasterCard ☐ DISCOVER

ACCOUNT #: _____

EXPIRATION DATE: _____

SIGNATURE: _____

Send this card along with $2.00 shipping & handling to:

**Leisure Western Book Club
20 Academy Street
Norwalk, CT 06850-4032**

Or fax (must include credit card information!) to: 610.995.9274.
You can also sign up online at www.dorchesterpub.com.

*Plus $2.00 for shipping. Offer open to residents of the U.S. and Canada only.
Canadian residents please call 1.800.481.9191 for pricing information.
If under 18, a parent or guardian must sign. Terms, prices and conditions subject to change. Subscription subject
to acceptance. Dorchester Publishing reserves the right to reject any order or cancel any subscription.

JOIN NOW!

Vado. But as the morning progressed, Slade came to the conclusion that only one of the two Comancheros was in camp.

A Comanchero was caste conscious, the leader setting himself apart by the opulence of his wagon. Among the ragtag band of wagons below, only one could house the leader of the Comancheros. That wagon was a converted Conestoga with a flat top of black-and-white cowhide.

But who lived in the wagon? Vado, the follower? Or Diaz, the leader?

The sun burned down from directly overhead when Paleto took his turn. Slade lay back on the cool rock floor and immediately fell asleep.

Muted screams penetrated his deep slumber. Paleto looked around when Slade stirred. The Apache brave's face was impassive. He nodded to the camp.

Below, the Comancheros were holding an Indian woman down and taking turns abusing her. Her guttural cries grew weaker and weaker. Slade's face turned to granite. "The hell with the gold," he muttered harshly, referring to the nuggets he had brought to buy Catheryn.

"Ay, Busca," said Paleto, slipping his knife from its deerskin sheath. "I will take much pleasure in making him speak."

When the Comancheros finished with the woman, they left her lying on the hot sand and went to the chuck wagon where they took turns drinking from large jugs of whiskey. They laughed drunkenly at the woman who slowly pulled together the pieces of her torn garments and struggled to sit up.

"They have not finished with her."

Slade eyed his brother. The Apache's wiry muscles rippled under his taut skin. *Paleto*—Apache for "clown," One-Who-Laughs. Never, thought the young half-breed, had he heard a name so consummate in Apache irony as this one. In all of the years he had known Paleto, the somber man had smiled no more than a handful of times.

Living with the white man for the last seven years, Slade had picked up many of their mannerisms and idioms. But after a short time with Paleto, the quiet young man slipped easily back into the Apache vernacular without being aware of doing so. It was the language of his formative years with the Apache.

"That is the way of things, my brother," he said, sensing that Paleto had troubled thoughts. "There is nothing we can do to help the woman. We must remain hidden if we wish to take the white woman."

Paleto turned his impassive eyes on Slade and made a throwaway gesture with his hand. "The Indian woman does not bother me. She is a Pimo. They are all dogs."

"Then what troubles you?"

He turned his solemn eyes on Slade. "As you slept, I thought of things."

"What things?"

"Of things I do not like to think about."

Slade frowned.

Paleto continued. "There is much out there . . ." He made a sweeping gesture with his hand to indicate the world outside. "Much that is changing. I have heard it from Cochise. Yes, even from Geronimo. The Apache must change if he is to survive. As I sit here and think on it, I am troubled."

He paused, stared at the ground, then turned his black eyes defiantly on Slade. "I do not want to change.

156

My life is full. I go where I wish. Food is plentiful. I have many enemies to fight. Why should such pleasures be forsaken?"

Slade looked at his brother with compassion. He knew exactly of what Paleto spoke, but he also knew change was inevitable. He had seen much of it in the East during the war. "Even our fathers faced change. Are we not men such as they?"

Paleto shook his head slowly. "Our change will be much more. So much I fear that my son and his son will never know of the pleasures I enjoyed."

Slade leaned back against the wall of the cave. What could he say—that the time would never come when the Indian would be forced to live as the white man? No. That was a lie, and lies only added to the pain.

Before Slade could reply, Paleto continued. "I had a dream, a strange dream. In it, I spoke with a holy man of the Paiutes who was said to have the power to bring dead people to life as well as to bring back the buffalo."

A frown knit Slade's forehead. "But buffalo are plentiful. The prairies are black with their numbers."

"That also puzzles me. Why dream of bringing back what is already here? Nevertheless, in my dream the holy man gave me a cup of liquid that took my life. I found myself in a new and beautiful land. My father and his father met me. Game was plentiful. The grass was green and high, and all of the Indian nations lived as one. Then the holy man brought me back to life.

"He taught me a new dance, a new song, and a new prayer. With it, he gave me sacred red paint. Back among my people, I spoke of my experience, of the dance, the *Wanagiwachipi*."

"Ghost dance?"

The solemn brave nodded. "We danced. On our clothes were painted the sun, the moon, the stars, and magpies. We danced through the night as if in a swoon, glorying in the new world we had been shown." He paused. His black eyes grew mournful. "Then the soldier came. With great guns he killed us."

For long moments, silence hung like an oppressive cloud over them. Slade cleared his throat. "It was but a dream."

Paleto nodded. "A dream, yes. But look around you, my brother. Our life is not the happy thing today it was when you and I were young."

"Perhaps not, but in other ways, we are happier." Slade did not really believe his own words, for Paleto's vision disturbed him.

"We had much fun, is that not so?" Paleto asked suddenly, waving his arms about his head, trying to frighten the gloom from his shoulders as you would scare buzzards away from carrion.

"Much fun."

And they spoke of days past, when as young boys they shared dreams, hunted game, played at being great warriors. It was a day of both happiness and sadness for Slade. Many of his old friends were dead. Others still lived, still fought. Deep in his heart, he knew that the days of his people were few, that they must be swallowed up by the coming changes. He, himself, had witnessed the strength and the power of the white man.

His thoughts returned to the present, to the Comancheros camped below. Within hours, the man for whom he had searched for years would be at his mercy.

The sun dropped below the western horizon. Still they waited. Finally, during the darkness before moonrise, they slipped into the camp. Paleto moved like a wraith, but the years in the white man's world had dulled Slade's skills. His foot rolled on some small rocks. The sound, though faint as the whisper of a lizard's feet over sand, nevertheless aroused the attention of a guard. Slade melted into the shadows at the base of a saguaro.

Blocking out the stars, a dark figure appeared in silhouette against the horizon. Crouching lower, Slade slipped his knife from its sheath and waited, muscles tense.

The guard drew closer.

Out of the corner of his eye, the wiry young man saw another movement to his right. It was Paleto slithering through the underbrush. Slade gripped his knife tightly. If the guard continued, he would stumble right over Slade.

Just as the guard reached the giant cactus, a tiny moan sounded to the right. Immediately the guard spun and jerked his rifle to his shoulder.

With the speed of a striking snake, Slade leaped forward, jammed his forearm around the guard's throat and crushed the man's windpipe into jelly.

He slammed the double-edged knife between the guard's ribs, deep into his lungs. The man tried to scream but no sound came from his throat. Violently, Slade worked the blade, reaming out a gaping hole in the struggling man's lungs.

The man's legs buckled. Slade stepped back. The guard slumped to the ground, blood bubbling from his lips. Paleto appeared by Slade's side. The two disappeared into the sparse underbrush surrounding the camp.

Moments later, they spotted the Conestoga. The side drapes were tied open to allow the night breeze to play over the elaborate four-poster bed in which the Comanchero leader slept. Four sentries guarded the wagon.

There was no way Slade and Paleto could slip in undetected. Two of the guards might doze, perhaps even three, but all four— Slade shook his head.

He felt the light touch of Paleto's hand on his arm. The Apache sniffed the air. They picked up the thick odor of human waste on a vagrant breeze from off the desert.

Like a ghost, Paleto disappeared into the darkness. Slade stayed at his heels. Why hadn't he thought of that? The Comancheros, as did the majority of the Indian tribes, always specified a particular area in which members relieved themselves. And such an area was never posted with guards.

The two men ducked behind the underbrush and waited. Sooner or later, Vado or Diaz would show up. Before he had time to ease himself into a comfortable position, Slade saw the Mexican clamber down from the wagon and head in his direction. Paleto disappeared in the shadows at the base of a creosote bush.

When the Comanchero passed the bush, Paleto cupped his hand over the Mexican's mouth and jabbed the needle tip of his knife under the frightened man's chin.

Slade moved next to him in the darkness and whispered. "One sound, and my friend here slices your fat throat."

NINETEEN

Paleto led the fat Mexican into the night, where Slade bound the burly man's hands behind his back and looped a strip of rawhide around the Comanchero's fat neck.

Stealing a horse for himself, Paleto led the way back to the cave, where they picked up Slade's buckskin.

Still leading his horse, Paleto then guided the small party to a dark and narrow crevice in the granite mountain overlooking the camp. The faint smell of rotted flesh assailed Slade's nostrils. Ignoring the odor, Slade looped a lariat around the Comanchero's neck and gave the other end to Paleto.

Groans of fear escaped the Mexican's gagged lips as he stumbled forward in the darkness. With each step, the odor grew stronger. The cave twisted through the mountain. Several times the Comanchero fell. Slade yanked him to his feet and shoved him forward. The blackness of the mountain was complete.

"We are here." Paleto's whisper bounced off the silent walls. The only sounds were of the scrape of the lariat being untied and a *thunk* as it dropped to the cave floor. "I will return," Paleto said.

Slade waited. The consummate blackness of the cave pressed in on him—suffocating. The fetid odor of rotted meat was thick and heavy.

The Mexican gagged.

Tiny sparks punched holes in the darkness. Paleto was building a fire. How often had the Mimbre Apache been in here, if he could move so surely through the darkness? Slade wondered.

A spark ignited a wisp of tinder. A flame flared, lighting the large room in which they stood. The Mexican prisoner groaned and staggered back against Slade. That's when the half-breed saw why Paleto was so familiar with the cave. It was a room of torture.

White bones littered the floor. Squealing rats scurried through a row of grinning skulls set on a stone ledge spanning the back wall. At the end of the row were two heads, one Mexican, one Indian, with maggot-covered chunks of flesh still clinging to the skulls, the source of the putrid odor permeating the room.

Paleto rose from the fire. He approached the Comanchero menacingly, his knife drawn. Slade stepped around in front of the Mexican for a good look at him. It had been fourteen years, but he was convinced he would still recognize the man who killed his mother, kidnapped his sister, and shot him.

He stopped in surprise. The Comanchero was not familiar. His nose was hooked from being broken. That must have been what both the pistolero and the Apache meant about the nose. "Damn," he muttered.

"This is not the one, Busca?" asked the Mimbre Apache.

"No. The one for which I search has part of his nose

missing. Right here," he said, drawing a line across the bridge of his own nose.

"Perhaps so," the Indian whispered, taking another step toward the Comanchero. "But this one might know of the one you seek." In a movement too quick for the eye, Paleto punched the point of his blade under the Comanchero's chin. "I think he will tell us what we wish to know." With his free hand, he whipped the gag loose.

"What do they call you?" asked Slade.

"Vado," the Mexican said hoarsely.

Slade eyed the burly Comanchero, who, sensing he was not to be immediately murdered, stared back defiantly. "You heard who I'm looking for. The Comanchero with the top of his nose missing. He is the murderer of my mother and the thief of my sister. Do you know him?"

The man pressed his thick lips together tightly.

"I asked you if you know the man."

The Comanchero remained silent despite the bubble of blood appearing around the point of Paleto's knife.

Paleto grinned back at Slade. "He is stubborn. But I will make him not so stubborn."

Keeping the knife at Vado's throat, Paleto led him to a boulder with a flat top, like a table. Next to the table was a heavy post sunk in the ground.

Slade nodded. He had not been away from the Apache long enough to forget. He tied the Mexican to the post.

Paleto freed one of the man's arms and lashed his trembling hand to the rock table, palm down. He then tied a strip of rawhide around the first joint of each finger and stretched them into a fan shape.

163

Vado's eyes were wild with fear, but he refused to speak. Slade asked again, his voice filled with warning. "Were you with those who escaped from Fort Richardson?"

Arms folded across his chest and his face impassive, Paleto looked on. Vado swallowed hard and shook his head. Paleto's hand flashed.

In the next instant the Comanchero sucked in his breath, then screamed in shock when he saw his little finger bounce across the rock table. Blood spurted from his hand as the Mimbre Apache drew back his knife and wiped the blood on his bare thigh.

Slade narrowed his eyes. "You best give me an answer while you have any fingers left."

Vado nodded eagerly. Words tumbled from his lips. "*Si, si.* I tell you. I was there. I was there." He squeezed his eyes shut and groaned through his dry lips. "*Dios.* It hurts. How it hurts."

"Speak then. Where is the man with the top of his nose missing?"

He stared at them with pleading eyes. The flickering of the flames glistened on the sweat beading on his greasy forehead and fat brown cheeks. "In *Tejas.* Fort Richardson. Elizio Hernandez is the one you seek. *Por favor.* No more."

Slade's face twisted in anger. "You lie. He was not among those who escaped with you."

Paleto raised his knife threateningly.

"No, no," Vado blubbered. "Two weeks ago. Riders say a colonel by the name of Mackenzie captured him and took him to Fort Richardson."

The young half-breed's eyes narrowed. So Mackenzie was already in Texas. The Comanchero's explanation fit the information Slade had picked up at Fort Sill. "This Elizio Hernandez—how do you know he is the one I seek?"

"The nose is as you say." Vado nodded his head violently. "He is the one. *Por Dios*. He is the one. The top of his nose has been shot away."

Paleto lowered his knife as Slade said, "How can you be sure he is the one? Such could happen to many."

Vado answered hastily, his dark eyes on Paleto, wary of any move of the lithe Apache. "In camp, years ago, he bragged of the white girl he and Diaz and a third man had captured from an Indian squaw."

"And?"

"He also told of shooting a young boy, a breed."

Slade's face hardened. "I was the boy." Rage boiled up in him. He took a step toward the bound Comanchero, his hand on the hilt of his own knife. How simple, how easy to spill the bastard's bowels on the floor and let him rot here with the others. He struggled to control the fury pounding in his chest.

The Comanchero read Slade's thoughts. He cringed. "I was not there. I have been with Elizio for only these last four years."

"You spoke of a third one. Where is he?"

Vado cast a frightened glance at Paleto. "Dead. Elizio killed him in an argument."

Slade felt a surge of excitement. "And the child. Where is she?"

"Please, senor. I know nothing of the little ones. All I know of a child is that the friars at Altar took from Elizio a boy-child. But I do not know when. That is what Diaz has said. Of the girl, I know nothing."

"The white woman you stole from Black Mountain. Where is she?"

"I . . . I did not steal her. It was Diaz."

"Where is Diaz? Where is the woman?"

"I do not know. She—" He squealed like a pig as Paleto's knife flashed in the firelight, and another finger bounced off the table. "I tell you true. She is gone south. That is all I know."

Paleto raised the knife again.

Vado babbled. "*No lo quiera Dios!* I speak the truth. God forbid that I lie. All I know is that the Nednis had spoken of wanting a white woman. After we captured her, the one for whom I work, Senor Diaz, said he would take her to the chief." With each beat of his heart, blood spurted from the two nubs on his hand.

Slade studied the blubbering Mexican. Fourteen years had passed. Much changes in such a span. Was the man one of the three? He did not believe so. "It is enough."

Paleto slashed Vado's bonds. The swarthy Comanchero collapsed to his knees, clutching his bloody hand to his belly. Slade touched the tip of his knife to Vado's jugular. "I let you live now. I see you again, I will kill you and leave you for the buzzards."

"We go now," the Mimbre Apache said, swinging astride the mustang. "The Nednis live in the Sierra Madres east of the village of Arizpe." He dug his heels into his mustang's flanks and rode recklessly down the dark and narrow cave. Slade followed, having already decided on his next step.

Behind, the Comanchero, Vado, cried out, "*Dios.* Do not leave me. I beg of you. I beg . . ." His words faded away under the pounding of the horses' hooves.

It was midmorning when they rode out of the crevice

and headed east. Five miles beyond the Comanchero camp, Slade pulled alongside Paleto and signaled for him to halt. "Diaz took her to the Nedni. That's Juh, isn't it?"

Paleto grinned. "That is as we guessed." He pounded his fist with his chest. "See, Busca? We are very smart men." His face grew somber. "But there is a problem."

"What is that?"

"As you said, Juh is of the Nedni. They are brothers to the Chiricahua. Cochise will become very angry if I go with you. You are special. You are Busca, the One-Who-Seeks. That is your vision. The gods and the moon and the stars have given you the vision. We cannot forbid such. But I . . . That is not my destiny."

"I understand. I would not have you offend a brother Apache. But I will ask a favor."

"Ask."

"I go after Diaz. Return to Bent in Tucson. Have him wire Captain Anderson at Fort Sill in Oklahoma Territory and ask him to have the authorities at Fort Richardson hold Elizio Hernandez until I get there."

The Mimbre Apache nodded. "I will do as you ask."

Slade offered Paleto his hand. "You are a good brother and a good friend. I will not forget."

Paleto the Clown came as close to shedding tears as he had ever come in his life. "Take care, Brother."

Slade blinked back his own tears and nodded. As Paleto rode away, Slade thought of the young girl in the mission at San Diego of whom Alberto Munoz had spoken. He shook his head. Such miracles were impossible.

TWENTY

Slade pulled up in the angular shadows of a giant saguaro and stared across the grayish green sea of creosote bushes and yucca spikes at the forbidding peaks of the Sierra Madres.

He glanced over his shoulder toward Black Mountain, continuing to struggle with his conscience. He knew he had to find Catheryn Dubuisson, but every minute he spent on her rescue was another minute something could go wrong at Fort Richardson.

The best thing to do, he told himself for the tenth time, was to get the trip down to Juh's over as fast as possible. With a soft click of his tongue, Slade put the buckskin into a gentle canter.

The Sierra Madres extend from northern Arizona two thousand miles into Mexico and Central America. A hundred miles wide, the Madres are a tangle of serrated peaks, deep canyons, and broad valleys of volcanic dust as deep as a horse's belly.

A formidable fortress, the Sierra Madres are filled with natural hideaways and refuges as well as a menacing environment of rattlesnakes, mountain lions, and precipitous drop-offs with no bottom.

And secreted somewhere within their uninviting shadows sprawled the rancheria of Juh, chief of the Nedni Apache.

His volatile temper as well as his voracious appetite for white women was widely known among both the Indian and the white man. Juh took the women to live in his wickiup until he satisfied his own carnal desires. After tiring of a woman, he then sold her to lesser chieftains or braves.

Slade forced the thought of Catheryn being so abused from his head. He had to fabricate a plan, to shape a scheme that would force Juh to release Catheryn without a fight and without any loss of dignity for the Nedni chief. And such a plan would be a task indeed.

Getting into the camp would be no problem. He was reared Apache. All Apache tribes, the Jicarilla, the Mimbre, the Lipan, the Mescalero, the White Mountain, the Nedni, and the Aravaipa Apaches knew of Busca, the Chiricahua who sought his sister. Nedni hospitality would be extended him.

The next step was soliciting help without creating suspicion. The Apache feted visitors until the visitors offended them. So, he must appear open and innocent of guile. Yet he must find answers and solutions, and quickly. As far as he knew, Catheryn could already be in Juh's camp.

An idea struck him, one skewed to the Apache way of thought. He turned it over in his head, considering its good and bad points, balancing them against the principles and beliefs of the Apache. It might work—if she had not yet reached the rancheria. But, if she had . . .

He would have to be careful. He must be as cautious as the coyote, as wise as the owl, and as swift as the black cougar of his vision.

By midafternoon, the desert of yucca and creosote began to give way to the rocky inclines of the Sierras. The sun baked the saw-toothed slopes. Far back out in the desert, shimmering heat waves distorted the giant saguaros, whose mighty arms seemed to be wilting in the debilitating heat.

His eyes constantly quartered the rocky inclines surrounding him. He followed a faint trail, invisible to all but an Apache eye. It wound upward. The hair on the back of his neck rose. He reined up and raised his hand. The silence was so profound that crickets chirruped. "I am Busca, of the Chiricahua."

His voice seemed unnatural in the still air.

Moments later, three Apaches materialized from the boulders ahead of him. All wore similar garb—short loincloths; deerskin boots sagging around their ankles; and broad, colorful headbands to hold their long black hair away from their eyes.

Unable to still their curiosity, two braves cautiously approached. The third, an older one, did not move. All three carried bows at the ready. Within one second, all three could fire. Two seconds later, Slade would be dead.

He cleared his throat. "I am Busca. I have been away from my own many moons. I come now to pay respects to Chief Juh."

The two glanced back at the older brave, who nodded for Slade to come ahead. The third brave led the way while the two younger ones followed.

The route to the rancheria was circuitous, an Apache ploy that provided the camp with sufficient warning against surprise attacks. By the time an attacker traversed the numerous cutbacks, the tribe would have gained more than ample time to prepare itself.

The rancheria lay high in the peaks of the Sierras on a granite slab as flat as the prairie and as wide as the dry bed of the Red River. A scattering of wickiups constructed of brush lay on one side. On the next two sides were caves in which the majority of the Nedni Apaches opted to live. The deep caves provided shelter against the rain and, with small fires, warmth against the cold nights. Chief Juh himself lived in the largest cave with his three wives. The fourth side of the granite table looked out over the desert below.

Wearing baggy white trousers of muslin and the traditional boots, Juh rose from his sitting position just inside the mouth of the cave as Slade rode into the rancheria. He tugged at his buttonless cavalry blouse to straighten it over his broad shoulders, then majestically folded his arms across his chest. He was a stocky man with three white scars down the side of his head and neck. Whatever animal had scarred Juh, a bear or lion, Slade figured it had also taken the man's ear off.

Slade reined up at the mouth of the cave. With a deferential nod, he introduced himself again and explained that he was traveling deeper into Mexico and wished to rest for a few days. He gave no reason for the journey, nor would he be asked. He kept his eyes on the chief. For a guest to exhibit too much curiosity about the rancheria was considered offensive. But Slade watched out of the corner of his eyes for any sign of Catheryn.

Juh grunted. "I have heard of Busca. Whatever we

have is yours." He waved his wives forward. "Food and mescal for Busca of the Chiricahua. He is our guest." Apache hospitality was an obligation observed by every tribe. Juh had heard of the young man, and he was curious.

Just as Slade dismounted, a brave stepped from another cave. He called out.

Slade stiffened. He cut his eyes to the newcomer. A flush of relief washed over him. It was Nana, his brother who had shared the wickiup with Slade and Paleto when they were boys with the Mimbre and then later with the Chiricahua.

Nana rushed forward. The two men greeted each other warmly, each genuinely happy to see the other after many years. Slade said, "Paleto told me you were with the Nednis, my brother. I was surprised. You were with Cochise when I left to fight the army and search for my sister."

The Apache grinned and pointed to a slender woman kneeling in front of a small fire. "I took Young Deer as my woman."

"I understand," Slade replied. When an Apache brave married outside his tribe, he was expected to join the tribe of his wife. "She is like the moon."

The stocky Apache nodded briskly, his teeth gleaming in a proud smile.

Nana sat beside Slade during the meal in Juh's cave, after which the three men drank the fiery mescal. Throughout the entire period, Slade resisted the desire to look around the camp. There would be time for that later. Soon, both Juh's curiosity and Apache custom would be satisfied.

Rising to his feet, the chief dismissed his two guests. Nana nodded to his own cave. "Come. I have room."

Slade agreed and followed his brother across the granite plateau to the cave.

They sat in the darkness of the cave, drinking more mescal and speaking of the past and the future.

Nana asked of Slade's search for his sister, and the young half-breed quickly detailed all that had happened since their last meeting, even of the trip to Los Angeles and the conversation with Alberto Munoz. "The mission of Altar is where I must soon travel. Hernandez gave them a boy-child. Perhaps they saw my sister."

"You have searched long, my brother. Sometimes, we must face disappointments."

Slade looked deep into his brother's eyes. "I know of what you speak, but I believe she is alive, somewhere, just as is the young woman at the mission San Diego of whom I spoke earlier. Hernandez is in jail in Texas as we speak. There I must go when I leave you."

"I hope you are blessed by the sun and the moon. Now tell me of Paleto."

As Slade spoke, he studied the camp. He saw no white women. He wanted to ask of the Comancheros, to tell his brother that one of the men for whom he had searched was coming to the rancheria, but he could not decide how to broach the subject without creating suspicion.

Nana unknowingly came to his aid as Slade finished telling of their brother. Draining the last of the mescal from his gourd, the intoxicated Apache grunted and held up the empty cup. "This is good. It does not make me ill like the whiskey of the Comancheros. But it is not as sweet. I like the sweet of molasses even if I become ill."

"Did you not buy much when they last came?"

"Yes, but it has been long." His dark face brightened. "They return soon. You will stay. We will become drunk together, but not with the whisky that makes you ill. Diaz has good whiskey. That is what we shall buy."

Slade laughed with his brother. "We will see. If it is too long, I must go." He hesitated. Now was the right moment to put his plan into action. He lowered his voice. "I have an important task to accomplish, one such as you would understand."

Nana frowned and leaned forward, his black, stringy hair falling on either side of his pan-shaped face. His frown deepened.

Slade continued. "I have been told there is a man, perhaps a Comanchero, who has taken my woman."

The Apache sat back and stared quizzically at Slade as if to ask what a Comanchero wanted with an Apache woman.

The young half-breed explained. "She is white. Very beautiful. Several days ago at Black Mountain she was stolen from me. I want her back."

Nana eyed him suspiciously. "You think she belongs to Juh—that he sent for her?"

"No. I would not betray his hospitality by believing such an untruth. As I said, my brother, I am traveling south. I have been led to believe that the Comanchero is heading for Janos. After I leave, do you believe Chief Juh would consent to send word to me if he hears of her?"

Nana nodded solemnly. "I understand. Yes, I think he would. If you wish, I go with you."

Slade laid his hand on Nana's forearm. "Thank you,

but I will do it alone. Sometimes a lone wolf can kill more buffalo than the pack."

Nana grunted. It was dark out now. The tiny fire cast a flickering orange glow on his somber face. "Sometimes the buffalo turn on the wolf. Remember, I will help if you so desire me."

Guilt weighed heavily on Slade. Even though the Apache esteemed trickery and deceit above courage, he disliked lying to anyone, especially to his brother, but it was a small lie. And the lie had to be told, for the truth surely meant a fight between him and Juh, and that was one battle that Jake Slade could never win.

He dropped off to sleep with a grim smile on his face at the irony of his situation. He did not want to lie to Nana, but Nana would lie to him without hesitation if the stocky Apache were in his moccasins.

Well before false dawn, while the stars still twinkled brightly to the west, Slade rose and went out behind the camp and relieved himself. On a granite monolith far above, a dark figure sat. The camp sentry.

With a grunt, Slade raised his hand in greeting, and then climbed up the rocks to the young man. They spoke briefly. By now, shades of gray presaged the dawn. Slade turned to leave, but as he did, he spied a thin black string winding across the shadowy floor of the desert far below.

His pulse raced. Diaz! Slade did not react, gave no impression that he had even spied the wagon train. Quickly he hurried back to the rancheria, to Juh's, ready to put the next step of his plan into motion.

He repeated his story to the chief, who listened skeptically. "I told Nana of my search. He offered to travel with me, but my trip takes me south. I have no desire to take any of your warriors with me, but I would like to ask your help should you hear of my woman."

Juh eyed the younger man stoically. "How would you have me help?"

"I go to Janos. If you hear of her, send a rider. That is all."

Juh grunted and rose to his feet. Without a word, he left the cave. Slade remained seated by the fire. He knew where the old chief was going, to verify Slade's conversation with Nana. Minutes later, Juh returned and, crossing his ankles, sat by the fire. "One comes today," he announced abruptly.

Slade pretended surprise.

The chief continued. "He will be here soon. I do not know if he has a white woman or not, but if he does, and if she is the one of which you speak, she will be yours to claim." His words were a mixture truths and lies. The young man understood. Juh must retain his dignity.

If Juh claimed the woman, he must fight for her, an unnecessary and dangerous obligation that, Slade had hoped, the old chief had no desire to undertake. There were too many other white women within a few days' ride.

Rising to his feet, Slade nodded, his face solemn. "I will wait with my brother, Nana."

"That is best. I will speak with the Comanchero."

Slade would have preferred handling it differently, but he did not wish to offend Juh, remembering the mercurial chief's reputation for violent mood swings. "As you say."

Reluctantly the young half-breed retired to Nana's cave.

TWENTY-ONE

Within an hour, the wagon train, an ill-repaired collection of celerities, buggies, surreys, mule carts, and freighters' wagons rattled to a noisy halt in the middle of the camp. Apaches peered warily from their caves and wickiups.

A heavy-bellied Mexican in worn and dirty regalia rose from the seat of the lead wagon, a celerity with a top of red oilcloth. The tinsel cord was stripped away from his sombrero, and multicolored patches covered his once gaudy jacket. Soiled longjohns showed in the slit calves of his *calzoneras* as he held up his hand in a sign of peace to Chief Juh, who stood regally awaiting his visitor in the mouth of his cave. The two men exchanged greetings.

The Comanchero climbed down and went to stand before Juh. A bullwhip was jammed under the faded sash about the Mexican's waist, its whipcord frayed from long use.

Jake Slade squinted at the newcomer. His nose was intact. He was not the one with the bad nose, but the Mexican could be one of the three. He corrected himself when he remembered Vado's words—of the *two* remaining.

His eyes swept along the string of rundown wagons, searching for Catheryn.

Nana laid his hand on Slade's arm. "Be patient, my brother. If she is there, we will have her for you. Juh has promised."

As they watched, two Indians, Papagoes from their dress, appeared from the last wagon, pulling a subdued Catheryn Dubuisson after them. Slade started. Nana restrained him. "Not now. Juh will tell you when." Unconsciously, Slade's hand dropped to the .44 on his hip.

The Papagoes shoved Catheryn, sending her sprawling on the granite at Diaz's feet. A cry escaped her lips, and she buried her face in her arms. Juh's eyes remained on the Comanchero.

The words between Juh and the Comanchero did not carry across the rancheria to Slade despite the animated and violent gestures of the Mexican. Juh, unmoving, impassive as the mountain cedar, stared down at the Comanchero and nodded across the rancheria to the cave.

That was Slade's signal. Removing the rawhide loop from the hammer of his .44, he stepped out of Nana's cave into the sunlight. His gray eyes were like ice. His arms hung lazily at his sides. With measured steps, he started across the rocky clearing, every muscle in his body taut with anticipation.

His eyes darted to the Papagoes and Mexicans in the train. Beyond them, he saw Nednis who had unobtrusively positioned themselves in the proximity of the newcomers in case of trouble. He felt a glow of pride in his people.

Now all he had to worry about was the fat Comanchero himself.

Catheryn glanced up. When she saw Slade striding toward her, she gave a cry of happiness. The Comanchero spun on her and cursed as he tore the whip from his sash and raised it over his head.

Faster than an Apache arrow, Slade dropped into a crouch. His .44 roared three times, chopping the whip-stock into four pieces.

Diaz, his moon face black with rage, spun back to Slade, who jammed his .44 into its holster. A wild fury exploded in the young man. His ears roared. His head spun. Never before had he wanted so desperately to kill a man with his bare hands. He started toward the Comanchero.

A Papago raised his rifle, but a guttural cry from one of the Nednis stayed his finger. The band of Comancheros looked around. Without their knowing, they had now become the rabbits.

Slade dropped his gunbelt without breaking stride. In the same effortless motion, he palmed his knife. The smooth handle of the double-edged blade rested comfortably in his hand, like the warm burn of a large swallow of mescal in his stomach. His heart thudded violently against his chest.

The fat Mexican pulled his own knife, a wicked stiletto with a point like the spine of the cholla cactus. A crooked grin played over his fat lips. He was no fool. He had played this game for years. And he had always won. But as he watched the younger man draw near, he wondered. There was something about the approaching man that bothered him. He licked his dry lips. Instinctively Diaz's free hand crept toward his own pistol.

Juh's words stopped him. "He has only the knife."

Diaz knew then that he would receive no support from the Nednis. This newcomer seemed one of them. Yet, he was white. How could that be? Slowly he eased forward to meet the gringo.

Less than six feet separated them when Slade halted. His pulse raced. He studied the Mexican. Was he facing one of the three Comancheros who had murdered his mother and kidnapped his sister fourteen years earlier?

He studied the man closely. The chiseled forehead, the subtle cheekbones bore the evidence of aristocratic blood, but his thick lips and hooked nose testified that he was ejected from the womb of a slattern who plied her trade among the cantinas of El Paso or any of the other cheap saloons in the dirty towns sprawled along the border. The face, a common one among Mexican peons, seemed no more familiar than a thousand other Mexican faces. Still, the years had been long.

Slade paused. He felt the uneven granite slab through his moccasins. He shifted his weight and spoke. "You have my woman."

The Mexican arched an eyebrow. He remembered the gringo who had escaped back at Black Mountain. Silently he cursed his people for not being more thorough. "So you say." His tone issued the challenge.

"I will take her, with your permission or over your body."

The Comanchero dropped into an attack posture, knees bent, weight on the balls of his feet, knife extended, his other arm extended to the side for balance.

Slade remained in a careless, almost lazy posture, his knife at his side.

Diaz eyed his opponent. Either the gringo was very good or very stupid. He studied Slade. He outweighed the gringo, but the young man stood a head taller, and from the look of his shoulders, he also possessed much strength. A direct attack would be senseless. The Comanchero's eyes narrowed shrewdly. "She is not worth dying for," he said, stepping back in deference. He dropped his hands to his sides.

Juh's face stiffened.

Slade started to Catheryn. Out of the corner of his eye, he caught a motion. Immediately he spun, ripping his slouch hat from his head and swinging it like a roundhouse right.

Something caught the hat and jerked it from his hand. He stepped back and dropped into an attack posture, his own blade extended. On the ground before him lay his hat, a piece of the brim neatly sliced off.

The leering Comanchero waved the point of his stiletto blade slowly, like a fan. "You move fast, gringo. But not fast enough. No one takes my property." He feinted.

Slade stepped back.

The Mexican grinned as he dropped back into a fighting stance. He circled to the right. "Now I will carve you into small pieces and roast them over the fire for my dinner tonight."

"The boast of a fat man," Slade said with a sneer as he moved to his own right, balanced lightly on the balls of his feet. He felt the solid surface of the granite plateau under his moccasins. At least the footing was firm. He kept his eyes on those of the Comanchero. Always watch the eyes, he had been told in those childhood days with the Apache. They tell you what will happen.

Diaz feinted. Slade held back. Diaz slashed. Slade parried. Again the Comanchero faked a lunge, trying to pull Slade in. The young half-breed refused to take the bait, content to circle and wait.

Abruptly, the big-bellied Mexican attacked, slashing from the ground up to disembowel. Slade spun, using his blade to drive the thrust aside. In the same instant, he planted his feet and threw a left hook with every ounce of leverage he could muster, smashing his fist into the Comanchero's temple in a blow that would have felled a horse.

The heavy-set man grunted, shook his head, and turned back to face his opponent. He shuffled forward, bearing to his right. Slade circled, his eyes locked on the Mexican's.

A sudden lunge. The Comanchero's knife swept inches from Slade's belly, then slashed back at his face. The younger man had seen the move coming and parried the lightning-like cut with his speed.

The Comanchero was strong and not dismayed by the younger man's superior speed. He had experience on his side. A look of supreme confidence and gloating satisfaction filled his black eyes.

The expression on the Mexican's face arrested Slade's attention. The Comanchero sensed the younger man's sudden distraction and attacked with broad, sweeping strokes. Slade backed away, defending himself with deft parries and slashing ripostes.

The expression on the Comanchero's face triggered a

memory. Slade had seen that look before, the gleam in the eyes, the peculiar arch to the eyebrows. He remembered that very expression on the face of one of the Comancheros as the man raped his mother.

Was this one of the three? He realized he could not kill the man. He had to question the Mexican first. Backing away, he stumbled over the coals of a fire, but caught himself before he fell.

Anxious to take advantage of Slade's sudden distraction, the Comanchero dropped to one knee and scooped up a handful of coals and slung them into Slade's face.

With a yell of triumph, the large man charged. Slade leaped aside. The point of the blade ripped through his loose-fitting cotton shirt, slashed across his abdomen, and laid open the first two layers of tissue. The wound, though superficial, bled freely.

Diaz charged again. Slade sidestepped and struck at the bulging carotid artery in the Mexican's throat. At the last instant, remembering that the Comanchero could not die until he had answered some questions, the young half-breed pulled the blade at an oblique angle and slashed the Comanchero's face from chin to ear.

The bull-like Mexican screamed and grabbed his cheek. The flesh bulged open like a butchered hog. Blood poured down his flabby cheek and heavy jowls to soak into the dirty silk neckerchief about his neck.

With relief, Slade saw the flow was steady, not spurting.

Instead of another reckless charge, the Comanchero eyed his younger opponent with new respect. This was one to be reckoned with. He fell into a methodical thrust and parry routine. Shuffle right, feint, feint, then thrust and slash. Sweat poured into his eyes, burning the raw wound in his cheek and mixing with the blood dripping to the granite beneath his feet. He wiped the sweat from his eyes with his fat fist.

Slade stilled the excitement the smell of warm spilled blood sent coursing through his veins. Too much passion for the fight was dangerous. It created carelessness.

Skillfully, he parried, then attacked. He had to find a way to disarm the Mexican. He wanted information. Yet, deep down, he knew the Mexican would not quit unless he was either dead or unable to raise a blade.

He felt his own blood running down his legs into his moccasins, which were becoming soggy and slippery on the granite. Slade feinted, dodged, then made a riposte to the Mexican's forearm.

The Comanchero parried the thrust, whipping the blade in a backhanded slash that missed Slade by less than a frog's hair as the younger man skipped away.

Both men varied their attacks. Slade inflicted a shallow cut on the Comanchero's forearm. He took a superficial slash on the back of his hand.

The sun climbed to its apex. Sweat ran down their bodies, stained their clothes black, burned their bleeding wounds. Slade felt the stickiness of his blood on his groin and legs. The sun crept to the west.

By now, the Nednis and the other Comancheros had drawn closer, so swept up by the struggle between two obviously equal opponents that they had forgotten their previous hostilities.

Slade knew by now that the only way he could disarm the Comanchero was by severing the tendons in the man's fighting arm. To get in that close meant risking a blade himself. But it had to be done. He was losing much blood. Soon, he would grow weak.

The granite beneath their feet had grown slick with their sweat and blood. Slade began fighting more defensively, hoping the Mexican would believe he was tiring. Perhaps then the Comanchero would become overconfident, and careless. All the while, he studied the fat man, whose size belied both his hand and foot speed.

Regardless of the weapon used in a fight, the duelist searches for weaknesses in the opponent's style that will give him the advantage he seeks. The Comanchero studied Slade even as the younger man sought advantage through some weakness of the Mexican.

Slade continued his defensive fight. Then he noticed a possible advantage. Whenever the Comanchero made a riposte to Slade's left side, and the younger man skipped to the right, the Mexican moved to his own right and the two men faced off again.

The move had become habit with the Mexican, and the opening for which Slade had searched.

The next time the Comanchero lunged, Slade spun left. In the same instant, the Comanchero's blade bounced off Slade's ribs and slid under his skin, opening a gaping flesh wound in his side.

Fear filled the Comanchero's eyes when he realized his blunder. He tried to back away, but the younger man was too fast. Slade slashed down at the Comanchero's arm, laying it open from wrist to elbow. With a guttural scream, the Comanchero grabbed his butchered arm and dropped to his knees.

The younger man staggered to a halt and stared down at the blubbering Mexican. A wave of dizziness swept over him.

* * *

It was dark when Slade awakened. He stared into the blackness over his head.

He tried to move. Sharp pain lanced his abdomen. He groaned. Someone next to him under the blankets moved. It was Catheryn. She pressed her body against his, her hand on his chest. "How do you feel?"

"Sore," he whispered.

She laughed softly. "Everywhere?"

Suddenly, Slade wasn't so sore any longer. "Where are we?"

"In Chief Juh's cave. He ordered you brought here and told me to take care of you." As she spoke, she caressed his chest.

Slade chuckled. "Like that?"

She paused. "Complaining?"

He remembered their night together in the cave on the Red River. He had never met such a woman. "No. But you should know, your husband's alive."

Catheryn did not reply. She continued her ministrations in the dark. Several minutes later, she said, "You just lie still and let me do all the work. I don't want your wounds to open up again."

The young half-breed had forgotten all about his wounds by then.

TWENTY-TWO

Slade rose early the next morning. Their room was off the main cave. Light filtered through the opening between the two rooms. He looked down at Catheryn, who slept peacefully, her full breasts rising and falling regularly under the blanket. A smudge of dirt was on her forehead. Another on her nose. She looked right at home.

He made his way from the cave, stepping over the sleeping chief and his wives. He stepped outside and stopped. He blinked his eyes and stared in disbelief. The Comancheros had pulled out during the night!

Quickly he rushed to Nana's cave for his gear, cursing himself for not revealing his suspicions concerning the Comanchero's role in the murder of his mother. As far as the Nednis were concerned, Slade had his woman back, trading had taken place, and there was no reason to prevent the Comancheros from leaving.

Nana's brows knit with dismay when Slade told of his suspicions concerning his sister and murdered mother. "If I had known, my brother, I would have held him for you. I—"

Slade interrupted. "This is not the time for talk," he said, reaching for his saddle. He winced and dropped the saddle and grabbed his side.

"I will saddle your horse for you," the Apache said.

Grabbing his gun belt, Slade followed Nana across the clearing to the corral. "Tell my woman I will return soon. She is to remain here."

"I go with you," Nana replied, tugging the cinch tight. He then whistled for his own mustang and looped a rawhide lark's-head knot around the animal's lower jaw and swung astride the wiry horse.

Juh appeared in the mouth of his cave as Slade rode from the rancheria. Nana quickly told the chief what had happened, then set out after his brother.

The sun was a blistering orange ball on the horizon when Nana rode in leading the buckskin. Catheryn screamed when she saw Slade slumped in the saddle, his chin on his chest, his eyes closed.

"Ambushed," Nana explained as they carried the young half-breed inside.

Catheryn looked on helplessly as one of Juh's wives quickly undressed Slade while another brought a white, foul-smelling poultice. There were ugly blue holes in his left shoulder and above his right hip, and the wounds in his belly and side had opened again.

The Nedni woman cleaned the wounds quickly. She glanced up at her husband. "The bullets pass through."

Juh grunted. "Good."

The second wife urged Slade to sip the broth she had made while Juh's third wife knelt and gently packed the odorous poultice into Slade's wounds.

"To draw out the poison," Nana explained to Catheryn. "He will heal quickly." The white poultice quickly turned dark as it pulled the poison from the wounds.

Nana grunted and looked at Catheryn. "I go now to find the one who did this to my brother."

Catheryn was amazed at just how quickly Slade did heal. The next morning, he sat up, his eyes bright, his appetite keen. For breakfast, he devoured two large bowls of venison stew and drank almost a quart of fresh spring water.

After breakfast, Catheryn told him of Nana's mission. Slade became thoughtful. Then he said, "I reckon I'll have to get well fast."

And his wounds did mend rapidly, so rapidly Catheryn believed she could almost see the healthy skin covering the gaping holes.

"Apache remedies," Slade explained one night as they lay in each other's arms. "The white man laughs at them, but it is no matter. The Apache is on his feet and racing across the desert even as the white man continues to lie on his bed of illness."

Catheryn ran her hand over his hard body. She loved hard bodies. Phillip had been like that once, but now his body was growing soft. Her hand dropped lower. She caught her breath in surprise. "You're ready again."

He laughed. "Aren't you?"

She giggled and snuggled against him. She replied without guile. "I'm always ready, but how did . . . I mean, so fast."

Slade laughed again. "I told you. The Apaches have remedies for everything."

* * *

The next few days and nights, Slade would never forget. But he also could not forget just how close he had been to finding his sister. The thought constantly gnawed at him like a tiny mouse nibbling away at a loaf of sourdough bread. He knew that as soon as he could ride, he would have to take up pursuit of Diaz, the fat Comanchero.

TWENTY-THREE

Slade lay staring into the darkness, his arm around Catheryn's shoulders. He heard a contented purr deep in her throat, and she snuggled next to him. Her body was smooth and warm, but strangely, he did not thrill to her touch as he had days earlier.

While his body healed, he had been able to justify his inactivity. But now he was almost well and whole, and an unfamiliar restlessness disturbed him.

Part of him wished their life together could continue unchanged. The past days had been idyllic, carrying him back to the carefree and happy days of his child-hood with the Chiricahuas, roaming the rugged mountains, swimming in the pools of icy water, and laughing at the tiny sparrows harassing the much larger and more fierce hawks.

But a deep-seated force in his subconscious had nagged insistently at him to once again take up the trail of those he had sought, to deny himself pleasure, to continue with the task he had taken on years earlier when he left Cochise and the Chiricahua.

And that force had intensified the night before when

Nana rushed in as Slade sat by the fire. "Diaz is dead," he had announced.

Slade's hopes crumbled. "Are you sure? What happened?"

Nana nodded emphatically. "I saw it, and I saw him after they left. He is dead, but"—a grim smile curled his lips—"but the one who killed him is the Comanchero you seek."

"He is what?" Slade stared at the grinning Apache in disbelief.

The Apache brave nodded and drew his forefinger across the bridge of his nose. "This part of the vaquero's nose is missing."

"Hernandez!" Slade jumped to his feet. "But that can't be. He is in jail at Fort Richardson in Texas."

Nana's grin broadened. "That is what you told me. I thought my eyes played like the sneaky fox, so I waited until night, then I slipped into the camp. I saw him close. The nose is as you have said."

The Nedni Apache continued. "He was angry that Diaz lost the white woman. He now rides in the wagon of Diaz."

"Where do they go?"

"I do not know. I left when I knew he was the one you sought. But there was talk in camp that Diaz was to meet with the Kwahadi Comanches of Quanah Parker."

Slade studied his brother for several seconds. "He is going to Texas. In the morning, I must leave."

Nana glanced at Slade's shoulder. "You are not healed."

"I am well enough," he replied.

* * *

Catheryn stirred at his side. From the change in her breathing, he knew she was awake. And he knew she would be ready to make love. He had never met a woman like her. Even a fancy woman grew tired, but not her. How could Phillip Dubuisson, skinny, frail man that he was, satisfy a woman like Catheryn? Maybe he couldn't. Maybe not even Slade could. Maybe Slade was only one of a long string of men who had attempted to.

He blew softly through his lips. She was a hard one to figure. He wasn't sure he even wanted to understand her. He didn't believe he would like what he discovered.

With a mixture of relief and regret, he knew that their time together was over.

"You awake?" Her voice was a whisper.

"Yes."

Her hand caressed his muscular abdomen in tiny circles. "How do you feel?"

"Good." But his voice was not convincing.

They had spoken earlier of the time when he must take her back to Tucson, back to Phillip. No date was set. Each enjoyed this period in the scheme of his life when time stood still. They both knew, however, that sooner or later, their life together must end. Though neither spoke of it, the end was announced the night before when word came about Diaz and Hernandez.

A soft groan sounded in her throat. "Is it time to go back?" There was an edge of finality in her voice.

He tightened his arm about her, pressing her bare flesh into his, feeling the warmth of her body. "It is time."

* * *

Catheryn lay silent for several minutes. She had planned for this very moment since the day Slade had saved her from Diaz. While Phillip claimed to have discovered the canyon of gold, she did not want to risk everything on his being able to return to it. He was weak. For all she knew, he might have struck his head as he claimed and then imagined seeing the valley. No, she reminded herself as an old cliché popped into her head. A bird in the hand is worth two in the bush.

Slowly she traced her finger up his abdomen and twisted the fine hair on his chest between her fingers. "I don't know what Phillip and I will do. He isn't cut out for this life. I tried to make him see that last time, to leave this horrid country, but he refused."

By "last time," Slade knew she meant when he had given them the bars of gold. "You had enough gold to live on for many years." He did not accuse. He simply stated a fact.

"That's what I told Phillip, but he refused to listen. He gambled a lot of it away in an effort to make even more. Then he insisted on trying to find that valley you told us about."

"Which almost got both of you killed or worse. You've got no idea how the Indian treats a white woman."

"I know," she whispered, touching her lips to his chest. "If it had been just me, why, I would be back in Philadelphia right now."

He wondered. He knew her well enough by now not to believe every word she said, although she herself might believe each word at the time. She was one of those remarkable women who accommodate themselves to existing situations and always make whatever adjustments are necessary—and with a perfectly clear conscience.

When Slade didn't reply, Catheryn nudged him. "Did you hear what I said?"

"I heard," he replied, suddenly realizing the direction in which she had turned the conversation. He couldn't resist smiling, a smile Catheryn was unable to see because of the darkness, but a smile that reflected his own growing sophistication in the world of the white man, thanks to his time with Catheryn Dubuisson.

A year earlier, even six months, he would have innocently fallen into Catheryn's trap. Not now. It was his turn to dangle the bait. "What would you do in Philadelphia?"

"A dress shop," she said, too quickly. "A fashionable one for ladies with fine taste."

"I imagine something like that would cost a lot."

"Yes."

"What about Phillip? If he refused to leave once, wouldn't he refuse again?"

Catheryn sighed and snuggled against him. Her voice quivered with self-pity. "I don't care what Phillip does. He hasn't taken care of me for years—in any manner. In fact, I don't believe he even loves me any longer, so I'm not going to worry about him. I'll go back by myself if I have to."

"I have friends in Tucson," Slade said, deliberately testing her. "They could probably find you a job until you saved enough money to go back and start up your shop. Would you like for me to say something to them?"

He felt her stiffen, then relax. She was silent for several seconds. When she replied, her voice was syrupy as red sage honey. "That would be very nice, thank you."

Suddenly, Slade felt guilty about teasing her. After all, they had spent the last weeks together intimately. He felt he owed her something. But, he reminded himself, she had probably enjoyed his body a hell of a lot more than he had hers, even though their time together had carried him to heights beyond his wildest dreams.

"Well, you won't have to work." He paused.

Catheryn scarcely breathed.

He felt her tremble in anticipation. The silence was pregnant with expectation.

Slade broke the silence. "I will speak to my brothers, the Nedni. They have gold enough here. I will ask for enough to take you back to Philadelphia and start your dress shop."

"Speak? I don't understand. You know where the gold is. Why can't we—I mean, why can't you just go out and get it. I'll wait for you. Then together, the two of us—"

"It is not mine to give," he said, interrupting her. "It belongs to the Apache. It must be with their approval. If I were to take it without permission, I would be no better than those who come like the coyote and steal our belongings."

Catheryn stifled her impatience. "I understand. Who will give you permission?" she asked sweetly.

"Juh," the young man said simply. "This is his country. The gold here belongs to the Nednis." He hesitated. "If I do this, will you give your promise that you will return to Philadelphia?"

"But what about Phillip? I can't promise for him."

"Just you," said Slade. "Only your promise." A sly

grin spread over his face. "I think Phillip will follow you wherever you go."

"Well, I can't promise for him, but for me, yes. I promise."

Slade wondered. Could it be possible she was telling the truth this time? He hoped she was. "I will ask this morning."

She said nothing. Her slender finger traced small circles on his chest. "Why don't you go to Philadelphia with me? The two of us together would make a big splash back there. After all," she added, dropping her hand lower, "you and I have a lot in common."

He chuckled. Her suggestion piqued his curiosity. He wondered just how it would feel to be married to her, to be with her every day and night for the remainder of their lives. "What about Phillip?"

"He's a weakling," she said with a snarl in her voice. "I'm always taking care of him. The fool will stay out here until he kills himself."

Her sudden vehemence made Slade realize that being married to her would not be too pleasant. He didn't love her. Not enough to live his life with her as his brother, Nana, had chosen to live with Young Deer. He loved her body, but not her soul. Though he could not explain how he had learned so, her spirit was dark and filled with shadows. That was the reason, pure and simple.

"Well," she said, "what about Philadelphia?"

"I can't."

"Your sister?"

"Yes."

She giggled and squirmed her body against his. "Well, you know what you're going to be missing."

He laughed and pinched her bare rump. "That's my misfortune."

After a breakfast of roast pork, Juh agreed to Slade's request.

Three days later, Slade and Catheryn rode into Tucson, the young man on his buckskin and Catheryn on a borrowed mustang. Two parfleche bags filled with gold nuggets were tied behind the cantle of her saddle. Pausing at Doc Burk's, Slade learned Phillip was recuperating at the local boardinghouse, Mrs. Maclane's, one of the few frame structures in the village.

They pulled up to the hitching rail in front of the boardinghouse. Catheryn dismounted and, refusing Slade's offer to help her, untied the bags of gold and slung them over her shoulder. She staggered slightly under the load. She looked up at Slade. "Are you sure you won't change your mind? We could have a wonderful time."

He leaned over and picked up the mustang's reins. "Who knows? Maybe one day I'll visit Philadelphia."

Catheryn smiled sadly, but her smile did not fit with the look of triumph in her blue eyes. "Thanks—for everything. I wish you nothing but the best."

He nodded. "Same to you." Pulling the buckskin around, he headed down the dusty street to Western Union, strangely surprised the only emotion he felt over their parting was relief.

Inside the office, he found two messages awaiting him, dated a week apart. He knew their contents, but he skimmed both, then reread each slowly as the telegrapher, Finas Cole, an ex–army scout who had retired after losing his right arm, looked on.

The old man began sending. "Hope it's what you've been lookin' for, Jake."

Slade shook his head. "Good and bad, Finas. Good and bad."

TWENTY-FOUR

Three-Fingers Bent looked up from the reins he was patching. A grin stretched across his wrinkled face. "I'd about given you up for a goner until that 'Pache friend of yours brought me word."

Slade tossed his gear on his bunk and reached for the ever-present pot of coffee on the potbellied stove. Holding the handle gingerly as he filled a tin cup, he grinned at Three-Fingers. "It was kind of interesting down there for a while. Just got lucky, I reckon."

The old man's grin faded. "One thing for certain about luck. It'll always change." He turned his eyes back to the reins in his hand.

Slade eyed Three-Fingers over the rim of the cup. "Maybe not. She's doing okay by me." He told Three-Fingers about the telegram. "They had the Comanchero, but he escaped a week after they brought him in."

Three-Fingers frowned. "I don't see no luck there."

Slade's lips twisted in a wry curl. "Then he came to Mexico." Slade went on to tell Three-Fingers of the killing of Diaz. "The man who killed him was Elizio

Hernandez, the bastard I've searched for all these years."

Three-Fingers shook his head. "I reckon that was luck. Where's he at now?"

"On the way to Quanah Parker's bunch out on the Staked Plains."

The old man laid the reins at his side on the bunk. He rose and stretched his cramped muscles. "How'd you find out about that?"

"Nana heard it, but none of this would have happened if I hadn't gone up to Black Mountain when we got back in from Los Angeles." Slade went on to tell him all that had taken place since Black Mountain, except for the intimacies between Catheryn and him.

Three-Fingers cocked his head so he could hear well in his good ear. When Slade finished, he said, "You just be damned careful, you hear?" He opened the door to the stove and tossed in a couple of pieces of kindling. "You leaving in the morning, reckon I'll mix up a batch of corn dodgers for you to chew on."

"That'll help," said Slade. "I had another piece of luck," he added. "Captain Anderson at Fort Sill wired that that Texas Ranger, Jack Barker, came by." Three-Fingers frowned. Slade grinned and said, "He steered Barker clean over to New Orleans."

Three-Fingers grinned, revealing several gaps in his worn teeth. "Serves him right." He hesitated. His grin faded. "One day, you and Barker are goin' to have to settle your score."

With a shrug of his shoulders, Slade replied, "I reckon you're right about that."

"You're damned right I am."

* * *

Sunrise caught up with Slade ten miles east of Tucson.

The next evening, he reached Apache Pass and continued due east to El Paso before cutting back northeast so he could come into the Staked Plains from the southwest. The route was the same the Comancheros chose, their battered and cheapjack wagons unable to withstand the rigors of mountain trails. He traveled easy, not wanting to spend the buckskin.

On occasion, at night under the starlight, or during a particularly boring stretch of trail, Slade's thoughts turned to Catheryn Dubuisson. No question about it. She had provided a hell of a lot of excitement in his life. And of the few women he had ever been with, she was, without doubt, the one who most enjoyed the company of a man and knew how to please him.

Who could say? Maybe someday he would pay a visit to Philadelphia.

Soon he reached the Staked Plains, one square mile of which looked exactly like the next, whether the next was one mile or a hundred miles away. No trees. Few scraggly bushes. Sparse, wiry grass struggling in the gray soil. And flatter than Lutie's pancakes.

Spanish explorers had traversed its awesome spaces utilizing stakes placed in the ground to mark their back trail. That's how the wilderness got its name, the Staked Plains.

Slade had crossed the plains several times. He preferred night travel, for the stars guided him well.

When he reached the plains this time, he again traveled at night, hoping to spot the Comancheros before they saw him. Each morning at sunup, he camped, built a small fire for coffee, swallowed a mouthful of jerky, and dozed lightly in the shade of the buckskin. At noon, he pulled out, traveling slowly, always watchful of ambush. At nights, he moved faster.

Two days into the Staked Plains, the smell of rotting meat assaulted him. Soon, Slade found the source: dead longhorns. Two days later, he spied a cloud of dust on the northern horizon. He swung wide to the west. By noon, he had moved in front of the cloud. The length of the billowing dust and the way it hugged the ground, as well as the dead cattle a couple of days back, told Slade it was a cattle drive, one of those damned-fool gambles to move a thousand head of Texas longhorns to the railhead at Dodge City.

But why here? Experienced and knowledgeable cattlemen avoided the Staked Plains. Those men, Goodnight and Loving, drove through New Mexico Territory to the west. The others, Chisholm and the like, used the trails farther east. No one cut through the Staked Plains.

He turned the buckskin north of the herd. The chuckwagon should be a few miles ahead, the cook looking for the right place to pull up and fix supper. Another hour of easy riding, and Slade spotted the chuckwagon sitting in the middle of the empty plains, its tongue pointing generally north and the team munching on the sparse grass. The greasy belly busied himself over a buffalo-chip fire.

Slade rode in with his hand held high. "Howdy. Saw your dust. Figured I might do some chores for a hot meal."

The cook, a bandy-legged spool of wiry muscle, spat a stream of tobacco juice on the ground. He studied the newcomer for several seconds, then lowered his Winchester. "Light." He offered his hand. "Name's Corky.

One more mouth ain't gonna hurt none. 'Sides, I reckon I kin use the help with chips." He nodded to the lead bay in his team. "That damned nag yonder almost stove me up this morning. Leg's awful gimpy since."

Leaving the buckskin ground-reined, Slade gathered an ample supply of buffalo chips and dumped them on the ground by the fire and then set about filling the possum belly under the chuck wagon.

Dust rose to the south. "They be coming in directly," Corky said as he poured water into the great black pot over the fire. "Jess Tamberlane is the trail boss. Fair man. Does all the tallying back home for the big outfits."

Slade watched with appreciation as Tamberlane brought the herd in and gently turned it into a neat circle south of the camp. The swing riders moved out to help the flankers gentle the herd while the men on drag snugged up the stragglers. They knew what they were doing. No question about that.

"They're good," Slade said.

Corky looked up from the dough he was mixing. "Should be. They work together down on the coast." He pulled the coffeepot off the fire. "Grab a cup. Coffee's hot."

Slade grimaced, then quickly erased the frown on his face. He poured a cup and squatted by the fire, but his mind was racing. The trouble that Jack Barker was trailing him over had occurred on the Texas coast.

The greasy belly failed to catch the fleeting frown on Slade's face. "You know cattle?"

"Some," Slade replied. "Enough to see that this outfit knows what it's all about."

A grin spread Corky's lips. "Reckon you're right there."

Slade frowned. "What I can't figure is why you come through this part of Texas. Long way without water."

Corky shrugged. A deep frown furrowed his forehead. "Need to ask Jess about that."

Jess Tamberlane was a tall, raw-boned Texan whose fair complexion gave the impression of always being sunburned. He swung down from his saddle and handed the reins to the wrangler. "Howdy," he said, pausing to study Slade before reaching into the chuck wagon for a cup and squatting by the pot.

Slade introduced himself and hunkered down by the trail boss.

"You're a long ways from nowhere," Tamberlane said, studying Slade curiously.

Slade did not miss the regard Tamberlane paid him. Almost as if he recognized the young half-breed.

"Could say the same about you, Mr. Tamberlane. This part of the state's mighty rough on cattle, even those longhorns you're pushing. All bones and hide is what you'll soon have."

Tamberlane grinned sheepishly and flicked his gaze toward the old greasy belly. "That's what Corky keeps houndin' me about 'til I can't get no rest, but you see, the old boys I'm working for told me to chance it." He sipped his coffee and nodded to the north. "I don't know if you're familiar with this part of the country, but according to what we been told, there's a big canyon north of here full of belly-high grass and all the water we could want."

205

Again, Tamberlane regarded Slade curiously, but the younger man replied without hesitation. "Yep, whoever told you hit it square between the eyes, but what he didn't tell you was that canyon's also brimful of Comanches, Quanah Parker's band. They call that canyon home."

Tamberlane's face grew hard. His jaw muscles rippled under the taut skin. "We never heard tell about that. How do you know?"

"It's my business, Mr. Tamberlane. You don't believe me, put your scout farther out, but tell him to keep his eyes open if he wants to keep his scalp." Slade went on to tell the trail boss of his own search, and how it had taken him all over the Southwest. He did not miss the look that passed between Tamberlane and the cook when he mentioned Comancheros. It was a sliver of information he would file away until he knew the meaning of the look.

The only part of the story he left out was the purpose of his present journey. "I was through here less than a couple months back. In fact, four or five days' ride east of here, I run across a band of Kiowas heading for a parley with the Comanches over on the Red. Something's up, but I don't know what."

Jess Tamberlane didn't know whether to believe Slade or not. The newcomer could be part of a trap. By now, several of the riders had come in and were gathered around the two men.

"Why don't you let me ride out, Mr. Tamberlane," said a redheaded cowboy not yet twenty years of age. "I kin find Luke out there, and we can push on up to that canyon. See if this jasper's tellin' us honest."

Tamberlane nodded briefly. "Reckon you don't mind spending the night, Mr. Slade? Kinda like a hedge against what might be."

Slade hesitated. He eyed the trail boss warily.

TWENTY-FIVE

The rich aroma of the SOB stew curled under his nostrils. He grinned and nodded at the stew bubbling over the fire and the bread dough rising by the fire. "I figure that'd be mighty hospitable of you, Mr. Tamberlane. It'll be right choice to put myself around a solid meal and then get a whole night's sleep without worrying about getting my scalp lifted."

After Slade had packed two helpings of SOB stew away, he lay down on his spread-out soogan, content with a full belly and basking in the glow and warmth of the campfire. Tamberlane rolled out his bedroll nearby. From time to time, he cut his eyes toward Slade as if something was weighing heavily on his mind and he was trying to figure out just how to speak of it.

Slade looked around. An amused grin cracked the somberness of his face. "You look like you got something chewing at you, Mr. Tamberlane."

Tamberlane returned the grin. "Reckon I do, Mr. Slade. I'll just blurt it out, and if I be wrong, I figure you'll tell me so."

The tug of apprehension nagged at him, but he held himself motionless. "Wouldn't be fair to you any way else. What's on your mind?"

"You ever been down in Brazoria County, Texas?"

Every muscle in Slade's body stiffened. He shrugged. "I've been a lot of places. What's so peculiar about Brazoria County?"

"Nothing. To be honest, you looked familiar when I first met you. I—"

"So I noticed," Slade said, interrupting Tamberlane.

The trail boss chuckled. "Hell, and I thought I kept it purty well hidden."

"You did. But I was brought up Indian. We see much that you don't."

Tamberlane's grin broadened. "Well, like I said, you looked familiar, what with your being . . ." He hesitated. "I mean, your family . . ." He hesitated again.

Slade laughed and finished Tamberlane's remark. "A half-breed?"

Ducking his head, Tamberlane nodded. "Well, yeah."

"Don't feel bad, Mr. Tamberlane. I have the same trouble with you white people."

Tamberlane stared at Slade several moments, failing to comprehend the younger man's remark. Abruptly, he roared with delight. "I had it coming, Mr. Slade. I sure had it coming."

"Forget it. Now what about Brazoria County?"

"Well, I reckon it was someone else, but a couple years ago, a half-breed killed the son of a rich rancher. He managed to get away, which was a good thing 'cause he was fixing to be the onliest guest at a necktie party. Come to find out, about six months ago, a couple old boys come forward and admitted that they saw the fight.

That it had been self-defense." He paused and studied Slade carefully in the reddish glow of the campfire.

Slade's face remained guarded, but to the young half-breed, it seemed as if a three-hundred-pound hog had been lifted from around his neck. Of course, it could be a trick. No sense in showing his hand on just one man's say-so.

Tamberlane continued. "I don't figure that was you, but it might be that you'll run into that yahoo sometime and pass on the word."

"Never been down that way, but you can't tell, Mr. Tamberlane. I just might run into him. This world is full of strange things."

The next morning, the air was crisp and cool. Slade rose early and stirred up the banked fire. Corky grunted and slid the coffeepot to the edge of the fire. Slade scraped coals around the base of the pot.

"You up early, son," the cook commented.

"Habit, I reckon. Can't remember the last time I didn't watch the sun poke its nose over the horizon yonder." He patted his stomach. "That was a fine stew you whipped up last night."

Corky couldn't resist smiling. A cantankerous old man, he took great pride in his recipes. He poured water into some flour and cornmeal and began mixing batter for some Mormon johnnycakes. Four large spiders greased with buffalo fat sat by the edge of the fire.

"Next time I pass through," Slade said, grinning, "I'd sure take a pleasure for some of your Shivering Liz. It's been a spell since I had any jelly dessert."

"Come on back, Mr. Slade. I'll make it up special."

The cook poured thick molasses into the johnnycakes and stirred it in well. "There we go," he said, pouring the mixture into the three-legged spiders and clamping the lids on firmly. "Few minutes, you're going to have a treat."

"It already smells good." Slade complimented Corky as he reached for the coffeepot again.

"Yeah." Corky beamed. "Damned good, if I say so myself."

Slade had just poured himself another cup when Tamberlane squatted next to him. A few minutes later, the redheaded cowboy and Tamberlane's scout rode up. Their drawn faces reflected their weariness, but even the all-night ride could not erase the concern in their eyes.

"Mr. Slade was right. That canyon's chock full of Comanches."

The scout agreed. "We best cut east or west here, Jess."

"I'd head west if I was you," Slade said. "There's water, but better yet, there's no hostiles over there. Apaches're back south. There's cavalry at Fort Bascom and Adobe Walls should you run into problems."

The trail boss considered Slade's suggestion. "Like I said before, Mr. Slade. You know an awful lot 'bout what's goin' on. From the direction you seem to be heading, it appears to me that you're making directly for the canyon."

After the conversation with Tamberlane the night before, Slade had a feeling the lanky trail boss was one to go to the well with. He told the Texan the rest of his story. "A few weeks back, I ran across a Comanchero by the name of Ramon Diaz down in Mexico. He was

211

killed by another Mexican named Elizio Hernandez, who I been looking for a hell of a long time. He got away while I was laid up. I figure he's at the canyon," he added.

"This Comanchero, what'd he look like?"

"All I know is that he's got a chunk of his nose missing."

"Riding in a celerity wagon with a red top?"

It was Slade's turn to be surprised. He glanced around the campfire. The cook nodded. Slade remembered the look that had passed between the two men the previous evening. "You seen him?"

"Four days back," Tamberlane drawled. "But he wasn't heading to the canyon. He was going due east."

"East?" Slade frowned. What in old billy hell was the Comanchero heading east for? Parker was due north.

"Didn't take him for no Comanche lover though. He only had three outriders with him, all Mex."

Slade grunted. "That was all he wanted you to see. Reckon he spotted your dust and sent his other men ahead. But I can't figure out why he's heading that way unless he's got a parley with some Kiowa or Comanche hotbloods."

Tamberlane rose and stretched his lanky frame. "Whatever it might be, as long as they don't pay us no mind, I'm content. But you, Mr. Slade, if you go after him, you best sleep with both eyes open."

"Hell, Mr. Tamberlane. I was raised up sleeping like that."

Fifteen minutes later, they parted company. Jess Tamberlane and his cattle headed west for the Goodnight-

Loving Trail. The trail boss stopped by the chuck wagon. He and Corky watched Slade head south. "What about it, Jess? That him?"

Tamberlane shrugged. "Said he'd never been in Brazoria County, but, yep, I think that was him."

Slade rode slowly, still trying to figure just what Hernandez was up to. The Comanches and Kiowas were getting damned restless. Now, this Mexican was poking his nose in. Slade didn't want to believe it, but he had a sinking feeling that Elizio Hernandez was right in the middle of the impending Indian trouble. And that meant he could prove mighty difficult to capture.

He dug his heels into the buckskin's flank. "Don't really care," he muttered as the animal broke into a mile-eating gallop. "Just as long as I get my chance at him."

Slade rode back along the eastern side of the cattle trail hoping to cut wagon sign. It wouldn't be difficult to recognize.

At noon on the second day, he ran across the trail. A mile northeast, he found where a single horse had waited in a shallow arroyo. On the edge of the short-grass prairie three miles farther, he discovered where the Comanchero had met up with the remainder of his men. Dismounting, Slade studied the sandy ground. He pondered over the vague sign.

The sandy soil forced Slade to call on all of his tracking skills. Thicker soils held a sharp track, but on the prairie, sand poured immediately into the prints, leaving only shallow impressions.

After several minutes, he decided he had been right. The Mexican had sent his other men on ahead.

He had hidden his men just in case the opportunity arose to ambush the herd. Obviously when the Mexican saw how many trail hands Tamberlane had, he opted to just keep on moving. Slade looked up from the sign and stared to the west. "Mr. Tamberlane, you're one lucky man."

Mounting, he set out on the trail, keeping a careful watch on the country around him. The wind picked up, blowing the sand. Slade moved slower, not wanting to lose Hernandez's trail. He rode with every sense alert. There was little enough shrubs and grass on the Staked Plains, but he had been taught as a child how to hide in the open with even less cover. There was no reason for him to believe that the Comanches or Kiowas could not do the same.

He made a cold camp that night a mile off the trail just in case anyone did any backtracking. To travel at night so close to the Comancheros was foolhardy. Slade was well aware that the Comanchero would always do the unexpected. He could run like the jackrabbit or he could double back like the mountain lion or he could lie in wait like the rattlesnake. The night was long. Slade slept in snatches.

The next morning, Slade reined up when he saw tendrils of smoke on the horizon. The trail he was following led straight to the lazy columns. Whether the fire belonged to Indians or to the Mexican, Slade had to move carefully.

The plains had begun to roll more now, offering hiding places not only for the young half-breed as he cautiously rode toward the smoke, but for Indians and the Comancheros as well.

Slade made a wide sweep to the south, taking care to stay near the base of the rolling hills rather than crossing their tops and silhouetting himself for whoever might be watching. The tenuous columns of smoke appeared to be from two fires.

He paused just below the rim of a small mesa. The wisps of smoke were less than a mile away. Slade did not move. He just sat on the buckskin studying the country around him. He dared not take the horse any closer. The wind was at his back, and Indian ponies can pick up vagrant scents for miles.

He dismounted and slipped across the flat mesa to the far rim. He lay on his belly and stared across the prairie at the dying wisps of smoke. At first glance, he saw that whoever had built the fires had departed. When he looked closer, his blood ran cold.

The smoke issued from dark objects on the ground. Slade knew immediately what they were. Grimly, he made his way back to the buckskin.

Despite the savagery he had witnessed as an Apache and the butchery of the Civil War, he had to clench his teeth to still the churning of his stomach as he rode up to the two drifters spread-eagled on the ground. The stench of burned meat forced itself into his nostrils.

The men's sightless eyes stared in horror at the burning sun. A large fire had been built over their groins, leaving a gaping hole where their genitals had been. Wispy smoke curled from the charred bones and crisp meat.

Slade remained in his saddle, his cold gray eyes quickly reading the sign. Comancheros. He hissed between clenched teeth. "Bastards!" Forcing the lump in

his throat back down, he turned the buckskin to the
East after the slowly moving band.

He'd better be damned careful, he reminded himself.
He could just as easily have been lying back there a
those drifters.

TWENTY-SIX

The wind blew hot and steady, a plaintive moan twisting through the sagebrush, baking the sandy soil. Slade clung doggedly to the faint trail.

Two days later, dark clouds gathered far to the south in massive, bulging thunderheads, their gray woolpacks towering high into the sky. Despite the great distance, the churning turmoil within the clouds was obvious. Lightning flashed, and the dull rumble of thunder rolled across the prairie.

Glancing at the fast-approaching clouds, he knew that darkness would come early, and he was in for a wet night unless he found shelter quickly. The rolling prairie dropped away to a sprawling canyon that fell sharply two hundred feet and stretched several miles in breadth. To the east, the gaping maw of the canyon disappeared into the horizon.

He paused on the rim. The trail led down a worn path into the very middle of the canyon. The wary young man was reluctant to ride into the cluttered landscape of sandstone boulders and patches of scrub oak.

Dusk grew thicker. The wind picked up. A few splatters of rain plunked into the sand at his feet.

At low spots in the undulating hills surrounding the canyon, storms had cut deep arroyos that acted as natural flumes to funnel runoff water from the prairie into the depths of the canyon. Slade lifted his eyes to stare at that invisible point where the canyon met the eastern horizon. While this was his first trip through this particular canyon, he surmised it opened into the North Fork of the Red River.

In the encroaching darkness, the canyon had a wild and desolate look. The gusting wind howled through its cavernous depths like a pack of wolves. Spindly bushes waved black branches like wraiths. A premonition sent chills up his back. Suddenly, he knew without question that somewhere in those forbidding depths, Elizio Hernandez camped.

A spray of water struck his back. Behind him, a gray veil of rain approached rapidly, a shadowy curtain pulling the night behind it. Within minutes, he wouldn't be able to see five feet in front of him.

As distasteful as the idea was to him, Slade knew he had to drop down into the canyon for shelter. Into one of the arroyos, he decided. Break the wind. And he had his tarp. More times than he could remember, he had spent a dry night bundled in his tarp.

The first arroyo he explored overlooked the entire canyon. He found a washed-out cut under the bank that was large enough for him and the buckskin. Another cold camp, he told himself ruefully as he removed the saddle and jammed it against the sandstone wall. He looped one end of his lariat around the buckskin's neck and the other end to his saddle. Finally, he crawled between his blankets under the tarp.

Darkness poured over them even thicker than the molasses the old trail cook had poured into his Mormon johnnycakes. Flashes of lightning lit the canyon below with an eerie bluish glow. Slade leaned against his saddle, chewing on a strip of jerky and idly watching the awesome display of nature.

Suddenly he rocked forward, his eyes straining into the darkness. There it was again. In the distance, a campfire winked. Slade squinted into the night. Was it his imagination? No.

The fire blinked again.

He slipped from his blankets. To hell with the rain, he told himself as he threw the saddle on his horse and his slicker over his shoulders.

In the darkness, distance was deceptive. Slade rode along the edge of the rim where he could keep his eyes on the tiny campfire far down the canyon. After an hour of slow riding, he rode down into a twisting arroyo, dismounted, and tied the buckskin to a spindly scrub oak. He made his way down the winding gully in the direction of the fire, pausing during the bursts of lightning, then hurrying forward in the darkness between. Soon, he reached the perimeter of the camp.

The earlier intensity of the rain slackened, but it continued to fall steadily, keeping everyone inside the wagons. Slade hid behind a large sandstone boulder. He wore a black slicker, and when he pressed against the boulder, the eye could not discern where the man began and the boulder ended.

He surveyed the camp. A protruding sandstone ledge

sheltered the fire from the rain. Two guards squatted by the fire, rifles leaning against the rock wall. One slid a large coffeepot into the coals.

Heads drooping, the camp horses stood disconsolately in the rain, coats shiny in the flickering light. Slade noted that there was little trash around the camp, and that the bed of coals around the fire was too well contained to be more than a day old. Though the weather severely limited his vision, Slade saw no evidence of Quanah Parker or his braves.

He glanced over his shoulder. Parker wouldn't be moving tonight unless it was urgent, but you could bet your last plugged nickel that as soon as the rain let up or the sun rose, he and his men would be on the move, as would the Comancheros. If Slade was going to do anything, now was the time.

He studied the rest of the camp. Bobtail wagons, trail-worn surreys, and patched-up freighters' wagons were parked in no particular arrangement. Wherever the driver decided to halt was where the wagon stood. The celerity wagon with the red top was less than twenty yards from the fire, too close to slip in undetected. He had to take out the two guards first.

Only fifty feet separated him from the two Comancheros, but it was enough that they could raise the alarm before he reached them. A grim smile curled his lips when he remembered his slingshot. Give an Apache brave a handful of iron balls and his slingshot, and he had a weapon not only as deadly as any percussion lock, but much more dependable, and silent.

Slade quickly found suitable stones, as round and smooth as possible. From experience, he had determined that flat stones would sail on him, and pointed stones would flare unexpectedly.

Fortunately, sandstone was a soft rock. Within brief minutes, he had rounded the stones to his satisfaction.

The guards still squatted by the fire, their backs against the sandstone wall, their heads together in hushed conversation. Slade loaded the slingshot and waited. The rain slackened. One of the guards rose and reached for the coffeepot.

This was Slade's chance. Stepping into the clearing, he planted his feet and spun the slingshot over his head several times until he heard the familiar whining hum of the rawhide thongs in the air. Lightning flashed, illuminating Slade like a specter in the eerie blue light. The squatting guard saw him. Before the man could react, Slade released one of the thongs.

The stone whistled through the air. With an inaudible sound, it struck the guard on the forehead. With a grunt, he settled back against the wall, his head resting on his shoulder.

The second guard looked around at the grunt. For a moment confusion froze him. In that instant, Slade slammed a stone into his temple. He dropped like a poleaxed hog.

Silently Slade slipped into the celerity wagon and stared down at the sleeping Comanchero. The bulk under the blanket appeared even greater than that of Ramon Diaz, outweighing Slade by at least fifty pounds. And remembering how Diaz had shrugged off his blow back at Juh's camp, the young half-breed slammed his fist into the Mexican's temple twice. "That'll keep you," he muttered, straining every muscle to throw the heavy man over a horse before leading the animal into the rainy night.

To the east, the sky lightened, but the rain continued to fall. Back at his own horse, Slade mounted and led the way out of the canyon through rising water, hoping to put as many miles behind them as possible before stopping.

Ahead, a wall of water slammed around a bend and, like a 2-8-0 freight locomotive, roared down the arroyo toward him. Leading the mustang carrying Hernandez, Slade kicked the buckskin up a steep incline to the canyon rim just in time to avoid the flash flood.

Slade dismounted to check the rigging of the horses. A grunt spun him around just in time to see a silver-heeled boot flashing in his face. He dodged and grabbed for his revolver, but not before the sharp rowels on the Comanchero's spurs slashed open the skin on Slade's jaw, sending him spinning to the ground. His .44 flew into the boiling waters hurtling down the arroyo.

He rolled when he hit. Just in time. The large Mexican drove his boot heel into the ground where Slade's head had been. Pivoting on his hip, the young half-breed kicked the Comanchero's feet from under him, but before Slade could take advantage of his move, the larger man had rolled away and leaped to his feet.

The two circled each other warily. Slade said through clenched teeth, "I have waited long for this. Today, you will die."

Hernandez's eyes glittered with cruelty. "So the whelp thinks to best Elizio Hernandez." He laughed. "I have heard you sought me, and I remember the wolf-bitch who was your mother and the whelp who was your sister. I took my pleasure with them, and then I killed them."

A rage of anger and despair rushed through Slade's veins, but he forced himself to remain calm, to ignore the Mexican's taunts. He could not afford to make any foolish mistakes with this formidable adversary.

They continued to circle. Hernandez said, "I killed them, and I will kill you."

Slade refused to listen to Hernandez. He feinted, then drove a hard right into the Mexican's big belly.

Hernandez merely grunted and slammed his meaty fist down on Slade's back, driving the lighter man to the ground. In the same instant, the Comanchero brought his knee up, catching the young half-breed square in the face.

Stars exploded in Slade's head. He felt the bridge of his nose bend, then snap, followed by a wrenching pain that seemed to bulge his eyes from their sockets. Warm blood poured over his lips and down his neck.

Hernandez grinned cruelly as the younger man climbed to his feet, almost blinded by the intense pain. "Do not whine, gringo. Your mother whined and begged. Your sister whined and begged. Is there no courage in the blood of your family?"

Drawing on the extraordinary self-discipline instilled into every Apache brave during his strenuous apprenticeship as a boy, Slade forced the throbbing pain from his head. If he hoped to best this Mexican, Slade told himself, it would have to be with brains, not brawn.

The Mexican squared his shoulders. "This time, I will cut your head from your shoulders. You will be dead when I leave." He lunged at Slade who stepped aside at the last moment and drove a fist into the heavier man's kidney.

With a grunt, the Comanchero spun and threw himself at Slade, driving them both to the ground. Arms and legs tangled, they rolled in the mud, each grasping for leverage. They twisted and fought to the edge of an arroyo down through which runoff water surged in a violent backrush of deadly whirlpools, roaring like a tornado as it exploded against sandstone walls and ricocheted into the canyon below.

The Comanchero rolled on top of Slade. Using his massive fist like a club, he battered at the younger man's face. After the first few blows, the pain dulled.

Slade jammed the heel of his hand under the fat man's jaw. Lightning flashed, and Slade's eyes met the pig-eyes of the Mexican. He looked into the eyes of the man who had raped and murdered his mother and sister.

With a cry of rage, Slade forced the Comanchero's head back. With his free hand, he drove his fist into the side of the Mexican's neck.

Momentarily numbed, the Mexican collapsed on Slade, who squirmed from beneath the fat man's bulk and stumbled to his own feet. Quickly shaking off the blow to the side of his neck, the bulky Mexican rolled to his feet. The two men eyed each other warily. A cruel grin twisted the Mexican's lips. He threw a roundhouse right that Slade easily stepped under to drive a sharp left and right to the fat man's heart.

Before he could step back, a solid blow caught him in the side of his head. Stars exploded. His ears rang, and he stumbled back, trying to keep his balance. He heard the Comanchero give a war cry. Instinctively, he jumped aside as the large Mexican slammed into him.

Grabbing the Mexican's arm and pulling it over his shoulder, Slade pivoted and threw his hip into the on-coming man. With a scream of alarm, the Comanchero flipped over Slade's shoulder, landing with a splash in the slippery mud.

Abruptly, the Comanchero slammed his heel into Slade's knee, knocking him backward toward the ar-royo. The rain-soaked edge of the arroyo crumbled un-der Slade's weight. He threw out his arms for balance, but the ground gave way, caving into the churning wa-ters below and carrying Jake Slade with it.

TWENTY-SEVEN

Slade struggled to the surface, coughing up the gallons of water he had swallowed, but the raging current and treacherous whirlpools in the bends of the arroyo kept pulling him back under. Swirling debris slammed into him.

He swam with the current, instinctively realizing that he could not fight it. The sides of the arroyo offered no handholds, nothing he could use to pull himself from the angry waters.

The current swept him down the arroyo, bouncing him against the steep walls. Suddenly, the water fell away, dropping him fifteen feet into the confluence of several other streams. He plunged underwater, and for a moment the roar of the raging flood disappeared. Choking for breath, he fought to the surface even as the churning waters hurled him down the deep and narrow cut that sluiced to the Red River many miles beyond.

In the dim light of early morning, Slade spied a small cave just above the waterline on the opposite side of the arroyo some fifty feet ahead. A thin stream of water ran over its lip into the arroyo.

Summoning all of his strength, he fought through the heavy current to the cave. Just as the water swept him past, he shot out his hand and dug his fingers into the soil. Gasping for breath, he clawed his fingers deeper into the red clay, reminding himself that there could be some unpleasant inhabitants of the cave also seeking refuge from the flood.

Painfully, he pulled himself up to peer into the small cave. The cave was less than ten feet deep. A tiny hole in the ceiling emitted light and water from above. He breathed a sigh of relief. No snakes. He crawled in and, hoping the roof would hold, collapsed on his back in the mire. Despite the throbbing in his head and the muddy bed on which he lay, exhaustion overcame him. He fell asleep.

Voices awakened him. He lay motionless, giving his senses time to orient themselves. His eyes and nose throbbed dully. Outside, the sky was gray and heavy with the portent of more rain. The wind whistled around the corner of the small cave. The voices grew closer, a mixture of Comanche and Papago and Spanish. Suddenly, like a flash of lightning, Slade realized that the Comancheros were searching for him! He listened as the ponies splashed through the mud below.

He turned his head to the opening and froze. In the mouth of the cave coiled three rattlesnakes, their beady eyes locked on him. With deliberate caution, he eased into a sitting position and slipped his knife from its sheath. His heart thudded.

The voices grew louder.

He kept his eyes fastened on the snakes. Their tongues flicked the air, testing, smelling. One began loosening its coils, ready to ease forward. Slade held his breath.

He glanced at the opening in the roof of the cave. He slipped his free hand into the hole in an effort to determine the thickness of the roof. His hopes sank.

The roof was several inches thick. To burrow through would take time, and the amount of dirt spilled into the cave would certainly aggravate the rattlers.

He would just have to wait, and hope.

The searchers were below the cave now. Maybe they would not look up.

They did.

"Up there," said one voice.

"Too high," another voice replied.

There were a few grunted assents. Slade heard the searchers sloshing through the mud and water as they moved on down the arroyo. Finally, the sounds of the retreating Comancheros disappeared. He remained motionless, his eyes locked on the immobile rattlesnakes.

Now all he had to do was get rid of the serpents, which, in such small confines, was easier said than done. He couldn't wait them out. Sooner or later, they would explore the object they sensed in the rear of the cave. That was their nature.

He scraped some mud from the wall of the cave. If he could irritate them just enough without stirring them into an attack frenzy, maybe he could drive them away. He knew they would not strike unless provoked. Like people, rattlesnakes went out of their way to avoid trouble. The trick was knowing just how much aggravation they would take before deciding to retreat or attack.

Moving his hand from the wrist down, he flipped the mud at the rattlesnakes. The dirt struck one on its spade-shaped head. Its rattles hummed. The other two joined in. Slade flipped a few more grains of mud. The humming intensified.

He tightened his grip on his knife.

The one nearest him slid a loop forward. Despite the muddy floor, the serpent was growing curious.

Slade flicked some more mud.

It struck the rattlesnake just below its raised head. For several seconds, the snake stared at Slade. Finally, it dropped its head and quickly slithered to the mouth of the cave, where it dropped over the edge.

He heard the sound of the snake hitting the mud and water below.

The other two rattlers followed quickly.

Slade released his pent-up breath and crawled to the mouth of the cave. The last of the rattlers disappeared into a pile of broken branches on the far side of the arroyo.

Quickly Slade dropped to the ground and hurried up the arroyo in the opposite direction the Comancheros had gone. Overhead, the clouds remained thick and ominous, promising more storms.

Slade doubted if the searchers would backtrack, but he refused to chance it. He wanted to put as much distance behind him and the Comancheros as possible. Once out of the canyon and into the rolling hills, he could relax.

They had taken his horse. His revolver and war club were lost. All he had was his slingshot and knife, but he was still Apache enough to live off the land and kill Kiowas and Comanches and Comanche lovers.

Thirty minutes later, Slade lay beside a sagebrush on top of a small rise. His face throbbed. He touched a finger to his nose. The skin was taut, and his nose had swollen to three times its normal width.

From his vantage point on top of the hill, he could see for miles. Heavy storms were all around him, dotting the prairie with gray columns falling from a black ceiling. The prevailing winds pushed the great, opaque pillars of rain across the prairie.

In the distance, a storm cell rolled over the Comancheros as they moved out of camp, almost obliterating them. Slade followed, his heart aching with the loss of his sister and his steps slowed by the beating he had endured. But he followed, driven by a fierce determination for revenge and a savage thirst that would be quenched only by the blood of Elizio Hernandez.

All day and into the dusk the band pushed forward despite the storms. Slade's eyes narrowed when he realized the Comancheros planned on traveling through the night. Wherever they were going, they were in a damned big hurry.

The thunderstorms grew heavier and more frequent. Finally the wagons circled and stopped.

Slade lay under a sagebrush on top of a hill and watched, oblivious to the rain pelting down on him. His eyes burned. He dug his knuckles into them. His body ached with exhaustion. He lay his head on his arm and tried to rest, but the bitter thoughts tumbling through his mind and the intense weather, the crashing thunder and the brilliant lightning, gave him no respite.

During the night, the storm abated. Slade slept. At dawn, the sound of rattling wagons awakened him. The Comancheros pulled out. He followed at a distance, not sure just what he should do next. All he knew was that he had to keep Hernandez in sight.

The wind held from the west, quickly drying the prairie. For two days, Slade followed. The second night, driven by thirst and hunger, he slipped through the darkness toward the fires. Momentarily careless, he approached the perimeter of the camp from upwind.

A sharp whinny cut through the silence of the night. Slade fell to his belly and waited. Murmurs came from the camp. Several figures appeared carrying torches, venturing into the darkness around the camp.

Slade quickly drew back, cursing himself for his carelessness, knowing that the camp would remain alert throughout the long night.

The caravan pushed out at first light. Slade continued to follow, but with no water and his only food a small rabbit he had eaten raw, the wiry man grew weak.

Two nights later, he drew his knife. With Apache brashness, he vowed that he would take food and water even if he had to kill for them. He glided through the sagebrush like a ghost.

Guards patrolled the outskirts of the camp.

Slade paused in the darkness, his eyes taking in the camp and his brain planning his next steps. His breath came hard. He had extended his body to the breaking point, and it was telling him so. A wave of dizziness swept over him. He tried to shake the lightheaded feeling.

Suddenly the crunch of footsteps in sand sounded behind him. He rolled over in time to see a startled Papago stop and stare down at him. Calling on the last of his reserve strength, Slade leaped on the surprised Indian and knocked him to the ground.

In the same movement, he drove his knife at the Papago's throat. The Indian caught Slade's wrist in a steel grasp. To the young half-breed's astonishment, the smaller Indian forced the blade away from his throat, at the same time crying out for help.

A chorus of shouts erupted from the wagon train.

With a curse of his own, Slade drove his left fist into the Papago's jaw and dashed into the darkness. Behind him, confused shouts and sporadic gunfire echoed through the night. Several hundred yards into the prairie, Slade dropped, gasping, to his knees, his cold eyes on the dark figures moving about the fire.

A voice called across the prairie. "Gringo. Next time, you won't be so lucky. Next time, I kill you. You hear, Gringo?" Hernandez's taunting laughter echoed through the darkness.

Later that night, Slade reluctantly made his decision. A week earlier, he could have manhandled the small Papago, but now his body was growing weaker although his determination had never wavered. He had to have food and water. The Comancheros knew he was about. Their camp would remain well guarded.

He had no choice. He turned east for Zeb's ranch.

If he could reach his old friend, outfit himself with a horse and food, maybe he could pick up Diaz's trail again before the sandy stretches of the vast Texas prairie swallowed the Mexican. His belly growled. He forced the hunger pangs from his mind. It would be a long run to Zeb's.

It was longer than he expected.

His shattered nose and the years he had spent forking a horse caught up with him within the first hour. Swollen tissue clogged his nostrils. Through his gaping mouth, he sucked air into his burning lungs and slowed his pace, remembering the long-ago counsel of Gokhlayeh as the somber-faced Apache watched the novices complete their twenty-mile run. "The hawk glides on the wind, saving his strength until he is ready to strike. Let it be so with you."

The slower pace revived Slade although each step sent sheets of fiery pain through his head. Soon, even that pain dulled, and he drifted into his own world.

Throughout the day and into the night, he ran, a single object in the middle of a vast and empty prairie. He closed his mind to his privations, focusing all of his energy on Zeb Walker's ranch, allowing no distractions in his mind.

It was a discipline every Apache youth either acquired or died in the effort trying to. That discipline was responsible for the tenacity and ferocity of the Apache, a ferocity that prompted General George Crook to label the Apaches "Tigers of the Southwest."

The Apache began learning self-discipline as an infant. Every aspect of his life was colored by that teaching. The degree to which the Apache practiced that trait is what set him apart from other tribes, from other men.

Slade had been exposed to enough of the white man's ways to understand that they had no comprehension of the degree of self-discipline the Indian exercised—to tolerate excruciating pain without a whimper, to deny the body food and rest until a task was completed.

Very few white men possessed that same discipline.

An ironic grin curled his lips. Those white men who did possess that trait, however, were the very ones responsible for Manifest Destiny, that westward expansion that drove the Indian from his ancestral home.

At midnight, he stopped and slept, but not before repairing his moccasins with squares of buckskin cut from his vest.

False dawn broke in the east. Slade set out again. The second day was as the first. He ran with the precision of one of those newfangled farm machines he had seen in pictures back in Tucson, mechanically, automatically, his physical torments forgotten. He was beyond sweat and pain now. The wind cooled his lean body. His legs pumped. He still breathed through his mouth, but his breath came easy and regular.

At dusk, Slade topped the rim overlooking Zeb Walker's valley. Without hesitation, he dropped off the hill and cut across the broad prairie toward the ranch. Smoke curled from the chimney.

Slade saw that the corrals were full. Business must be good. Maybe someday, when he found his sister, he would take Zeb up on his offer to go into business with him, breaking horses for the cavalry.

Suddenly, he stumbled to a halt, realizing what he had been thinking. A tear formed in his eye, and a great emptiness filled his soul. His sister was dead. All these years of searching had been in vain. But then a cold fury replaced the anguish. Slade repeated his own promise. Sooner or later, he would kill Elizio Hernandez.

A dark figure appeared in the open door to the main house. It was Zeb. Slade would know that tassel of gray hair anywhere. The old man stood without moving, his Winchester cradled in the crook of his arm. Finally, he turned back into the house. He had recognized Slade.

The next morning, after seeing Slade's face in the light of day and making one or two ribald comments about how the younger man had better watch out for angry husbands, Zeb picked out a spry bay for Slade. "He's gelded. Smart too. He'd bring a good price from them army fellers."

Slade nodded, his expert eyes playing over the animal. Zeb had taken good care of this one. His tail had been thinned and shortened, and his hooves were trimmed and shod.

"He could be a good night horse," Zeb said as he slipped a half-breed bit in the horse's mouth. "He's easy going and sure-footed. Just what you need goin' back after that Mex."

Ignoring the low-grade pain pounding inside his skull, Slade swung into the saddle and rode the bay around the corral, putting the animal through its paces. The bay had rough edges but quickly picked up some of the young half-breed's expert leads. Slade grunted with satisfaction after a few minutes. Zeb was right. With the right training, the bay would turn into a fine animal.

He nodded his satisfaction at Zeb when he passed. The old man grinned like a wolf in a chicken house. Slade winked. Zeb winked back and shuffled over to the gate and threw it open. "Got some grub packed up for you," he called over his shoulder. "Best fill a couple canteens with well water. It's goin' to be another steamy one today after all the rain we've had."

Tying the bay to the hitching rail outside the main house, Slade followed his old friend inside and reached for Zeb's razor. He started when he saw his face in the piece of mirror nailed to the wall. Staring back at him was a black cannonball with two gray eyes and a set of swollen lips. Gingerly he lathered his cheeks and quickly shaved what sparse beard he had.

Zeb said, "Like I told you last night, look out fer them Kiowas. Word is they been meetin' regular-like with Quanah's Comanches. Something's goin' on at the reservation."

"Don't worry. I'd trust a rattlesnake before I'd relax around them." Slade rolled up the bedroll Zeb had put together for him. "I don't figure they're up to doing much this late in the year."

"Reckon you're right about that. Way I see it, they're figuring on breakin' off the reservation, but they won't until spring. I suspicion they'll let the army take care of 'em this winter."

Slade grinned. "Can't say as I blame them." He paused and gazed thoughtfully at Zeb, who poured them one last cup of coffee before Slade pushed off. "If the white man would just stop moving in. There's game for ever'one. Buffalo are all over the plains. Antelope are thick as longhorns. As long as the white man pushes on in and wipes out these animals, the Indian will fight."

A wistful look filled Zeb's old eyes as he remembered his own childhood. He knew of what Slade spoke, for he had grown up in a country even more pristine and idyllic than his younger friend's.

"It's always changing, son," he said softly. "I recol-

lect my old pap tellin' me about all the beaver an' fox
an' ermine the old-timers brought in. The West was a
land of plenty, and you damn sure hit it spang on the
nose when you say if we used it right, it would take care
of us. Why an old she-wolf couldn't nurse her whelps
no better than this country would care fer us."

Slade looked at Zeb in surprise. He had never heard
the old man say more than half a dozen words about
any subject. Now he was delivering a sermon like one
of those circuit-riding Methodist preachers.

Zeb continued, his face growing hard. "But the
white man is a taker. He ain't goin' to stop and consider what he's done to the country. Not for years will
he stop and consider. By then . . ." He made a sweeping gesture with his hand. "All this is going to be ru-
ined. There won't be no more buffalo, no antelope, no
wolves." He looked deep into Slade's eyes. "And no
more Injun."

The younger man shook his head. "I sure hope to hell
you're wrong, Zeb." He drained his coffee. "But I can't
do nothing about it now. I got to find me a Comanchero."

"Good luck, son," Zeb said, rising and extending his
hand. Last night when Slade spoke of his sister's death,
the old man refused to believe it, saying instead that
Hernandez had lied.

Not once had Zeb referred to the girl as being dead.
"When you find that sister of yours, come on back and
the three of us'll build a ranch that'll put them down on
the coast to shame."

For a moment, Slade remained silent. He knew what
the old man was trying to do, but it wouldn't work.

237

Laura Ann was dead, and the sooner Slade accepted that fact, the better off he would be. Zeb was just trying to ease Slade's pain. He nodded to the old man. "You take care, hear?"

Five minutes later, Slade rode away, outfitted with grub, one of Zeb's old navy .36's and a beat-up Winchester '66. To polish off his complement of weapons, he had his slingshot and his knife.

He headed east, hoping to pick up Hernandez's trail. By the time he reached the general area, the sand had covered all traces. Vainly he searched, casting in widening circles for sign.

At the end of each fruitless day, he cursed himself for leaving the Comanchero's trail, but deep down, he knew had he not gone to Zeb's, he would be dead now, either by starvation or thirst or at the hands of the Comancheros.

After several days, he decided to head back to the arroyo where he had run across the Kiowa powwow that night months earlier. He had as good a chance at cutting the Comanchero's sign there as anywhere else.

Days passed, became weeks. Jake Slade scoured the Texas Panhandle and Indian Territory between Adobe Walls and Fort Sill, then west to Palo Duro Canyon. Hernandez had dropped from sight. The few Kiowas or Comanches with whom Slade powwowed denied having seen the men he described.

Early autumn, Slade gave up. Weary of hardscrabble meals of roots and sage hens and snakes, he turned the bay south for one last visit to Fort Sill. He had covered so much ground so often in the last several weeks that he had a permanent map of the Texas Panhandle pounded into his skull.

Sooner or later, he told himself as he urged the bay into a comfortable six-mile-an-hour gait, he would find the Comanchero. And then he would make sure his mother and sister slept in peace.

TWENTY-EIGHT

During the weeks that Slade combed the Texas Panhandle for Hernandez, Zeb's prediction of reservation trouble became more substantial. The Indians Slade encountered were too close-mouthed. The Kiowas drew particular attention for they wore a single feather in their braided hair and rode horses covered with dots representing hailstones.

Twice Slade powwowed with a small band of two or three braves. Twice he asked if they had seen any Comancheros. Twice, they said no.

When the last party of three rode away, Slade was convinced that plans were being made for something big. Maybe Zeb's idea about the tribes bolting the reservation wasn't so far-fetched after all.

In Fort Sill, he discovered Anderson was out on patrol, so he told Captain Paul Sheridan of his suspicions and concerns.

"You're certain?" asked Sheridan as he poured Slade a drink of Kentucky bourbon from his own private store in his quarters late that night.

Slade leaned his elbows on the table and stared into

heridan's eyes. "War talk is the only explanation. If
hey had been after game, there would have been evidence of the hunt. None of the parties carried any
game. And the Kiowas rode their warhorses."

Sheridan frowned. "I don't understand."

The young half-breed grimaced. Sheridan was a good
man, a conscientious officer, but damned ignorant of
the ways of the Indian. How could he or any other officer be expected to contain the Indians to the reservation
if he didn't know anything about them?

Slade explained slowly. "The Kiowa has a work
horse, a warhorse, and a hunting horse. They treat the
animals like family. Even stable them in their wickiups."

"So what you're saying is that if the Kiowa had been
hunting, they would have ridden different horses,"
replied Sheridan.

"Yes."

"But how can you tell the difference?"

"Experience, Captain. Experience."

A wry grin spread over Captain Sheridan's weathered
face. He held up his glass in a toast to his companion.
"To experience, Mr. Slade. To experience."

That was one toast to which Slade drank. He added
one of his own. "Here's to living long enough to get the
experience."

"I'll sure as hell drink to that," exclaimed Sheridan,
taking another sip. "So you really think it means trouble?"

"No question. They'd even painted hailstones on the
horses."

Sheridan arched an eyebrow. "Hailstones?"

Again Slade explained. "The Indian believes hailstones make him invisible."

The captain shook his head, his forehead furrowed. After several thoughtful moments, Sheridan asked, "What kind of trouble do you think they'll cause us?"

Slade shrugged. "Friend of mine figures they're going to break off the reservation."

Sheridan nodded slowly as he studied the half-empty glass of whiskey in his hand. "I hate like old billy hell to hear that, but I'm afraid your friend might be right. The younger bloods are gettin' mighty restless. Some of them have been taking off for a short spell and then coming back. Claim to be out hunting, but after listening to what you've said, I remember now that they have been coming back empty-handed. Claim there's no game out there."

Slade drained his glass and pushed back from the table. "Reckon I'll light out now. Just wanted to let you know what I'd run across."

"When do you figure they're going to do something?" Sheridan gestured at Slade's empty glass as he asked the question.

The young half-breed shook his head. "One's plenty. As far as when you can expect trouble, I'd say come spring."

A frown wrinkled Sheridan's brow. "Why so long?"

"Hell, Captain." Slade laughed. "The Indians're not dumb. They're going to let you soldier boys feed them this winter; then they'll jump you."

Sheridan stared at Slade for several seconds, not comprehending the humor at first. Then his face broke into a wry grin. "I'll be damned." He laughed. "That is a joke on us. A damned good joke." He threw back his head and roared as the full realization of just how the Indians were using the white man became clear to him.

As his laughter subsided, he told Slade that Jack Barker had come back through on his return from the wild-goose chase down to New Orleans.

Slade arched an eyebrow. A faint grin ticked up one side of his lips. "And?"

Sheridan laughed again. "Fit to be tied. He was yelling like a wild steer with his balls caught in the fork of a tree."

The smile on Slade's lips faded. "Hope I didn't cause any trouble."

The captain's reply was all innocence. "No reason for any trouble. Seems like there's no record of Mr. Barker visiting the fort prior to his return from New Orleans, so any misinformation he received could not have come from here."

The two men's eyes locked. Slade said, "That's what I call efficient record keeping."

Sheridan's grin broadened. "We try."

Slade left the post ten minutes later, declining Sheridan's offer of a bunk for the night. "Ceilings spook me, Captain, but I appreciate the offer," Slade said as he mounted the bay and turned it west.

"Sorry your trip was for nothing. If I run across that Comanchero again, I'll lock him up for you 'til all hell freezes over. I know how to reach you in Tucson."

"Thanks, Captain."

"When you planning on coming back this way?"

"Who knows? Right now, I've got to get back to work, or I'll be out riding the chuckline."

Sheridan eyed Slade in the yellow light thrown from the open door. He had taken a liking to the young man with the serious face. "You ever decide you want to work for the army, come see me." He held out his hand. "I'll have a spot for you."

Slade shook it. "Thanks for the offer, Captain. I'll remember. Never can tell when something good is going to happen," he added with a note of optimism.

But for the first time in his life, Slade felt discouraged, empty. Now, he had nothing to look forward to. The last seven years he had spent searching for his sister. Now she was dead. He stared at the stars as he rode out of the fort. He spoke to the bay. "What now?" He drew a deep breath and tried to throw off the depression settling about his shoulders.

As he rode out of the fort, the local sutler went into the communications office, pausing momentarily to watch Slade ride out of the fort.

Out of habit, Slade cut northeast for a final swing through the canyons where he had found, then lost, Elizio Hernandez. "Who knows?" he muttered to his horse. "Could be he's like a rabbit and makes a wide circle."

He rode into the canyons four days later. As he expected, there was no sign of Hernandez. The only tracks in the sandy beds were animal.

To the west, the sun dropped to the horizon. Slade pulled into a small copse of elm and made camp. He slept with a small fire that night, too wearied by all that had happened to be concerned about security.

The next morning, Slade pulled out early, threading his way through the canyon as it made a great sweep to the south. He slouched indifferently in the saddle, oblivious to his surroundings.

Suddenly, a voice cut the stillness of the morning. "Hold it right there, Slade."

Instantly, the young man recognized the voice—Jack Barker, the Texas Ranger who had been trailing him for two years. Slade reined up. Without looking in the direction of the lawman, Slade said, "You got lucky, Jack."

Barker laughed. "No luck at all. I got me a wire from the fort. Figured to find you out here somewhere. You're gettin' careless in your old age. Your fire last night led me straight to you."

The crunch of the horse's hooves in sand drew closer to Slade. The wild and crazy idea of shooting it out with Jack Barker popped into his head, but then he reminded himself of Elizio Hernandez. If Slade was going to shoot it out with anyone, the Mexican was the one.

Barker rode in front of Slade and halted. Using the muzzle of his revolver, he tipped his hat back on his head, and then to Slade's surprise, dropped the revolver into its holster. "It's been a long chase, Jake."

The hair on the back of Slade's neck prickled. Something was wrong. He nodded to the revolver. "You seem to be mighty sure of yourself."

The lawman shrugged. "I am. I'm heading back to Brazoria County. But not with you."

Slade frowned. "You've gone and lost me now, Jack."

"After that wild-goose chase over to New Orleans, I ran into a friend of mine up north of here. He was coming back from a trail drive. Name of Jess Tamberlane. Seems like a couple witnesses come forward clearing you. Just to be certain, I wired home. Sure enough, old son. They tore up the warrants on you. Far as Brazoria County is concerned, you're a free man." He paused, then gave Slade a sheepish grin. "I'd been hounding you so long, I figured you had a right to know it was over."

For several moments, the young half-breed stared at the impassive lawman. "I'll be damned," he finally muttered. "So Tamberlane was telling the truth."

"Yep. He guessed you was the one, but he didn't figure you believed him."

"I didn't."

Barker shrugged. "Don't know as I blame you." He removed his hat and scratched his head. "Well, can't say I've enjoyed the last two years, Jake, but I'll admit, you're the hardest man to run down I've ever had the misfortune to take after." He studied the younger man for several moments, wondering if he could have taken Slade in a fair fight. A rueful grin played over his weathered face as he realized he was glad he hadn't found out.

He slapped his hat back on his head and nodded. "I gotta go. Brazoria County's a hell of a piece from here."

Slade watched the lawman head east. He was too tired, too weary to be angry with the man who had dogged his heels for the last two years. All he wanted to do now was go back home to Tucson and try to make some sense of his life.

When Barker disappeared over the rim of the canyon, Slade clucked his tongue, and the bay headed west for Tucson.

* * *

The ride back to Arizona was uneventful. The few bands of Indians he ran across knew nothing, or revealed nothing, of Hernandez.

Nine miles out of Tucson, Slade rode toward a familiar landmark, the Jesuit mission of San Xavier del Bac. There he would pause for a drink of the mission's sweet and cold water. The sun beamed down from directly overhead, and the heat rose from the ground in waves, drying the skin, parching the throat.

The courtyard was empty when he rode in, not surprising because of the heat. Everyone with good sense was inside the adobe buildings, resting in the cool shadows. He pulled up at the water trough and dismounted.

He removed his hat and ducked his head underwater. He then shook his head like a dog and ran his fingers through his wet hair. The cold water running down his shoulders and back tingled.

A greasy voice broke the silence. "Do not move, gringo."

Slade stiffened, then turned to the voice, at the same time thumbing the rawhide loop off the hammer of his revolver. His blood ran cold. Elizio Hernandez stood just inside one of the arches of the mission's arcade. Next to him stood Vado, a broad sneer across his fat face. Both Mexicans held revolvers trained on Slade.

Vado held up his hand with the two nubs. "Before we kill you, gringo, I cut off all your fingers. Then you will feel the pain as I."

Slade kept his eyes on Hernandez. Vado continued taunting and gloating. "I am the third man, gringo. I rode with my uncle, Elizio. Now you will die at the hands of the same who killed your own mother."

The pounding of Slade's heart against his chest slowed. If a man must pick a time to die, he could do no better than now, Slade told himself. One of the three men who murdered his mother and sister was dead, Ramon Diaz. Now, he faced the other two.

The familiar bloodlust of the Apache surged through his veins. A sense of peace, a sense of the inevitable came over him. He spoke in a soft, chilling voice. "Perhaps I die, but I promise, you also will die on this day."

The gloating sneer fled Vado's face. Hastily, he jerked his revolver up and fired.

Slade's hand flashed for his navy .36.

Hernandez fired.

For several seconds, the courtyard rang with the explosions of gunfire. Acrid smoke filled the air. Slade stood rooted to the ground, firing carefully. Slugs whined past his head. Two tugged at his shirt. One tore his hat from his head, another slammed into his shoulder, but the long years of searching kept his feet planted firmly on the ground as he made each of his six shots count, three for each man, the last payment on a fourteen-year debt.

When the smoke drifted away, Slade remained standing in front of the water trough. Blood stained his sleeve, running from a ragged furrow cut into the deltoid muscle. Another slug had nicked his ear, but a grim smile played over his lips as he slowly approached the prostrate Comancheros.

Elizio Hernandez and his nephew, Vado, lay sprawled on the tiled arcade. With the toe of his boot, Slade turned each Comanchero over and stared down at the two for several seconds. He dropped his .36 back into its holster and slowly slipped the rawhide loop over the hammer of his revolver. "Now, it's over," he said, turning back to his bay.

TWENTY-NINE

As he rode toward Tucson, he was filled with the inexplicable feeling that he had failed in all he had striven to achieve despite having slain those he had sought for so long. He was empty inside. Not the way he had expected to feel.

Three-Fingers Bent patched Slade's shoulder and daubed some coal oil on the younger man's ear. Later in Mildred's Café, Slade stared wordlessly at the cup of coffee cradled in his hands. The two men had just put themselves around a plateful of fried potatoes and a thick steak and washed it all down with coffee. Bent was in a jovial mood.

"Don't worry, boy. What you need is to git back to work. We'll pull out tomorrow at one thirty. Word is a couple of them Eastern highbinders has been spotted along the road. Need to keep an eye for them. Don't know why they come out here. We got trouble enough with our own hijackers and owlhoots."

Slade looked up at his old friend, who was warming up to one of his favorite subjects. Bent was right about one thing: hard work always helped a man clear his head and straighten his thinking. "Suppose you're right. It's still not easy to believe it's all over."

With a cluck of his tongue, Bent shrugged. "Not ever'thing be over."

The young half-breed frowned across the table at his old friend.

Bent explained. "There's a chance you might have that woman to worry about."

A surge of excitement shot through Slade, tingling his skin. "What woman are you talking about?"

"That blonde with the stove-up husband. You remember. They might still be around."

The young man tried to act casual, not seem too excited over the news. "Around? They were supposed to go back to Philadelphia."

Three-Fingers signaled the waitress for another cup of coffee, into which he poured a dollop of rye from the pint bottle he always carried in his hip pocket. "Don't know about that, but I do know as quick as that man of hers got where he could travel, they pulled out in a buckboard with as fine a pair of matched bays I've ever seen."

"How long ago?"

"A couple weeks after you went back to Texas."

Slade's eyes narrowed. "They traveling or prospecting?" He knew the answer. He hoped he was wrong. He hoped they planned to go overland to Soldier's Farewell or on to El Paso. But what would they do there? Stagecoach connections to Philadelphia could be made in Tucson a hell of a lot easier than traveling to either of the other villages. Besides, no one spent money on matched bays just to ride to another town and then sell them.

The older man considered the question. "Don't know, but knowing how people be, I'd guess prospecting. That's why I said your worries ain't over. 'Course, there's one or two good things down the road too."

Struggling against sudden despair, Slade ignored the older man's last remark. Muttering a curse, he shoved back from the table.

"Where you goin'?"

"Doc Burk's. Dubuisson stayed with him a spell. Maybe he told Doc something."

The old man arched a skeptical eyebrow. "Maybe so. See you back at the shack."

With a grunt of assent, Slade left the café and made his way down the narrow dirt streets of Tucson. Laughter and sounds of merriment erupted from the open doors of the saloons that lined either side of the litter-strewn street.

Doc Burk lived in a large adobe on the outskirts of town. A young Mexican boy in baggy white trousers and a floppy jacket opened the door and ushered Slade into the Doc's office.

An older man pushing fifty, Doc Burk listened as Slade explained his concern. "Well, Mrs. Dubuisson did spend a good deal of time with her husband," he replied. "But never in my presence was anything said of them going back to Philadelphia."

He opened a humidor and extracted a long black cigar. He offered one to Slade, who declined. After lighting his stogie, Doc Burk continued. "She dressed expensive. She had money. I guess from the gold you mentioned. They never came right out and said it, but I'd wager a twenty-dollar gold piece that they were going out to look for more gold."

He paused to blow a stream of smoke into the air. "I could be wrong, but I don't think so."

Slade's hopes sank. He rose and thanked the doctor. The older man's thoughts confirmed his own.

Back in his adobe, Slade told Three-Fingers to find another shotgun for the morning ride. "I'm going to look for Dubuisson and his wife."

"Dammit, boy. You can't do that. Old Bill Harnden needs you. We ain't got nobody 'cept that redheaded shanty Irishman, O'Toole. He's drunk half the time."

Slade frowned. O'Toole was a part-time regular. What was Three-Fingers's worry now? The Irishman functioned as well drunk as he did sober. "Look, Bent. Tomorrow's Monday. I'll be back in plenty time for the Friday run." He paused. When he continued, his voice carried an ominous fatality. "I don't think this will take long. I know where to look."

Quickly throwing some grub into a parfleche bag, he saddled the bay and rode out, heading for Black Mountain. Confused thoughts tumbled through his head. Why? After all of the gold he had given them? Why throw away their lives? He found no answer. But then, they were white. And maybe that was the answer.

At sunrise, Slade paused on the rim of a mesa overlooking a broad valley of huge boulders. The air was crisp and cool, a tonic for the lungs. The cry of a hawk cut through the stillness. The breaking of the sun over the horizon and the subsequent burst of oranges and reds filling the cloudless sky never ceased to fill Slade with wonder.

At that moment, he came as close as he would for many years to comprehending the difference between the Indians like him and the white people like Catheryn and Phillip Dubuisson. The Indian was as one with nature, going with its ebb and flow, drawing on its strength, adjusting to its violence, living and dying with it, and in that way, the Indian gave value to nature as well as to his own life.

The white man contested nature, despised its forces, opposed its violence, refused to accept its strength, and pitted his own puny cunning against the unforgiving whims of nature.

As in the flood-ravaged arroyo, you either swam with the current and survived, or you fought against the current and died.

The bay pranced, restless to continue the journey. Slade clicked his tongue and tapped the reins lightly against the animal's neck.

Two times throughout the afternoon, Slade encountered Apache sentries. Both times they recognized him and returned his greeting.

Halfway up the trail to the canyon, Slade spotted a wrecked buckboard at the bottom of a two-hundred-foot drop. There were no bodies in the wreckage.

Back in his saddle, he drew a deep breath, steeling his nerves for what he knew he was going to find when he reached the canyon. He couldn't keep from hoping that he was wrong, but Catheryn and Phillip had violated the Apache home too many times to hope for any forgiveness now.

He wasn't wrong. The curse still held.

He found them, what was left of them, just outside the canyon. From his saddle, he read what had happened.

The attack had been sudden. Phillip's bones, the few remaining after wolves and coyotes had worried over them, and the turkey buzzards and shinned hawks, and even the little kingbirds had picked them clean, lay at the edge of a clearing. Apparently he had been hit just as he dismounted from the wagon. A gust of wind rattled two arrows still between the white bones of his ribs. A thighbone lay in the remnants of his denim trousers.

Farther into the canyon lay Catheryn's bones. She had made a run for the creosote, hoping to hide in the fissure behind the shrubs.

Slade grimaced at the crushed forehead of her skull. An Apache must have been hiding in the cedars, and when she rushed by, he stepped out and killed her.

The slow click of many hooves on granite sounded behind Slade. He did not turn. Then a single set of clicks drew close.

"I am sorry, Busca, my brother."

Slade recognized Nana's voice. His eyes remained on Catheryn's bones. "It was the will of the gods."

"Perhaps. She was a woman of much trouble. Her soul was dark. You are fortunate that she was not yours."

Slade glanced at Nana, wondering idly what had brought his brother up from Mexico.

The Apache wore a crooked grin.

"You knew that I was lying at Juh's?"

Nana's grin broadened, revealing bright white teeth. "Juh also knew. But the Comanchero, he is a pig. It was great fun tricking him. And you are my brother. Whatever you ask, I will do. Besides, she was only a white woman." He reined his horse around. "Come. We camp near."

"Can't," Slade replied, sorely tempted. "I've got to make the Friday run to Fort Yuma."

Nana laughed. "Bent will not mind. You can go next trip. You have traveled far and fought long in the last months. It will do you well to be with family."

A long sigh escaped Slade's lips. "I wanted them to go back to Philadelphia," he said, speaking his thoughts. "And I wanted to find my sister, but she is dead. I failed everybody."

"No, Busca. You failed no one. The whites did not want your help."

Slade looked around, his forehead wrinkled in pain. "Maybe they didn't, but my sister is dead."

The grin on Nana's face broadened. Slade frowned. The Apache tipped his head, gesturing behind them.

Five riders faced them—Bent, Bill Harnden, Paleto, and two strangers. One was a tall, handsome Californio, and the other, a winsome young senorita. They all wore wide grins.

Slade frowned at Nana.

The Apache nodded. "It was a girl-child the friars at the mission Altar took from Hernandez, not a boy-child. Later she was sent to San Diego."

Disbelief rocked Slade back on his heels. "You mean . . . that she . . ." The words clogged in his throat.

The next thing he knew, he was running across the clearing, and Little Butterfly, Laura Ann, his sister, was running to meet him.

The entire party returned to the rancheria of Cochise. Slade refused to let Little Butterfly out of his sight as Bent explained how Nana had come to Paleto and him, and the three had then gone to Bill Harnden. The four of them followed the clues Slade had provided. The young Californio was her betrothed, Don Alvarez de Lopez, heir to a sprawling estate near the great waters to the west.

Later that night, when all slept and peace lay over the mountains, Slade went into the night and stared up at the glistening stars.

With a deep sigh of contentment, he spoke to the stars and moon. "Sleep well, Mother. Our Butterfly is home."

Back at Black Mountain, a gust of wind blew the remnants of Phillip Dubuisson's trousers across the road, where they came to rest against a dead stump.

RIDERS TO MOON ROCK

ANDREW J. FENADY

Like the stony peak of Moon Rock, Shannon knew what it was to be beaten by the elements yet stand tall and proud despite numerous storms. Shannon never quite fit in with the rest of the world. First raised by Kiowas and then taken in by a wealthy rancher, he found himself rejected by society time after time. Everything he ever wanted was always just out of his grasp, kept away by those who resented his upbringing and feared his ambition. But Shannon is determined to wait out his enemies and take what is rightfully his—no matter what the cost.

LOREN ZANE GREY

AMBUSH FOR LASSITER

Framed for a murder they didn't commit, Lassiter and his best pal Borling are looking at twenty-five years of hard time in the most notorious prison of the West. In a daring move, they make a break for freedom—only to be double-crossed at the last minute. Lassiter ends up in solitary confinement, but Borling takes a bullet to the back. When at last Lassiter makes it out, there's only one thing on his mind: vengeance.

MAX BRAND®

JOKERS EXTRA WILD

Anyone making a living on the rough frontier took a bit of a gamble, but no Western writer knows how to up the ante like Max Brand. In "Speedy—Deputy," the title character racks up big winnings on the roulette wheel, but that won't help him when he's named deputy sheriff—a job where no one's lasted more than a week. "Satan's Gun Rider" continues the adventures of the infamous Sleeper, whose name belies his ability to bury a knife to the hilt with just a flick of his wrist. And in the title story, a professional gambler inherits a ring that lands him in a world of trouble.

ZANE GREY

RANGLE RIVER

No name evokes the excitement and glory of the American West more than Zane Grey. His classic *Riders of the Purple Sage* is perhaps the most beloved novel of the West ever written, and his short fiction has been read and cherished for nearly a century. The stories collected here for the first time in paperback are among his very best. Included in this volume are two short novels and two short stories, plus two firsthand accounts of Grey's own early adventures in the territories that he so notably made his own. Zane Grey was an author who experienced the living West and wrote about it with a clarity and immediacy that touches us to this day.

Dorchester Publishing Co., Inc.
P.O. Box 6640 ___5212-1
Wayne, PA 19087-8640 $5.99 US/$7.99 CAN
Please add $2.50 for shipping and handling for the first book and $.75 for each additional book. NY and PA residents, add appropriate sales tax. No cash, stamps, or CODs. Canadian orders require $2.00 for shipping and handling and must be paid in U.S. dollars. Prices and availability subject to change. **Payment must accompany all orders.**

Name: _____

Address: _____

City: _____ State: _____ Zip: _____

E-mail: _____

I have enclosed $_____ in payment for the checked book(s).

CHECK OUT OUR WEBSITE! www.dorchesterpub.com
____ *Please send me a free catalog.*

#45
WILDERNESS
IN CRUEL CLUTCHES
David Thompson

Zach King, son of legendary mountain man Nate King, is at home in the harshest terrain of the Rockies. But nothing can prepare him for the perils of civilization. Locked in a deadly game of cat-and-mouse with his sister's kidnapper, Zach wends his way through the streets of New Orleans like the seasoned hunter he is. Yet this is not the wild, and the trappings of society offer his prey only more places to hide. Dodging fists, knives, bullets and even jail, Zach will have to adjust to his new territory quickly—his sister's life depends on it.

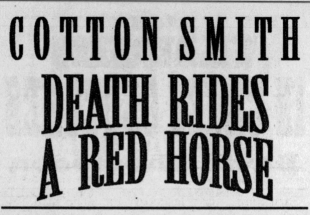

COTTON SMITH

DEATH RIDES A RED HORSE

What started as a simple trip for supplies has turned into a race against time and a fight to survive. Cole Kerry almost single-handedly broke up a raid on the town by a gang of outlaws. But one of them grabbed Cole's wife as they rode off, and Cole himself was shot in the back when he tried to track them down. Now it's up to his older brother, Ethan, to find Cole and rescue his wife—if they're still alive. It's a tough enough job for any man. Ethan isn't about to let the fact that he's blind stand between him and what he needs to do.

MANHUNT

Tim McGuire

Living as a wanted man for the past six years has been mighty tough for Clay Cole. The man known far and wide as the Rainmaker has been running from the law for a crime he didn't commit. Now Clay's stopped running. The Rainmaker is determined to clear his name once and for all. But the law has something far more dangerous in mind for Clay. A brutal killer has escaped from prison with the aid of his gang and a Gatling gun—and he's taken Clay's friend as a hostage. The sheriff knows the Rainmaker is the perfect man to track down a killer. And Clay will do anything to rescue his friend…even if it's the last thing he does as a free man.
